Texas! Lucky

Texas!
Lucky

Sandra Brown

Bantam Books

TEXAS! LUCKY

A Bantam Book / Published by arrangement with Doubleday

PUBLISHING HISTORY

Doubleday edition published July 1990
Bantam mass market edition published February 1991
Bantam hardcover edition / January 2009

Published by
Bantam Dell
A Division of Random House, Inc.
New York, New York

Book design by Glen M. Edelstein

Bantam Books is a registered trademark of Random House, Inc., and the colophon is a trademark of Random House, Inc.

ISBN 978-0-553-80403-4

Printed in the United States of America
Published simultaneously in Canada

www.bantamdell.com

10 9 8 7 6 5 4 3 2 1
BVG

Texas! Lucky

Chapter One

There was going to be trouble, and, hell, he just wasn't in the mood for it.

Lucky Tyler, seated on a barstool, was nursing his second whiskey and water. Bothered again by the rough, masculine laughter coming from one corner of the tavern, he glanced irritably over his shoulder to look in that direction.

"Might've known Little Alvin would sniff her out," the bartender said.

Lucky only grunted in response. Turning back to his drink, he hunched his shoulders and sank a little deeper into his slouching position on the barstool. He reasoned that if the broad hadn't wanted the attentions of Little Alvin or any other guy, she wouldn't have come into the lounge alone.

Describing the place as a lounge sure was euphemistic, he thought. The place was a bona fide honky-tonk. It didn't possess a single feature that would elevate it to any higher caliber of drinking hole than that.

It had first opened during the boom, fifty or so years earlier. Before the bar had a flashing neon star out front, before it had indoor plumbing, the place had served bootleg liquor to roughnecks, wildcatters, and the ladies of the night who comforted them when the wells turned up dry or who took their money when they struck black gold.

The highway tavern hadn't had a name then that anybody could remember, and it didn't have one now. It was simply known to locals as "the place," as in, "Meet'chu at the place after work for a drink." Respectable men frequented it alongside those who weren't respectable.

But a respectable woman wouldn't be caught dead inside. If a woman came to the place, she was there for one reason and one reason only. The instant a woman alone darkened the door, hunting season commenced. It was understood.

That's why Lucky wasn't too concerned about the welfare of the woman being hassled by Little Alvin and one of his least savory companions, Jack Ed Patterson.

However, when another burst of laughter erupted from the corner, Lucky swung his gaze around again. Several things struck him as odd. A long-neck beer stood on the chipped Formica table in front of the woman, along with a half-filled glass. A glass? She must have requested it, because at the place long necks weren't usually served with a glass even to a woman. Strange that she had asked for a glass.

She wasn't exactly dolled up either. Oh, she was good-looking, all right, but her makeup was conservative, and her clothing upscale and chic. She wasn't your ordinary gal-about-town on the prowl or even a housewife looking for a distraction from the daily grind or revenge on an inattentive husband. He couldn't quite pigeonhole her, and that intrigued him.

"How long's she been here?" he asked the bartender.

"Got here 'bout a half hour 'fore you came in. Know her?"

Lucky shook his head no.

"Then she sure as hell ain't from around here." The bartender guffawed, implying that Lucky kept a more accurate account of the local female population than the Census Bureau. Which was the truth.

"Soon as she came in and ordered her beer, she drew everybody's attention like flies to honey. 'Course, the rest backed off when Little Alvin showed more than a passing interest."

"Yeah, he's a real ladies' man, all right," Lucky said sardonically.

Little Alvin had been so dubbed merely because he was eighth of the eight offspring born to the Cagneys. Standing 6' 5", he weighed about 290, 30 pounds of it put on since he had left the NFL several years earlier.

He'd been playing first-string linebacker for the Denver Broncos when he caused a league controversy. One of his quarterback sacks had left a rookie Dolphins player with blurred vision, stuttering speech, and a retirement pension.

The tackle had been so unnecessarily rough, Little Alvin himself had suffered a dislocated shoulder. The team management had used his injury as its reason for not picking up his contract at the end of that season, but it was speculated that management was glad of the excuse to get rid of him.

Upon his suspension, Little Alvin had returned home to East Texas and picked up where he'd left off years before as Milton Point's meanest bully. He still considered himself a superstud football hero.

Tonight neither his dubious charm nor his fame were working on the woman he'd set his sights on. Even from across the dim, smoky lounge, Lucky could see that she was growing more agitated by the minute.

The George Straight ballad blaring from the jukebox prevented him from hearing the words they exchanged, but when Little Alvin laid a meaty hand on the woman's shoulder, there was no mistaking how she felt about his romantic overtures. She shrugged off his hand and reached for her purse. She attempted to slide out of the booth, but 290 pounds of Little Alvin Cagney, along with his sidekick, Jack Ed Patterson, who had recently done time in Huntsville State Prison for assault with a deadly weapon, blocked her escape.

Lucky sighed. He was going to have to do something

about this, and damned if he was in the mood for it. It had been a hell of a week. Business was rotten, and a loan payment was only weeks away from coming due. Susan was dropping hints about a diamond ring for her left hand. The last thing he needed was a run-in with a couple of lowlifes like Little Alvin and Jack Ed.

But what if their quarry had been his kid sister, Sage? He would like to think that some decent guy would come to her aid. Of course, Sage was smart enough not to get herself into a sticky situation like this. But you couldn't decline to protect a woman's virtue just because she was dim-witted.

His daddy had drilled into him and Chase, his older brother by a year and a half, that when a lady said no to a pass, the answer was no. Period. No questions asked. The woman might not be very nice for leading a guy on and then changing her mind at the last minute, but the answer was still, unequivocally, *no*. And his mother expected him to treat every woman chivalrously, no matter how trashy she was.

His ears still rang whenever he recalled the lecture his mother had given him in the ninth grade, when he brought home the delicious gossip that Drucilla Hawkins had "done it" at the drive-in the previous Saturday night. What had gone on in the backseat of her boyfriend's blue Dodge was the talk of the school.

Laurie Tyler wasn't interested in the juicy details of Miss Hawkins's fall from grace. She had sternly warned her younger son that he had better not be overheard defaming any girl's reputation, no matter how reliable the source of the gossip was. He'd been admonished to treat every woman—and her reputation—with respect and dignity. It had been such a scalding lecture that he remembered it to this day, nearly twenty years later, at the ripe old age of thirty-two.

He muttered another foul curse beneath his breath, and tossed back the remainder of his drink. Some things you had to do whether you wanted to or not. Defending a woman from Little Alvin and Jack Ed was one of those things.

One booted foot, then the other, unhooked its heel from the chrome rung encircling the legs of the barstool. Lucky swiveled around on the maroon vinyl seat, worn slick and smooth by too many rear ends to count.

"Careful, Lucky," the bartender warned. "They've been drinking all afternoon. You know how mean Little Alvin gets when he's drunk. Jack Ed's bound to have his knife handy, too."

"I'm not looking for trouble."

"Maybe not, but if you cut in on Little Alvin's action, you'll get trouble."

Apparently everyone else in the place smelled trouble, too, because the moment Lucky left his stool at the bar, bells on the pinball machines fell silent for the first time in hours. The row of video games still beeped and burped and flashed a kaleidoscope of electronic colors, but those playing them turned curiously, instantly attuned to the sudden shift in the atmosphere. It was like the expectant stillness before a tornado struck.

Drinkers at the bar and those occupying booths ceased conversations to follow Lucky's swaggering progress across the room toward the booth where the woman was demanding that an amused Little Alvin get out of her way.

"I'd like to leave now."

Lucky wasn't fooled by the quiet calm in her voice. Her eyes were shifting nervously between the two men. Jack Ed was a fraction of Little Alvin's size, but in his own way he was intimidating. He had a ferret's eyes and the sharp, pointed grin of a jackal. They hadn't fallen for her phony defiance any more than he had.

"How come you're in such a hurry, honey?" Little Alvin cooed. He bent over her so far, she recoiled into the corner of the booth. "We're just startin' to have fun."

Jack Ed giggled at his friend's clever way with words. His laughter broke off when Lucky spoke from behind him.

"I don't think the lady's having any fun a-tall, Alvin."

Little Alvin came around with all the grace, agility and temperament of a bull whose tail had just been given a hard yank. Lucky was standing with one thumb tucked beneath his waistband, the hand casually curled over his tooled-leather belt, and the other braced against the tarnished brass hat rack mounted on the end of the neighboring booth. His feet were crossed at the ankles. He was smiling pleasantly. Only the cocky tilt of his dark blond head and the coldness of his blue eyes belied his friendly tone of voice.

"Bug off, Tyler. This is none of your b'iness."

"Oh, I think it is. Since a dumb slab of meat like you doesn't seem to appeal to the lady, she's still fair game, right?" Lucky looked down at the woman and gave her the warm smile and lazy wink that had coaxed a legion of women out of their better judgment and their clothing. "Hi. How're you doin'?"

Little Alvin growled his disapproval and took two hulking footsteps toward Lucky, whom he championed in size by three inches in height and a hundred pounds. He swung a ham-size fist toward Lucky's head.

Lucky, for all his seeming nonchalance, was braced and ready for the attack. He parried quickly to his left, ducking the blow and simultaneously catching Jack Ed under the chin with his elbow. Everybody in the place heard his lupine teeth smash together. Jack Ed careened into the nearest pinball machine, which set up a chorus of ringing bells.

Having temporarily dispatched Jack Ed, Lucky pivoted in time to place his right eye directly in the path of Alvin's ramming right fist. Lucky had been kicked in the head by a horse when he was twelve. The kick had knocked him cold. It hadn't hurt nearly as much as Alvin's punch.

His whole body shivered with the pain of the impact. If he'd had time to indulge it, his stomach would have rebelled by heaving up two glasses of whiskey and water. As it was, he knew he had to either get back into the fight or die at the enraged hands of Little Alvin Cagney.

Bar patrons were cheering him on, except those who feared reprisal from Alvin. Knowing all he had on his side were dexterity and speed, he lowered his head and drove his shoulder into Alvin's gut, knocking the larger man off balance.

A sudden shout warned him of Jack Ed's recovery. Spinning around, he barely had time to suck in his midsection before Jack Ed took a swipe at it with his infamous knife. He kicked the extended knife out of Jack Ed's hand, then gave him a quick chop in the Adam's apple with the edge of his hand. The ex-con toppled into a table; it crashed to the floor. Jack Ed sprawled beside it, unconscious, lying in a puddle of spilled beer and broken glass.

Lucky came around again to confront Alvin. Looking like the provoked giant in a Grimm's tale, the former linebacker was crouched in an attack stance.

"Stop this!"

The woman was out of the booth. Hands on hips, she was furiously addressing both of them, though Lucky seemed the only one aware of her. Little Alvin's eyes were red with fury. His nostrils were receding and expanding like twin bellows.

"Get out of the way or you'll get hurt!" Lucky shouted to her.

"I want this to stop. You're behaving like—"

Little Alvin, giving her no more regard than he would a pesky housefly, flicked his hand at her, catching her lip and drawing blood. She fell backward.

"You son of a bitch," Lucky snarled. Any brute who would strike a woman didn't deserve a clean fight. Swinging up his booted foot, he viciously caught the other man in the crotch.

Instantly Little Alvin was stunned motionless, seemingly held upright by the gasps that rose from the onlookers. Then he clutched the injured area and dropped to his knees, rattling glassware throughout the building. At last, eyes crossing, he went over face first into the puddle of beer beside Jack Ed.

Lucky gulped in several cleansing breaths and tentatively dabbed at his swelling eye. Stiffly he approached the woman, who was attempting to stanch her bleeding lip with a paper napkin.

"You all right?"

She flung her head up and glared at him with vivid green eyes. Lucky, expecting tears, admiration, and gushing gratitude, was startled to see naked enmity on her face.

"Thanks a lot," she said sarcastically. "You were a big help."

"Wha—"

"Lucky," the bartender called to him, "here comes the sheriff."

Lucky blew out a gust of breath as he surveyed the damage the fight had caused. Overturned tables and chairs

Chapter Two

Sheriff Patrick Bush shook his head in dismay as he observed Little Alvin and Jack Ed. Alvin was rolling from side to side, groaning and clutching his groin; Jack Ed remained blessedly unconscious.

The sheriff maneuvered the matchstick from one corner of his mouth to the other and looked up at Lucky from beneath the wide brim of his Stetson. "Now, how come you went and did that to these boys, huh?"

"Might've known I'd get blamed for it," Lucky grumbled as he plowed his fingers through his thick hair, raking it off his forehead.

The sheriff pointed toward Lucky's middle. "You hurt?"

Only then did Lucky notice that his shirt had been ripped and was hanging open. Jack Ed's knife had left a thin red arc across his stomach. "It's okay."

"Need an ambulance?"

made the place look as if it had sustained storm damage. Broken glass, spilled beer, and capsized ashtrays had left a disgusting mess on the floor where two battered bodies still lay.

And the ungrateful tart, whose honor he had stupidly defended, was mad at *him*.

Some days, no matter how hard you tried, nothing went right. Placing his hands on his hips, his head dropping forward, he muttered, "Hell."

"Hell, no." He swabbed at the trickle of blood with his tattered shirt.

"Start cleaning up this mess," the sheriff ordered his accompanying deputy. Turning to Lucky, he asked, "What happened?"

"They were coming on to her, and she didn't like it."

Bush looked at the woman, who had been standing nearby, silently fuming. She had tried to leave earlier, but had been instructed to stay put until the sheriff got around to asking her a few questions.

"You okay, ma'am?" The sheriff was looking worriedly at her lip. It was slightly swollen, but no longer bleeding. Despite the unnatural fullness, it was pulled into a tight, narrow grimace.

"I'm perfectly fine. I was perfectly fine when Sir Galahad here took it upon himself to interfere."

"Sorry," Lucky snapped, "I thought I was helping you out."

"*Helping?* You call this *helping?*" She flung her arms wide to encompass the damage done to the place. "All you did was create an unnecessary ruckus."

"That true, Lucky?" the sheriff asked.

Barely controlling his temper as he glared down at the woman, Lucky said, "Ask the witnesses."

The sheriff methodically polled the bystanders. All murmured agreement to Lucky's version of what had taken place. The woman gave each one a disdainful glare. "Am I free to go now?" she asked the sheriff.

"How'd your lip get busted, ma'am?"

"The gorilla did it," she said, nodding down at Little Alvin and corroborating Lucky's account of her injury.

"What was your business here?"

"You didn't ask what *they* were doing here," she argued, gesturing to the men surrounding her.

"I know what they were doing here," Bush replied. "Well?"

"I was having a beer," she answered curtly.

"You didn't lead these men on, did you? You know, wink, flirt, anything like that?"

She didn't deign to answer, and only stared at him with open contempt for even suggesting such a thing. In Pat Bush's estimation she didn't look like a typical bar pickup. During his twenty-year tenure as sheriff he'd broken up enough barroom brawls to recognize a troublemaking broad when he saw one.

This one wasn't typical. Her clothing wasn't provocative. Neither was her demeanor. Rather than inviting male attention, she put out vibes that said *Do Not Touch* and seemed about as approachable as a lady porcupine.

More out of curiosity than anything, he asked, "You from around here?"

"No, from out of town."

"Where 'bouts?"

"I was just passing through Milton Point," she replied evasively, "on my way to the interstate highway."

Sheriff Bush tipped his hat forward so he could scratch the back of his head beneath it. "Well, ma'am, the next time you're just passing through, find another place to have a beer, a place more suitable for ladies."

Lucky made an unflattering snorting sound, implying that he didn't believe she fit the distinction.

"I'll take that into consideration, Sheriff." She gave Lucky another chilling glare. Then, slipping the strap of her handbag over her shoulder, she headed for the door.

"You don't want to press charges for the busted lip?" Sheriff Bush called after her.

"I only want to get out of here." Moving purposefully toward the door, she went out into the waning twilight without looking back.

Every eye in the room followed her departure. "Ungrateful bitch," Lucky muttered.

"What's that?" the sheriff asked, leaning toward Lucky.

"Nothing. Look, I gotta split, too." A glance through the dusty window showed her getting into a red compact car, one of those square, lookalike foreign numbers.

"Hold your horses, Lucky," Sheriff Bush said sternly. "I warned you last time that if you got into any more fights—"

"I didn't start this, Pat."

Though Pat Bush was acting in an official capacity, Lucky addressed him like the family friend he was, one who'd bounced Lucky on his knee when he was still in diapers. So while Lucky respected Pat's uniform, he wasn't intimidated by it.

"Who're you going to believe? Me or them?" he asked, gesturing down to the two injured men.

The red car was pulling onto the two-lane highway, its rear wheels sending up a cloud of dust. Losing his patience, Lucky again confronted Pat, who kept such a watchful eye on the Tylers that very few of their escapades got past him.

He had caught Chase and Lucky pilfering apples from the A&P supermarket when they were kids, and turning over portable toilets at a drilling site one Halloween night, and throwing up their first bottle of whiskey beneath the bleachers at the football stadium. While driving them home, he'd given them a sound lecture on the evils of drinking irresponsibly before turning them over to their daddy for parental "guidance." He'd been a pallbearer at Bud Tyler's funeral two years before, and had cried as hard as any bona fide member of the family.

"Am I under arrest or not?" Lucky asked him now.

"Get on outta here," the sheriff said gruffly. "I'll wait here till these skunks come around." He nudged Little Alvin and Jack Ed with the toe of his lizard boot. "Do something smart for a change, and stay outta their way for a day or two."

"Sure thing."

"And you'd better let your mama take a look at that cut."

"It's fine."

In a hurry, Lucky tossed a five-dollar bill on the bar to

cover the cost of his drinks and dashed out the door. He had noted that the red car had turned west onto the highway and remembered the woman saying she was headed for the interstate, which was several miles away. He vaulted into his vintage model Mustang convertible and took out after her in hot pursuit.

Miss Prissy wasn't going to get away with brushing him off like that. He'd risked his life for her. Only good fortune and well-timed quick-stepping had prevented him from getting more than the tip of Jack Ed's knife. His eye was swollen nearly shut now, and his skull felt as if a drilling bit were going through it. He would look like hell for days on account of this ungrateful redheaded chippy.

Redheaded? He thought back. *Yeah, sorta red. Dark reddish-brown. Auburn.*

How was he going to explain his battered face to his mother and Chase, who just this morning had stressed to him the importance of keeping their noses absolutely clean?

Tyler Drilling Company was faced with bankruptcy unless they could persuade the bank to let them pay only the interest on their note and roll over the principal for another six months at least. Lucky shouldn't be seen around town sporting a black eye. Who wanted to extend credit to a brawler?

"Since Daddy died," Chase had said that morning, "everybody's been skeptical that you and I can run Tyler Drilling as well as he did."

"Hell, it's not our fault the price of crude fell drastically and has stayed so damned low."

It was an argument that didn't need voicing. The faltering oil market and its disastrous effect on the Texas economy weren't of their making, but they were suffering the consequences just the same. The equipment Tyler Drilling leased out had been so inactive over the last several months, they had joked about storing it in mothballs.

The brothers were frantically trying to come up with an idea for diversification that would generate business and income. In the meantime the bank was becoming less and less tolerant of any outstanding loans. Though most of the board members were lifelong friends, they couldn't afford to be sympathetic indefinitely when so many banks across the nation, and particularly in Texas, were failing.

"The best we can do," Chase had said, "is show them our intent to pay when we can, try to drum up business, and stay out of trouble."

"That last remark is aimed at me, I guess."

Chase had smiled good-naturedly at his younger brother. "Now that I'm settled down with a loving wife, you're the tomcat of the family. You're expected to sow a few wild oats."

"Well, those days might be coming to a close," Lucky had remarked unhappily.

His brother, shrewdly picking up on the veiled reference, asked, "How *is* Susan?"

Being reminded of her now made Lucky groan. Or maybe he groaned because, when he turned the Mustang onto the entrance ramp of the interstate highway and pushed it through the forward gears, the cut across his belly pulled apart again and started to ache.

"Damn that woman," he cursed as he floorboarded the convertible in order to close the distance between him and the winking taillights he was following.

He wasn't sure what he was going to do when he actually caught her. Probably nothing more than demand an apology for the snooty way she'd treated him after he'd risked life and limb to protect her from sexual harassment.

However, thinking back on the contemptuous way she'd looked him over, as if he were a piece of bubble gum stuck to the bottom of her shoe, he figured an apology wasn't going to come easily. She didn't seem the simpering type.

Women. They were his bane and his delight. Couldn't live with them. Sure as hell couldn't live without them. He had vowed to abstain numerous times after particularly harrowing love affairs, but he knew it was a vow he'd never keep.

He loved women—their clothes, their paraphernalia, their scent. He liked their giggles and their tears, and, even though it often drove him to distraction, their persistent attention to detail. He liked everything about them that made them different from himself, from their maddening habit of paying with change in favor of breaking a bill to the way their bodies were made. In Lucky's educated opinion, about the best thing God ever created was a woman's skin.

But out of bed they were a royal pain.

Take that young divorcée in Marshall, for instance. She was a complainer, and could whine until the sound of her voice was as offensive as fingernails on a chalkboard. The only time she wasn't griping about something was when they were in bed. There, she purred.

Another of his most recent liaisons had been with a gold digger. If he didn't bring her a gift each time he saw her, any kind of trinket, she swelled up with affront. Only hours of loving could coax her back into a good mood. Then there was the clerk at the drugstore. In bed she was clever and innovative. Out of it, she wasn't as smart as the nearest fence post.

Susan Young was just the opposite. She was smart. Maybe too smart. He suspected that she was withholding sexual favors not because of any moral scruples, but because she wanted him standing at the altar all dressed up in a tuxedo and watching her as she glided down the aisle of First Methodist Church in a long white gown to the tempo of the wedding march from *Lohengrin*.

After his discouraging meeting with Chase that morning, Lucky had kept his lunch date with Susan at the home she shared with her parents. Her father, George, was CEO of the bank that held Tyler Drilling's note. They lived in an impressive home on one-and-a-half perfectly manicured acres in the center of town. As soon as the maid had cleared away the dishes, George had returned to the bank and Mrs. Young had excused herself to go upstairs, leaving Lucky alone with Susan.

He had pulled her into his arms and kissed her. Smacking his lips when they pulled apart, he sighed. "Better than Clara's strawberry shortcake," he said, referring to the sumptuous dessert the housekeeper had served.

"Sometimes I think all you want from me is kisses."

His eyes moved over her, taking in her affected pout and the small, impudent breasts that jutted against her blouse. He covered one with his hand. "That's not all I want."

Susan squirmed away from him. "Lucky Tyler, will you behave? My mama's upstairs, and Clara's in the kitchen."

"Then let's go someplace else," he suggested on a burst of inspiration. Their house was formal and somber and unpleasantly reminded him of a funeral home, which put a damper on romance. In that environment it was little wonder Susan was holding out. "I've got to drive over toward Henderson this afternoon and see a man on business. Why don't you come along?"

She declined with an adamant shake of her head. "You drive too fast. With the top down, my hair gets blown all over the place."

"Honey, with what I have in mind, it'll get messed up anyway," he drawled, pulling her against him again. This time she participated more actively in their kiss. By the time they came up for air, Lucky was hot and ready.

Then Susan had ruined his arousal by mentioning her father.

"Promise not to get mad if I tell you something." Experience had taught him that those words usually prefaced

something that was going to make him mad, but he gave her
his promise anyway. She didn't meet his eyes as she played
with the buttons on his shirt. "Daddy's worried about me
spending so much time with you."

"Why's that? He seemed polite enough at lunch."

"He's always polite. But he's still not thrilled about our
going out lately."

"Why not?"

"You *do* have a reputation, you know. A reputation that
nice girls like me aren't even supposed to know about."

"Oh yeah?" She wasn't so nice that she balked when his
hand ventured beneath her full skirt and stroked the back of
her thigh. "He asked me what your intentions were, and I
had to tell him that I honestly don't know."

He was already bored with the topic of George Young
and entranced by the expanse of smooth thigh he was caressing, but the word "intentions" set off alarms inside his
head. He withdrew his hand and took several steps away
from her. While she had his undivided attention, she drove
home her point.

"Of course, Daddy never discusses his banking business
with me," she said with a calculated batting of eyelashes,
"but I get the distinct impression that he's afraid to extend a
loan to a man who isn't settled down. You know, married
and all."

Lucky hastily consulted his wristwatch. "Gee, it's getting late. If I can't talk you into going with me, I need to get

on the road. Don't want to miss that appointment." He headed for the door.

"Lucky?"

"Hmm?"

Moving to face him and looping her arms around the back of his neck, she arched the front of her body against his. She came up on tiptoe and placed her lips near his ear, whispering, "Daddy would almost have to extend your loan if you were family, wouldn't he?"

He had given her a sick smile and beat a quick retreat, after promising to join them for dinner that evening at seven-thirty. He wasn't ready to get married. Not to Susan. Not to anybody. Not by a long shot.

He liked Susan well enough. He wanted to get her into bed, but mainly because he hadn't yet managed to. She was spoiled and would be hell to live with. Besides, he strongly suspected that she wouldn't be all that great a lover. He believed that for her, sex would be a form of currency, not pleasure.

He liked his women willing, active, and enjoying the tumble as much as he did. Damned if he wanted a wife who swapped him favor for favor, or one who withheld bedroom privileges until she got her way.

No, he hoped Susan Young wasn't holding her breath until he got down on bended knee and asked for her hand in marriage. She would turn blue in the face before that ever happened.

And as soon as he could get to a phone, he would need to call and cancel their dinner date. She would be upset, but he sure as hell couldn't show up at the Youngs' dinner table with his face looking the way it did.

"Women," he muttered with disgust as he took the exit ramp behind the saucy red compact.

clerk who rang up his purchases. He bought a pint bottle of whiskey, a tin of aspirin, and a raw steak. Because the gray meat was turning green around the edges, it had been marked down. It was unfit for human consumption, but that wasn't what he had in mind anyway.

"Does the other guy look better or worse?" the curious clerk asked.

Lucky gave him a lopsided grin. "He looks okay, but he feels a hell of a lot worse."

Returning to his car, he slumped in the white leather seat behind the wheel, uncapped the bottle, and washed down three aspirins with his first swig of whiskey. He had just un-wrapped the smelly steak when he saw the woman emerge from the restaurant. Because he had been anticipating how good it was going to feel to place the cool meat on his throbbing eye, he was cursing beneath his breath when he reached for the car door handle, prepared to open it.

He paused, however, when she walked down the side-walk and entered the check-in office of the motel. Within a few minutes she came out with a room key.

Lucky waited until she had backed out and driven her car around the corner before following her. He rounded the building just in time to see her entering a room on the ground floor about midway along the west wing of the motel.

Things were looking up, he thought with satisfaction as he pulled his Mustang into a parking slot. He preferred their confrontation to be private. That was why he hadn't

Chapter Three

Lucky pulled into the paved parking lot about ninety seconds behind the woman. The roadside complex comprised a U-shaped, two-story motel, a restaurant boasting the best chicken-fried steak in the state—which he seriously doubted—a gas station with dozens of pumps, and a combination liquor and convenience store.

She had gone into the restaurant. Through the plate-glass window Lucky watched a waitress show her to a table. In a short while she was brought what appeared to be a club sandwich. How could she think of food? He felt like hell. Eating was out of the question.

Easing himself out of his car and keeping away from the window so she wouldn't see him, he limped toward the convenience store.

"What happened to you, buddy? Get hit by a Mack truck?"

"Something like that," Lucky replied to the cheerful

followed her into the restaurant. Unwittingly she was playing right into his hands.

Pocketing his car keys in his jeans, and taking the steak, aspirin, and whiskey with him, he sauntered toward the door she had just closed behind her and knocked.

He could envision her pausing in whatever she was doing and looking curiously at the door before moving toward it cautiously. He grinned into the peephole. "You might just as well open the door. I know you recognize me."

The door was jerked open. She looked as volatile as a rocket about to launch. "What are you doing here?"

"Well," he drawled, "I was following you, and this is where you ended up, so here I am."

"*Why* were you following me?"

"Because you've got something I want."

At first taken aback, she then regarded him closely. Her wariness was immensely satisfying. She wasn't as tough as she wanted everybody to think. Still, her voice was haughty enough when she asked, "And what might that be?"

"An apology. Can I come in?"

Again his answer threw her off guard, so she didn't initially react when he moved toward the door. However, when his foot stepped on the threshold, she braced a hand against his chest. "No! You cannot come in. Do you think I'm crazy?"

"Could be. Why else would you come into the place all by yourself?"

"What place?"

He glanced down at her hand splayed across his sternum. She hastily dropped it.

"The *place*. The bar where I courageously defended your honor this afternoon."

"My honor didn't need defending."

"It would have if Little Alvin had got his slimy paws on you."

"That weaselly little man?"

"No, that's Jack Ed. Jack Ed Patterson. Little Alvin is the one you called a gorilla. See, they call him Little Alvin because—"

"This is all very interesting, but I just want to forget it. Rest assured that there wasn't a snowball's chance in hell of them getting their 'slimy paws' on me. I had the situation under control."

"Is that right?" he asked, giving her a smile that said he didn't believe her for a minute, but he admired her spunk.

"That's right. Now, if you'll please excuse—"

"Uh-uh." He flattened his hand against the door she was about to shut in his face. "I don't have my apology yet."

"All right," she said irritably, shoving back a handful of auburn hair he wouldn't mind having a handful of himself. "I apologize for . . . for . . ."

"For not thanking me properly for rescuing you."

Gritting her teeth, she emphasized each word. "For not thanking you properly for rescuing me."

Propping his shoulder against the doorjamb, he squinted

at her. "Wonder how come I don't think you really mean that?"

"Oh, I do. I truly do. From the bottom of my little ol' heart." Resting her right hand on the left side of her chest, she fluttered her eyelashes as she made a pledge. "If I ever get hit on in a bar again, you'll be the first one I call to defend me. I'll even recommend you to my fragile, feminine friends. How's that for gratitude?"

Ignoring her sarcasm, he raised his hand and touched the corner of her mouth with the tip of his index finger. "Your lip is bleeding again."

Turning her back on him, she rushed into the room and bent over the dresser top to check her reflection in the mirror. "It is not!" When she turned back around, Lucky was standing inside the closed door with his back to it, grinning like a hungry alley cat who'd just spotted a trapped mouse.

She drew herself up straight and said in an overly calm voice, "You don't want to do this. I'm warning you that I'm capable of defending myself. I'll raise such a hue and cry, I'll bring this building down. I know how to use physical force. I'll—"

Lucky started laughing. "What did you think I had in mind, ravishing you? All I want to do is hear a sincere apology from you, then I'll be on my way. In the meantime I'm going to borrow your bed for a minute."

Setting the whiskey, aspirin, and packaged steak on the nightstand, he hopped on one foot while pulling off his boot, then got rid of the other one the same way. He stretched out on the bed and piled both pillows against the headboard, sighing with relief as his head sank into them.

"If you don't get out of here this instant," she shouted angrily, "I'll call the management! I'll call the police!"

"Will you quiet down, please? My head's pounding. And whatever happened to all that self-defense you were threatening me with?" Removing the steak from its Styrofoam tray, he laid it against his battered eye. "If you'll bring the glasses over, I'll share my whiskey with you."

"I don't want any of your whiskey!"

"Fine. But could you please bring me a glass?"

"All right, if you won't leave, I will."

She marched toward the door and yanked it open. A jangling sound brought her head around. Her car keys were dangling from the end of Lucky's finger. "Not yet, Miss . . . uh, what's your name?"

"Go to hell!" she yelled, slamming the door closed again.

"Hmm. Named after your mother or father?"

"Give me my keys." She thrust out her hand.

"Not until you apologize. While I'm waiting, how about that glass?" He nodded toward the dresser where an ice bucket and two glasses were wrapped in sterile paper.

"If you want a glass, you can get it yourself."

"Okay." He sighed. But when he tried to sit up, the skin across his stomach stretched and the knife wound reopened. Wincing, he fell back onto the pillows. When his hand came away from reflexively touching the area, it was stained with fresh blood.

She gave a soft cry and quickly moved to the side of the bed. "You really are hurt."

"Did you think I was faking it?" Lucky was smiling, but his lips were pale and taut. "And I rarely go around in a shirt that's been sliced to ribbons."

"I . . . I didn't think . . ." she foundered. "Shouldn't you go to the hospital?"

"It'll be okay once it closes and stays closed."

Bending over him, she raised the hem of his ripped shirt. The extent of the cut made her gasp. It wasn't deep, but it arced from beneath his left breast to the waistband of his jeans on his right side. In places his tawny body hair was clotted with dried blood. The thin red line was seeping.

"This might get infected if it's not seen to." The resolution on her face barely had time to register with him before she said, "Better take off your shirt."

He hesitated, because in order to remove his shirt, he'd have to set aside her keys. She sensed the reason for his hesitation and said with asperity, "I wouldn't desert a man who is broken and bleeding."

Lucky dropped her keys on the nightstand, undid his shirt buttons, and eased up far enough to pull the fabric off his wide shoulders. She assisted him, negligently tossing the tattered garment to the floor and focusing only on his wound. "That wretched little man," she said, shuddering.

"Jack Ed? Yeah, he's a real scumbag. I'm relieved to know your flirtation with him wasn't anything serious."

"I wasn't flirting, and you know it," she said crossly. Leaving the bed, she went into the adjoining bathroom. A moment later she was back with a washcloth soaked in warm water. Nudging his hip with hers, she sat down on the bed beside him and applied the cloth to the cut. He sucked in a sharp breath.

"Does it hurt?" she asked in a gentle tone.

"Dumb question."

"I'm sorry, but it really should be cleaned. Lord only knows where that knife has been."

"I wouldn't even want to hazard a guess."

Before, he had been too angry at her to concede what a looker she was. Now he did. She wore her dark auburn hair shoulder length and loose, and probably tried to control its natural tendency to wave. Green eyes were now surveying his wound sympathetically, but he knew firsthand those eyes could be as frigid as a brass doorknob in January.

Her lean face had well-defined cheekbones, but a mouth with a soft, full lower lip. As a connoisseur, with vast experience of lips, he recognized them right off as extremely kissable. Her plush lower lip was a dead giveaway that this was a woman with a sensual nature.

That was probably something else she tried to control. She certainly tried repressing it with tailored clothing that didn't quite conceal a noteworthy figure. Not voluptuous. Not model-skinny either. Somewhere in between.

Slender but curved. Spectacular legs. He couldn't wait to see her out of her suit jacket, with nothing covering her breasts except the silk blouse she was wearing beneath the jacket.

First things first, however. He was assured of success, but this woman was going to be an exciting challenge, something rare that didn't come along every day. Hell, he'd never had anybody exactly like her. Rules of the game might have to be adjusted as he went along.

"What's your name?"

She raised deep forest-green eyes to his. "D-D-Dovey."

" 'D-D-Dovey'?"

"That's right," she snapped defensively. "What's wrong with it?"

"Nothing. I just hadn't noticed you stuttering before. Or has the sight of my bare chest made you develop a speech impediment?" He suddenly wanted her face nuzzling in his chest hair. Badly.

"Hardly, Mr.—?"

"Lucky."

"Mr. Lucky?"

"No, I'm Lucky."

"Why is that?"

"I mean my name is Lucky. Lucky Tyler."

"Oh. Well, I assure you the sight of your bare chest leaves me cold, Mr. Tyler."

He didn't believe her, and the smile that tilted up one corner of his mouth said so. "Call me Lucky."

She reached for the bottle of whiskey on the nightstand and raised it in salute. "Well, Lucky, your luck just ran out."

"Huh?"

"Hold your breath." Before he could draw a sufficient one, she tipped the bottle and drizzled the liquor over the cut.

He blasted the four walls with words unfit to be spoken aloud, much less shouted. "Oh God, oh hell, oh—"

"Your language isn't becoming to a gentleman, Mr. Tyler."

"I'm gonna murder you. Stop pouring that stuff— Agh!"

"You're acting like a big baby."

"What the hell are you trying to do, scald me?"

"Kill the germs."

"Damn! It's killing *me*. Do something. Blow on it."

"That only causes germs to spread."

"Blow on it!"

She bent her head over his middle and blew gently along the cut. Her breath fanned his skin and cooled the stinging whiskey in the open wound. Droplets of it had collected in the satiny stripe of hair beneath his navel. Rivulets trickled beneath the waistband of his jeans. She blotted at them with her fingertips; then, without thinking, licked the liquor off her own skin. When she realized what she'd done, she sprang upright. "Better now?" she asked huskily.

When Lucky's blue eyes connected with hers, it was like completing an electric circuit. The atmosphere crackled.

Matching her husky tone of voice, he said, "Yeah, much better. But warn me next time, okay?"

"I think that'll be enough to prevent any infection."

"I'd rather have risked infection. Although," he added in a low voice, "having you blow on me was worth it."

Because that flustered her, she raised her militant shield again. "Your eye looks terrible." The steak was now lying on the pillow where it had tumbled when she surprised him with her whiskey disinfectant. She picked it up by her thumb and index finger, holding it at arm's length. "This thing stinks to high heaven." Returning it to the Styrofoam tray, she rewrapped it in its plastic covering and tossed it into the trash can. "Stay where you are. I'll go get some ice."

Taking the plastic bucket with her, she left the room. Lucky liked the rear view of her too. Nice calves, nice bottom. If he didn't feel so bad . . .

But he did. During the fight, a rush of adrenaline had prevented him from feeling every punch. Now he was beginning to bruise in places he didn't even remember getting struck. His head was throbbing. He was feeling woozy, too, probably from the combination of the aspirin and that last shot of whiskey.

So while the thought of thawing Dovey was enthralling, he had to be content to fantasize. He certainly wasn't in any physical condition to take it further.

She returned with a bucket of ice, and filled the center of another washcloth with a scoop of small cubes. Knotting the corners over it, she brought it back to the bed and gently laid the makeshift ice pack on his eye.

"Thanks," he mumbled sleepily, realizing that he might be a little drunk as well as hurt. Her hand felt so comforting and cool, the way his mother's always had whenever he was sick with fever. He captured Dovey's hand with his and pressed it against his hot cheek.

She withdrew it and, in a schoolmarm's voice, said, "You can stay only until the swelling goes down."

A crude comeback sprang into his mind, but he resisted saying it. She wouldn't appreciate the bawdy comment right now. Besides, a reference to another swollen member of his body might be the very thing that would cause her to kick him out.

"I don't think I'll be going anywhere a-tall tonight," he said. "I feel like hell. This is all I want to do. Lie here. Real still and quiet."

"Good idea. You can have this room. I'll get another one."

"No!" he cried, dislodging his ice pack. "I mean, I can't take your room."

"Don't worry about it. It's paid for. It's the least I can do after what you did for me this afternoon."

"I'm not worried about finances," he said sharply. "But at least now you're admitting that I rescued you from Little Alvin and Jack Ed."

"Just so you could put in your bid for me?"

"Huh?"

"You 'rescued' me from them, but you're no better. Your technique simply has more polish."

"You think . . . think . . ." he stammered. "You think I want to share this room so— Come on, lady. Do I look like I'm in any condition to have sex?"

He followed her gaze down the length of his body and realized that he *did* look as if he could have sex. He was shirtless, bootless, and sprawled in the center of a motel bed. His recent vivid fantasies had created a bulge behind his fly that he hoped she wouldn't notice.

Immediately he fell back against the pillows with a great moan, not entirely faked, and replaced the ice pack against his eye. Waving his hand weakly, he said, "Go on. Do whatever you want. I'll be okay."

He watched through slitted eyes as she picked up her purse and headed for the door. "All my injuries are probably external," he mumbled just as she placed her hand on the doorknob.

She turned. "You think you might have internal injuries?"

"How the hell do I know? I'm no doctor." He placed a tentative hand on his side. "I thought I felt some swelling here, but it's probably nothing. Don't let me hold you up any longer."

Putting aside her handbag, she returned to the bed and gingerly sat down on the edge of the mattress. It was difficult for Lucky to look pained rather than give in to a complacent smile. He expected her to murmur sympathetically. Instead, she said nothing.

When he turned his good eye to her, she was staring down at him skeptically. "If you're conning me—"

"I told you to leave. Go on. Get another room. If I need you, I can call you through the motel operator."

She pulled her full lower lip through her teeth several times, which caused Lucky to groan for an entirely different reason. "Where do you feel the swelling?"

She had missed her calling. She could have been a great vaudevillian straight man. She was feeding him cues to which he had terrific punch lines. Again resisting the impulse to say aloud what he was thinking, he took her hand and guided it to his side.

"Around here somewhere. Feel anything out of the ordinary?"

She probed the taut skin for several moments, working her fingers up and down his side from waist to armpit. "No. I don't think so."

"That's a relief." She withdrew her hand. "I just hope no ribs are broken," he said hastily.

"Which side?"

"Same one."

Her fingers walked up his ribs cautiously, gradually feeling their way, until they reached the hair-matted, curved muscle of his chest. It might have been the feel of his chest or of his distended nipple that caused her to pull her hand back quickly.

"You're probably just stiff and sore," she said.

You can say that again, Dovey. "Good."

"But maybe I'd better not leave you alone," she surprised him by saying.

"Oh gee, that's terrific."

"I wouldn't want your death by internal bleeding on my conscience the rest of my life."

He frowned, saying drolly, "I wouldn't be crazy about that either." Removing the dripping ice pack from his eye, he handed it to her. "I'm drowning from this thing."

She took it away, and a few minutes later brought him a replacement. "Maybe by the time this one soaks through, your eye won't hurt so bad."

"Maybe. Could I please have a glass now? I think I'm entitled to a drink."

She poured each of them one. He tossed his back. It made him cough, but the liquor spread an anesthetizing heat through his midsection that made his discomfort more bearable.

Dovey went into the bathroom to add water to her cup, then dropped in a couple of ice cubes and sipped the drink like a lady. He remembered the glass she'd poured her beer into. Classy broad, he concluded muzzily. Not pretty in the soft, cushy, baby-doll sense, but certainly striking. She would turn heads on any sidewalk in the world.

Through a mist of pain and booze, he watched her remove her jacket and drape it over the back of a chair. Just as
he'd thought—high, round breasts.

Oh yes, quite a looker was Dovey. But that wasn't all.
She looked like a woman who knew her own mind and
wasn't afraid to speak it. Levelheaded.

So what the hell had she been doing in the place?

He drifted off while puzzling through the question.

Chapter Four

The room was in total darkness when Lucky awakened. He tentatively opened one eye, after trying to open both reminded him that his right one would be black-and-blue and swollen shut for a day or two.

There was artificial light coming from the parking lot through the crack between the drape and the wall. It was still night, but he didn't care enough about the time to try to check his wristwatch.

His muscles were cramped from lying in one position for so long. He stretched, wincing and moaning slightly, and attempted to turn onto his side. When he did, his knee bumped into another.

He mumbled, "Dovey?"

"Hmm?"

He often awakened in the middle of the night with a woman in bed with him, so he responded as he usually did, by curving his arm across her and pulling her closer. Their knees automatically straightened, bringing their bodies together. Her hair brushed his cheek, and he turned his face into it, inhaling its honeysuckle scent and mindlessly kissing the strands that fell across his lips.

That felt so good, so right, he pressed his lips against her smooth forehead, then let them trail over her brows to her eyelids. Her lashes feathered his lips. He kissed her cheekbone, her nose, then her mouth.

Reflexively she drew back. "Lucky?" she whispered.

"Yes, baby," he whispered back before seeking her mouth again.

Her lips separated slowly. His tongue slipped between them. The inside of her mouth was delicious, but unfamiliar. He didn't remember ever kissing her. He explored deeply, leisurely, thoroughly, before biting gently on her lower lip—*that* he remembered craving to do—and sucking it into his mouth.

Making a small sound, she stirred against him restlessly. Her hands landed softly on his bare chest. As his tongue glided across her lower lip, he felt her fingers combing through his chest hair and her nails gently raking his skin. It struck him as odd that all her responses were so tinged with shyness. Then her fingertips glazed his turgid nipple, and his analysis ended. He had no thoughts beyond the taste and feel of her.

Rolling partially atop her, he lowered his hand to her breast, but became confused when he encountered clothing. It was silk, true, but what was she doing in bed with clothes on? It suddenly occurred to him that he was still wearing his jeans. No wonder he was so uncomfortable.

Befuddled, he reached for the top button of his fly. When it and the others were undone, he eased himself free, sighing with relief. The pressure had been almost painful.

Using his personal system of radar, his lips found her neck in the darkness and began dusting it with kisses as his hand moved to her breast again. The barriers of buttons and her brassiere clasp didn't deter him in the slightest, and soon his hand was filled with warm, malleable woman flesh.

Now we're back on track, he thought.

Everything was as it should be. Her breast was full and soft as his hand gently reshaped it. When he drew his thumb across the tip, it responded as he expected, becoming tight and hard. He sandwiched it between two of his fingers, enjoying the small wanting sounds that issued from her throat each time he applied the merest pressure to her nipple.

Eventually he took it into his mouth. His tongue circled and stroked and teased until her hands were clutching at his shoulders and his own body was burning like a furnace.

"Sweet, sweet," he whispered as he moved aside her garments and hungrily kissed her other breast. "So sweet."

Hose. Pantyhose, he thought miserably when his hand slipped beneath her skirt to caress her knee. He despised the things, and wished he had five minutes alone with the sadist who had invented them.

Moments later, however, he was delighted when his

stroking hand discovered satiny smooth skin above her stockings. Apparently she was delighted, too, because at the touch of his hand against her inner bare thighs, her back arched off the bed and she released a staggering sigh of pleasure . . . and mounting need.

He tracked the lacy suspenders up to the V of her thighs. Inside her panties there were myriad textures to explore and fluid heat to drown in—he wanted badly to taste her. But he didn't have the time. His body was compelling him to hurry.

Had he ever had this woman before? No. He couldn't have. Otherwise he wouldn't be experiencing the contradictory urges to hurry and to loiter. He resented the time it took to fumble in his pocket for the foil-wrapped prophylactic and slip it on. The same desire that compelled him to position himself in the cradle of her thighs was prompting him to wait.

But he was already there, hard and hot and pressing toward sweet deliverance. And she was moist and soft and snug and sweet.

He heard himself say hoarsely, "I'm sorry. I'm sorry," but he wasn't even sure why.

All he was sure of was that he could never get enough of this woman. He gathered her beneath him, stroked her expertly, then buried himself deep within the sheath of her body. He wanted to sustain the pleasure, but it was so immense, he was helpless to stop the climax that claimed him, shook him, drained him.

It left him depleted. Totally spent, he laid his head on her breasts, making kissing motions against her nipples with his lips and lightly grinding his stubble-rough cheek against the soft mounds. Tenderly he palmed the nest of damp curls at the top of her thighs.

She touched his hair. Feeling the caress, he smiled. Then he drifted off to sleep again, wondering why, since it had been so damned good, he'd never made love to her before.

No matter how much Lucky drank the night before or how late he caroused, he always woke up at daybreak. His father had had chores for Chase and him to do before school. The habit of waking up early had been ingrained in him.

When he first became conscious, his head felt like a bowling ball stuffed with cotton, which might roll off his shoulders at any moment. It was an effort just to open his one functioning eye. Nevertheless, when he saw through the slit that he was alone in the bed, it came fully open. Stretching out his hand, he touched the imprint her body had left.

Grunting and groaning from the whipping he'd taken from Little Alvin, he sat up, switched on the nightstand lamp, and groggily surveyed the room. No suit jacket. No keys. No purse. No sign that she'd ever been there.

Maybe she'd just gone out for coffee.

He swung his feet to the floor, swearing liberally as pain rocketed up through the soles of his feet straight to the crown of his head. Dizzily he stood up and hobbled toward the window. With as dramatic a flourish as his battered body would allow, he flung back the drapes, startling a middle-aged couple walking down the breezeway.

The woman uttered an astonished gasp and hastily averted her eyes from Lucky's semi-nudity. Her husband gave him a reproving look before taking his offended wife's elbow and ushering her toward their camper parked at the curb.

Lucky automatically began rebuttoning his jeans while staring hard at the empty space where Dovey's red car had been parked the evening before.

"Damn!"

She had made a clean getaway. Sneaked out like a thief. That thought sent his hand plunging into his jeans pockets for his money clip. He found it intact.

She *had* been here, hadn't she? She wasn't just a figment of his imagination? No, of course not. He couldn't have imagined eyes that unusual shade of green. If he had dreamed her, it had been one hell of a dream. One he wished he could have every night and never wake up from.

He limped into the bathroom and switched on the un-kind, unflattering fluorescent light. The image the mirror over the basin threw back at him belonged in a monster movie. Not only was his hair a mess and his lower jaw dark with stubble, but, as predicted, his eye was black-and-blue and swollen almost shut. There was a bruise as big as a baseball on his shoulder, probably where he had gouged

Little Alvin's middle. The cut across his belly had closed, but was still a bright red line.

Then something incongruous caught his eye, something reflecting the blue-white glare of the fluorescent tube. He pulled a long, dark red strand of hair off his chest. It had become ensnared in his chest hair. Spurred on by that discovery, he returned to the bedroom and checked the wastepaper basket. He found what he was looking for.

Sinking down onto the bed, he held his aching head between both hands. She'd been real, all right. He hadn't imagined her. Nor had their lovemaking been a dream, except in the metaphorical sense.

Unsure whether that made him feel better or worse, he returned to the bathroom and showered. As soon as he was dressed, he left the room and got into his Mustang. He'd been negligent to leave it uncovered and unlocked all night, but thankfully it hadn't been vandalized. He drove it around the building to the office and went in to speak to the motel clerk—not the same one who had been there the evening before.

"Mornin'." His smile was almost as big as his ears. "Have some coffee."

"Good morning. Thanks." Lucky poured himself a cup from the pot brewing on a hot plate. "My name's Lucky Tyler. I spent last night in room one ten. The room was registered to a young woman."

"Yeah?" The clerk propped his elbows on the counter and leaned forward eagerly.

"Yeah. Would you please check your register for her name?"

"You don't know it?"

"Dovey something."

"Must've been some night. She do that to you?" He nodded toward Lucky's black eye and torn shirt.

"What's her name?" Lucky's tone of voice prohibited further speculation or comment.

The clerk wisely checked his files. "Smith, Mary."

"Mary?"

"M-a-r-y."

"Mary Smith?"

"That's right."

"Address?"

"Two hundred three Main Street."

"City?"

"Dallas."

"Dallas?"

"Dallas."

"Two hundred three Main Street, Dallas, Texas?"

"That's what it says."

Lucky was familiar enough with the city to know that the two-hundred block of Main Street was downtown in the heart of the commercial district. He suspected Ms. Smith of duplicity. And Smith! Mary Smith, for crying out loud. Not even very original. Where had "Dovey" come from?

"Did she give a phone number?"

"Nope."

"Car tag?"

"Nope."

"Which credit card did she use?"

"Says here she paid with cash."

Lucky swore. "Driver's license number?"

"Nope."

"Great."

"Sounds to me like the lady was covering her tracks."

"Sounds that way to me too," Lucky mumbled, his mind on where and how he might pick up her trail. "When a guest pays with cash, isn't it procedure to get some form of identification?"

"It's procedure, but, you know," the clerk said, shrugging, "we don't always do it. I mean, people traveling together get the hots, check in for a quickie, things like that. Most times they don't even stay overnight."

Knowing the clerk was right, Lucky combed back his hair with his fingers. He'd washed it with bar soap, and it was drying in a helter-skelter fashion. "What time does the other guy come on duty? The one who works this desk on the evening shift."

"Four."

Lucky tossed his empty disposable coffee cup into the wastepaper basket and ambled toward the door. "Thanks."

"You bet. Come again," the clerk called cheerfully.

Lucky shot him a withering look before he went out into

the bright, new East Texas sunlight that was just breaking over the tips of the tall pine trees and spearing through his eyeballs straight into the back of his skull.

He slipped on the sunglasses he'd left on his dashboard the day before and pointed the Mustang toward home. He would start tracing her at the place later this afternoon. Not only did she owe him an apology, but now he was due an explanation as well. In the meantime he couldn't devote the whole day to tracking her. Even though there wasn't much work to do, he and Chase felt better about business if they looked and acted busy.

The drive home would normally have taken an hour, but Lucky was anxious for more coffee and some breakfast, since he hadn't eaten the evening before. He floorboarded the Mustang, and in a little over thirty-five minutes was turning off the farm-to-market road into the lane leading to his family's home.

The narrow blacktop road was lined with pecan trees. In summer, when they were in full leaf, their branches formed a thick green canopy over the road that sunlight could barely penetrate. The only time he didn't appreciate the trees was in the fall, when his mother sent him out to pick up the crop of nuts that covered the ground. Still, the effort became worth it when the pecans showed up in homemade fudge and pies.

They raised only enough cattle to keep them in fresh beef, and stabled a few riding horses. Sage had spoiled them and turned them into pets, and they offered little challenge to hellbent riders like Chase and Lucky. As he sped past, Lucky honked at the small herd grazing on the thick grass that grew on the acreage surrounding the house.

The two-story structure was built of painted white brick, and had black shutters on the windows opening onto the deep front porch. His father had built the house when he and Chase were youngsters, but Lucky never remembered living anywhere else. When Sage came along, quite unexpectedly, another three rooms had been added on to the back side to accommodate the Tylers' growing family.

It was a handsome house, and homey. Lucky knew the day would come when he would marry and move out as his brother had two years earlier, but he dreaded thinking about it. This was home. His fondest memories were directly connected to this house.

He knew every nook and cranny of it. He knew which stairs creaked when someone stepped on them. His initials were carved on every peach tree in the orchard. He'd smoked so much of the grapevine that grew along the fence, it was a wonder there was any of it left.

He could almost recall each individual Christmas, and one particular Easter stood out in his memory because he and Chase had replaced the hard-boiled eggs his mother had dyed for Sage's Easter basket with raw ones, and had got a spanking for ruining her day.

"Oh hell."

This morning he was none too happy to see Chase's car parked in the curved drive in front of the house. It was early for him to be out. Lucky had hoped to give the swelling around his eye a few hours to go down before confronting his older brother.

Resigned to the inevitable interrogation, followed by a lecture about maturity, image, and responsibility, he parked his Mustang and loped up the front steps.

Entering the wide, airy foyer, he followed the smell of fresh coffee toward the kitchen situated in the southeast corner of the house. At this time of day the sun bathed the pale walls with butter-colored light.

"Lucky, is that you?" his mother called through the rooms.

"None other. What's for breakfast?"

He entered the kitchen and was surprised to see Tanya, Chase's wife, sitting with him at the kitchen table. Small and blond, she perfectly complemented his tall, dark brother. Lucky liked Tanya immensely, and often teased her by saying that if she ever got smart and left his brother, he had first dibs on her. That would never happen. She was devoted to Chase, which was one of the main reasons Lucky liked her so much.

When he walked in, she gave him one of her sweet smiles, which turned into open-mouthed gaping when he removed his sunglasses. His smile disfigured his face even more.

Laurie Tyler, attractive even in middle age, flattened her hand against her breasts and fell back a step when she saw Little Alvin Cagney's handiwork on her son's face.

"Good Lord, Lucky, we heard you'd been in another fight, but I didn't expect anything this bad. Did that Cagney brute do that to you?"

"Yeah, but you ought to see him," he quipped as he headed for the coffee maker and poured himself a cup.

"Where the hell have you been?"

Lucky blew on his coffee and looked at his brother through the rising steam. "Are you in another lousy mood today? It's not even time for me to be at work yet, and already you're on my case."

"Lucky, something's happened," Laurie said, laying a hand on his arm. Her eyes were a similar shade of blue, and almost as bright and youthful as her son's. Now, however, they were clouded with concern.

"Happened?"

Just then Sage came barreling through the back door. Here lately, Lucky was startled every time he saw his kid sister. She wasn't a kid any longer. Only a few weeks earlier they'd attended her graduation from the local junior college. Next fall she would be studying at the University of Texas in Austin. She no longer looked like an adolescent. She was a woman. And it seemed she'd become one overnight.

"I was in the stable and saw his car pull in," she said breathlessly, as though she'd been running. "Have you told him yet?"

"Told me what? What the hell is going on?"

"We had a fire last night," Chase said grimly.

"A fire?"

"In the main garage." Chase left his chair and went to the coffee maker to pour himself a refill.

"Jeez." Lucky suddenly felt nauseous. "I'm sorry I wasn't available. How bad was it? Nobody was hurt, I hope."

"No, nobody was hurt, but the building burned to the ground. Everything in it was destroyed."

Lucky dropped into a chair and dragged his fingers through his hair again. What Chase had told him was inconceivable, but the grim faces surrounding him confirmed that it was the truth. "How'd it start? What time did all this happen? Did they get it put out?"

"The first alarm came in about two-thirty. They fought the blaze till around four. It's out now. Hell of a mess though."

Chase returned to his chair across from his brother. Once he was seated, Tanya rested her hand on his thigh in a silent, wifely gesture of sympathy and support.

"Thank God we've kept up our insurance premiums," Lucky remarked. "As hard as it's been to rake together the cash for—" He broke off when he intercepted the exchanged looks that went around the kitchen. "There's more?"

Chase sighed and regretfully nodded his head. Laurie approached Lucky's chair as though she might, at a moment's notice, have to render maternal consolation. Tanya stared down at her hands.

Sage was the one who finally spoke up. "There's a whole lot more. Who's going to tell him?"

"Be quiet, Sage."

"But, Mother, he's got to find out sooner or later."

"Sage!"

"You're suspected of setting it, Lucky."

Chapter Five

Lucky's gaze swung toward his brother.

"Did she say 'setting it'? The fire was set?"

"It was arson. No question."

"And somebody thinks I set it?" Lucky snorted incredulously. "Why in hell would I do that?"

"For the insurance money."

Lucky's disbelieving gaze moved around the room, lighting briefly on all four faces, which were watching him closely to gauge his reaction. "What is this, April Fool's Day? This is a joke, right?"

"I wish to hell it was."

Chase leaned forward and folded his hands around his coffee mug as though he wanted to strangle it. His light gray eyes shone fervently in his strong face. He was as handsome as his younger brother, but in a different way. While Lucky had the reckless nonchalance of a cowboy of a century ago, Chase had a compelling intensity about him.

"I couldn't believe Pat would even suggest such a thing," he said.

"Pat! Sheriff Pat Bush? Our *friend*?" Lucky exclaimed. "I saw him yesterday evening at the place."

"And that was the last anybody saw of you."

"We heard all about your fight with Little Alvin and that scummy Patterson character," Sage said. "People said you were fighting over a woman."

"Exaggeration. They were moving in on her. She didn't welcome their advances. All I did was step in." He gave them a condensed version of the altercation. "You would have done the same thing, Chase."

"I don't know," he remarked dubiously. "It would take some kind of woman to get me in a tussle with those two."

Lucky sidestepped the reference to Dovey. "Jack Ed got me with his knife. That's how my shirt got ripped."

"He came at you with a knife!"

"Don't worry, Mother, it was nothing. Just a scratch. See?" He raised his bloodstained shirt, but the sight of the long, arcing cut across his middle didn't relieve Laurie.

"Did you have it seen to?"

"In a manner of speaking," he grumbled, remembering how badly it had stung when Dovey poured whiskey along the length of the cut.

"Who was the woman you fought over?" Sage asked. Her brothers' escapades with women had always been a source of fascination to her. "What happened to her?"

"Sage, I don't think that's significant," her mother said sharply. "Don't you have something else to do?"

"Nothing this interesting."

Lucky was unmindful of their conversation. He was watching his brother and gleaning from Chase's somber expression that the situation wasn't only interesting, but critical.

"Pat can't possibly believe that I started a fire, especially in one of our own garages," Lucky said, shaking his head to deny the preposterous allegation.

"No, but he warned me that the feds might."

"The feds? What the hell have the feds got to do with it?"

"Interstate commerce. Over fifty thousand dollars' worth of damage," Chase said, citing the criteria. "A fire at Tyler Drilling qualifies for an investigation by the Bureau of Alcohol, Tobacco and Firearms. Pat stuck his neck out by warning me what to expect. It doesn't look good, Lucky. We're in hock at the bank. Since Grandad Tyler started the company, business has never been as bad as it is now. Each piece of equipment is insured to the hilt." He shrugged. "To their way of thinking, it smells to high heaven."

"But to anybody who knows us, it's crazy."

"I hope so."

"Why me?"

"Because you're the family hothead," Sage supplied, much to the consternation of everyone else present.

"So far," Chase said after directing a stern frown toward his sister, "we can't account for your whereabouts after you left the place last night, Lucky."

"And that automatically makes me a suspect for arson?" he cried.

"It's ridiculous, but that's what we're up against. We've got no problem if we provide ironclad alibis. The first thing they asked me is where I was last night. I was home in bed with Tanya. She confirmed that."

"Do you think they believed me?" she asked.

Chase smiled at her. "You couldn't lie convincingly if you had to." He dropped a light kiss on the tip of her nose. Then, giving his brother his attention again, he said, "You didn't spend the night at home. They're going to ask where you were all night."

Lucky cleared his throat, sat up straighter, and cast a guilty glance toward his mother. Sensing his discomfort, she resorted to her standard cure-all. "Would you like something to eat?"

"Please, ma'am." His mother could make him feel humble and ashamed when no one else could. She turned toward the stove and began preparing him a meal of eggs and bacon.

"Naturally the first person we called this morning was

Susan Young," Sage informed him, dropping into a vacant chair at the table.

"Oh terrific," Lucky mumbled.

"She was mighty p.o.'d when—"

"Sage," Laurie said warningly.

"I didn't say it. I just used the initials."

"It still sounds so unladylike."

Rolling her eyes, Sage turned back to her brother. "Susan wasn't too thrilled to find out you'd stood her up at dinner to go tomcatting."

Lucky muttered a curse, careful to prevent his mother from hearing it over the sizzling sound of frying bacon. "I forgot to call her."

"Well," Sage said importantly, twirling a tawny strand of hair around her finger, "you'd better be thinking up a sympathetic story, because she is steamed." Pinching her light brown eyes into narrow slits, she made a sound like steam escaping the tight lid of a kettle.

"We have much more to worry about than Susan's jealousy," Chase said.

"Besides," Laurie added, carrying a plate of food to the table, "Lucky's affairs are no concern of yours, young lady."

Lucky attacked the plate of food. After a moment he realized that the sound of his fork scraping across his plate was the only noise in the kitchen. He raised his head to find them all staring at him expectantly.

"What?" he asked, lifting his shoulders in a slight shrug.

"What?" Chase repeated more loudly. "We're waiting for you to tell us where you were, so that if the badge-toting guys in the dark suits and opaque sunglasses come asking, we'll have something to tell them."

Lucky glanced back down into his plate. The food no longer looked appetizing. "I, uh, spent the night with a lady."

Sage snorted as derisively as Lucky had when Pat Bush had called Dovey that. "A lady. Right."

"What lady?" Chase asked.

"Does it matter?"

"Ordinarily not. This time it does."

Lucky gnawed on his lower lip. "Y'all don't know her."

"Is she from out of town?"

"Yeah. She was the, uh, the one Little Alvin was hitting on."

"You picked up a stranger at the place and spent the night with her?"

"Well, who are you to get so righteous, Chase?" Lucky shouted, suddenly angry. "Before Tanya came along, you weren't above doing the same damned thing."

"But not on the night one of our buildings was torched!" his brother shouted right back.

Tanya intervened. "Chase, Lucky didn't know what was going to happen last night."

"Thanks, Tanya," Lucky said with an injured air.

"Oh, Lucky, that's such a foolhardy thing to do these days."

"I'm not stupid, Mother. I took the necessary precautions."

Sage grinned, her eyes twinkling wickedly. "Aren't you the good Boy Scout. Do they give merit badges for taking 'the necessary precautions'?"

"Shut up, brat," Lucky growled.

Thanks to Tanya, Chase had reined in his temper. Sparks often flew between the two brothers, but the grudges lasted no longer than the temper flare-ups. "Okay, all you need to do to clear yourself is get the woman to vouch for you."

Lucky scratched his stubble-covered jaw. "That might be tricky."

"Why? When she tells the authorities that you spent all night with her, they can eliminate you as a suspect and start tracking down the real arsonist."

Chase, believing their dilemma had been resolved, started to stand. Lucky pointed him back into his chair. "There's a slight problem with that, Chase."

Slowly Chase lowered himself back into his seat. "What problem? How slight?"

"I, uh, don't know her name."

"You don't know her name?"

"No, sir."

This day would go down in Lucky's private annals as one of the worst in his life. His head still felt as though it had a flock of industrious woodpeckers living in it. His vision was blurry in the eye that had connected with Little Alvin's fist. Every muscle in his body was screaming at the abuse it had taken. He was suspected of setting a destructive fire to his place of business. Everybody, including members of his own family, was treating him like a leper because he'd spent the night with a woman he couldn't identify.

And he had thought yesterday was bad.

According to their expressions, neither the sheriff and his deputies nor the federal investigators believed him any more than his family had that morning.

One of the investigators turned to Pat Bush. "You didn't get her name at the scene of the fight?"

Pat harrumphed. "No. It occurred to me later that I had failed to, but there didn't seem any need for it at the time. She wasn't interested in pressing charges."

A skeptical "hmm" was the agent's only response. He turned to Lucky again. "Didn't you think to ask her her name?"

"Sure. She told me it was Dovey, but—"

"Would you spell that please?" The request was made by another agent taking notes in a spiral notebook.

"Spell what?"

"Dovey."

Lucky blew out a breath of exasperation and looked

toward Pat Bush for assistance. The sheriff's terse nod merely indicated that Lucky should go along with the ridiculous request. Lucky succinctly spelled the name. "At least I think that's right. She registered at the motel as Mary Smith of Dallas." He snapped his fingers and raised his head hopefully. "Listen, the clerk there will remember me."

"He does. We already checked."

Earlier Lucky had provided the investigators with the name of the motel on the interstate, located about midway between Milton Point and Dallas. "Then why the hell are you still busy with me? If I've been cleared, why aren't you out looking for the guy who burned our building?"

"The clerk could only testify to seeing you this morning," the senior agent informed him. "He didn't see you going into the room last evening. And even if he had, he couldn't vouch for your staying there all night without leaving."

Lucky glanced at his brother, who was leaning against a battered army-green metal filing cabinet in Sheriff Bush's office. Lucky shook his head as though to say that this was a lost cause, and he was tired of playing cops and robbers by their rules.

Meeting the agent's cold stare, he arrogantly asked, "Do you have any physical evidence connecting me with this crime?"

The agent shifted from one wing-tipped shoe to the other. "The exact cause of the fire hasn't yet been ascertained."

"Do you have anything linking me with that fire?" Lucky repeated.

Backed against a wall, the agent replied, "No."

"Then I'm leaving." Lucky came out of his straight chair and headed for the door.

"You'll be under surveillance, so don't even try to leave town."

"Go to hell," Chase told the agent on his way out, following his brother. "Lucky, wait up!" he called as he emerged from the courthouse a few seconds later. Lucky was already at the curb in front of the official building with his hand on the door handle of his car. He waited for Chase to catch up with him.

"Can you believe this crap?" he asked, angrily jutting his chin toward the first-floor office where the interrogation had taken place.

"It's crap, but they're serious."

"You're telling me," Lucky muttered. "The hair on the back of my neck is standing on end. I had enough of jail the night we got arrested for knocking down old man Bledsoe's fence. It was an accident! How the hell were we supposed to know his thoroughbred mare was in that pasture? Or that she was in season?"

Chase peered up at his brother from beneath his heavy brows, and, together, they started laughing. "He went nuts when that jackass raced in there and mounted her. Remember how he was jumping up and down and yelling? Never laughed so hard in my life."

"We stopped laughing the next morning when Daddy came to pick us up. As I recall, he didn't say a single word all the way home."

"The drive from town to home never seemed so long," Chase agreed. "We had all that time to fret about what our punishment was going to be. But you know," he said with a mischievous wink, "that mare's offspring was the ugliest damn mule I've ever seen."

They laughed together for several moments, remembering. Eventually, however, Lucky sighed as he slid his hands into the rear pockets of his jeans and leaned against the fender of his car.

"We've had our brushes with the law, but never anything like this, Chase. They haven't got a damn thing on me, so why am I so scared?"

"Because being accused of a felony like arson is scary. You'd be a fool if you weren't."

"In deference to the ladies in our family, I hope it doesn't become necessary, but a DNA-matching test would prove that I had sex in that motel room."

Chase winced.

"Right, it makes me squeamish too," Lucky said bitterly. "But even though lab tests would prove that *I* was there, they wouldn't prove that *she* was, or that I didn't leave at some point during the night, drive back here, set the fire, then return by daylight and make certain the clerk remembered me."

"The only one who can establish your alibi is the woman." There was an implied question mark at the end of Chase's statement.

Lucky looked chagrined. "It wasn't as sordid as it sounds."

"Sounds pretty sordid, little brother."

"Yeah, I know," he admitted on a sigh. "Look, I chased her down because she hightailed it out of the place without even thanking me for saving her from those two slimeballs. Made me mad as hell. I caught up with her at that motel and talked myself into her room.

"By that time, I was feeling the effects of Little Alvin's punches. A few shots of whiskey had made me woozy. I lay down on the bed. I think she got to feeling sorry for me then, 'cause she cleaned the knife wound and got an ice pack for my eye. I fell asleep."

"I thought you had sex."

Again Lucky looked at something besides his brother's inquisitive face. "Sometime during the night I woke up," he said quietly. "She has this really incredible dark red hair. And her skin is so creamy, translucent, you know." Suddenly he yanked himself out of the self-imposed trance and frowned at his own susceptibility. "She was classy, Chase."

"Then what was she doing causing a stir at the place?"

"Damned if I know. But she wasn't your ordinary barfly, willing to grant sexual favors in exchange for a few drinks. Not a party girl. If anything, she was uptight and . . . and . . . bossy. The kind of woman I usually avoid like the plague."

"You'd have done well to avoid this one."

Lucky was reluctant to agree. For some reason he hadn't yet had time to analyze, he wasn't sorry about the night before. Nor did he think it would be his only encounter with Dovey, or Mary, or whatever her name was.

The consequences of their night together had got him into more trouble than he'd ever been in. That was saying a lot. But inexplicably he didn't regret it. At least not as much as the situation warranted.

"So what's your plan?"

Chase's question pulled him out of his reverie. "To find her."

"How, if you don't even know her name?"

"I'll start at the place and work forward from there."

"Well, good luck."

"Thanks."

"If you need me, you know where to find me."

"I'll be glad to help you and the boys with the cleanup," Lucky offered.

"We can't start until they've finished their investigation. God knows how long that'll take, because they're sifting everything through a fine-tooth comb, looking for evidence. All you could do is what I'm doing, and that's standing around twiddling my thumbs.

"No, your time will be better spent clearing yourself.

The insurance company isn't going to pay us one red cent until we've been exonerated." Chase squinted into the sunlight. "Any ideas who might've done this?"

"My first guess would be Little Alvin and Jack Ed."

"Revenge?" Chase chuckled. "From what I've heard, you made Little Alvin sorry he was a man."

"He deserved it."

"Pat thought he might be a suspect, too, but he's got a whole tribe of Cagneys swearing that Little Alvin was playing cards with his brothers all night."

"With an ice pack on his crotch?"

Again Chase laughed. "Remind me never to get you really mad at me." His expression turned serious again. "Which I'm likely to do by saying this."

"What?"

"It might be a good idea to go see Susan Young. Her daddy's already called me twice today demanding to know what's going on."

Lucky swore. "You're right. I'd better get over there and smooth her ruffled feathers. We need to stay in good with the bank now more than ever. Besides, I truly did do Susan dirty by standing her up last night."

"And making it public knowledge that you spent the night with another woman." Chase eyed him speculatively. "She must've been some redhead."

Refusing to be baited, Lucky settled into the driver's seat of his convertible and turned on the motor. "In ten or

twenty years we'll be laughing about this the way we did
about Bledsoe's mule out of his thoroughbred mare."

She padded into her kitchen and opened the refrigerator.
As expected, it was empty. One of the hazards of living
alone was a bare cupboard. It was less of a hassle to do
without food than to prepare meals for one.

The thought of going grocery shopping on her return to
Dallas early that morning hadn't been very appealing.
Instead, she'd driven straight to her condo and, after taking
a long, hot bath to relieve her soreness, had gone to bed.

There she had stayed most of the day, telling herself she
needed the rest after her ordeal. Actually she had dreaded
the moment of accountability to her conscience for what
she had allowed to happen the night before.

There was about half a cup of skim milk in the bottom
of the carton. Sniffing it first to make sure it hadn't soured,
she poured it over a bowl of Rice Krispies. They were so
old, they barely had any snap, crackle, or pop left in them,
but they would line her empty stomach.

She went into the living room, curled into a corner of
her sofa, and reached for the TV's remote control. It was
too late for the soaps and too early for the evening news.
She was left with reruns of syndicated sitcoms.

In one, the male lead had dark blond hair and a mischievous, I'm-up-to-no-good grin. She quickly switched to another channel, unwilling to have anything remind her of

the stranger she had spent the night with . . . been intimate with . . . made love with.

The thought of it made her hand shake so badly she had to set the bowl of soggy cereal on the coffee table or risk spilling it. She covered her face with her cupped palms. "Dear Lord," she moaned. What in the world had caused her to behave so irresponsibly?

Sure, she could list a million excuses, starting with her emotional state yesterday and ending with the gifted way that man had kissed her when he drew her out of her dark loneliness and despair into his strong, warm arms.

"Don't think about it," she admonished herself, picking up the transmitter again and vigorously punching through the channel selector.

She had derided women who were susceptible to handsome faces, brawny physiques, and glib come-ons. She had thought she was smarter than that. She was far too intelligent, discerning, and discriminatory to fall for a pelt of gold-tipped chest hair and heavily lashed sky-blue eyes. His charm had melted her morals and feminist resolve. Lucky Tyler had succeeded in touching her where no other man ever had—her heart, her body.

Mortification made her whimper. To stifle the sound, she pressed her fingertips against her lips, then explored them tentatively, feeling the whisker burns. She had discovered those sweetly chafed places on her breasts, too, during her bath. They had brought back tantalizing sensations that swirled through her midsection.

When she had tried to sleep, squeezing her eyes tightly shut, she recalled the tugging motions his mouth had made on her nipples. Her lower body contracted with a pleasurable ache whenever she remembered that first, sweet piercing of her flesh, then the strength and depth of his penetration.

Now she crossed her arms over her lower body and bent at the waist in the hopes of eradicating both the mental and physical recollections. They made her hot. They made her want. They made her ashamed.

Lust for a total stranger? In a cheap roadside motel? What a stupid thing to have done! How reckless! How wrong! How unlike her!

But she hadn't exactly been herself yesterday, had she? Before one could pass judgment on her, one would have to understand the state of mind she'd been in twenty-four hours ago. One would have had to experience the same cruel rejection, traverse the same bleak corridors, feel the lingering sense of suffocation even after escaping those corridors.

One would have to experience the sense of futility and defeat she had felt upon learning that sometimes even making supreme sacrifices wasn't enough. Having reached the devastating realization that someone's love, or even gratitude, couldn't be won, she'd been at her lowest.

Enter Lucky Tyler—as gorgeous as an angel and as delightful as one of the devil's favored children. He'd been funny and sexy and needful.

Perhaps that had been his main attraction. He had needed her, fundamentally and simply, a man needing a woman. She had desperately needed to be needed. She had responded to his need as much as she had to the transporting caresses of his hands and mouth.

"Oh sure. Right," she muttered to herself impatiently. Rationalizations came a dime a dozen, and none was going to be sufficient justification. It had been a foolhardy thing to do, but she had done it. Now she had to come to terms with it.

Thank heaven she had had the foresight to use a phony name and pay in cash when she checked into the motel. He couldn't trace her. Could he? Had she overlooked something? In her haste to leave that morning had she left behind a clue that would lead him to her if he had a mind to find her?

No, she was almost sure she hadn't. As far as Mr. Lucky Tyler was concerned, she was totally anonymous. Only she would ever know about last night, and she would forget it.

"Starting now," she averred as she left the sofa. Giving the belt of her robe a swift tug, she moved into the spare bedroom that served as her office at home. She switched on the desk lamp and her word processor, slid on a pair of reading glasses, and sat down in front of the terminal.

Work had always been her salvation. Other people re-
lied on alcohol, drugs, sports, sex, to forget their troubles
and make life livable. For her—except for last night—
nothing worked like work itself. Besides, she had a dead-
line.

Once she got a clear screen on her computer, she referred to her notes and began typing. Her fingers flew over
the keyboard. She wrote well into the night, as though the
devil were after her . . . and rapidly closing in.

Chapter Six

Susan Young descended the stairs slowly, looking wounded, her mouth sulky. From her appearance, Lucky guessed that she had been crying most of the day, or at least wanted him to think so. Her eyes were watery and red. The tip of her nose had been rubbed raw by tissues. Her complexion was splotchy.

In lieu of hello she said, "Mama advised me not to speak to you." She halted on the third stair from the bottom.

Seeing a potential way out of this unwelcome encounter, Lucky asked solicitously, "Would another time be better?"

"No, it would not!" she replied tartly. "We've got a lot to talk about, Mr. Tyler."

Drat, he thought.

She descended the last three steps and swept past him into the formal living room. It smelled sickeningly of furniture polish. Afternoon sunlight was shining through the windows, dappling the pale blue carpet with patterns of light and shadow. It was a gorgeous day. Lucky wished he were outside enjoying it. He wished he were anywhere but where he was—in the Youngs' formidable living room, being subjected to Susan's hurt, chastising glare.

"Well?" she demanded imperiously the moment she had closed the double doors.

"What can I say? I did something terribly stupid, and got caught."

His demeanor was self-deprecating. He'd learned early on that the only way to handle a woman scorned was to assume all the blame and be as honest as was prudent. There had been those occasions, however, when honesty had been suspended because either castration or his life was at stake. He didn't think Susan's wrath had reached that level of danger . . . yet.

Looking properly contrite, he said, "Can you forgive me for standing you up last night, Susan?"

"Of course I can forgive you for that, although it was a tacky thing to do."

"It certainly was. I owe your parents an apology for it, too."

"We held up dinner for an hour and a half waiting on you. We didn't eat until nine."

That would have been about the time Dovey was blowing on his knife wound, cooling his flesh, and inflaming his passions with her soft breath. Damn, it had felt delicious, stirring his body hair, fanning his skin.

"I have no excuse for what I did."

The apologetic words were beginning to stick in his craw. If not for her father's position at the bank, he'd tell this spoiled brat that he wasn't accountable to her for whom he slept with, and that would be the last she'd see of him.

He was anxious to begin his search for Dovey, and was only going through the motions of stroking Susan because it was politic to do so. He hadn't needed Chase to spell that out to him. However, he rued the day he'd asked Susan for that first date several months ago. He wanted to lash out, reminding her that he'd made her no promises, certainly had made no commitments, and that whoever he slept with, whether it be one woman or a dozen, was no business of hers. Only a reminder of the loan payment coming due forced him to squelch his mounting temper.

Hoping that she wouldn't catch the hopefulness in his voice, he said, "You'd be better off refusing to see me again."

She gazed thoughtfully at the floor for a moment, then raised her shimmering eyes to his. "I've got a more forgiving spirit than that."

Damn! Women loved to be forgiving. It vested them with enormous power over the forgiven. They thrived on the poor sucker's guilt like carrion birds on a carcass, picking it clean.

"I can forgive you for skipping dinner with us," she said. "I can even overlook your engaging in a barroom brawl, because I know you have a volatile nature. I'll admit that's part of the attraction you hold over me.

"What I'm finding very difficult to forgive . . ." Here, her lower lip began to quiver and her voice became tremulous. "You've humiliated me in front of the whole town. They say you couldn't be located when the fire broke out last night because you were with a whore."

"She wasn't a whore." The application of that word to Dovey made him so angry that he was startled by the intensity of his emotion.

"Then who was she?"

"A stranger. I never saw her before last night, but she wasn't a whore." Susan was watching him shrewdly. He softened his tone. "Look, Susan, I didn't set out to sleep with anybody last night. It just sorta happened."

That was the truth. He hadn't wormed his way into Dovey's motel room with the intention of making love to her. He'd only wanted to provoke her as badly as he'd been provoked, get his apology, and then leave.

It wasn't entirely his fault that it hadn't quite worked out that way. He'd been half-asleep when he reached for her. She'd been fragrant and warm and soft and compliant. Her damp lips had been mobile beneath his, her body responsive. He couldn't be blamed for how naturally his body had responded to the sexy stimuli. Of course, it had been conditioned to respond.

". . . understand. You left here yesterday aroused. Right?"

He blinked to clear his vision, and tried to grasp what Susan had been saying. "Uh, right."

She approached him, gazing up at him through spiky,

wet lashes. Her mouth looked vulnerable. But for all her tears and sniveling, Lucky knew she was about as helpless as a barracuda.

"So you took your lust for me and spent it on a willing woman," she whispered, laying her hands on his chest. "I guess I should be flattered, though I'm still very hurt. The thought of you in bed with another woman makes me just want to die."

She looked closer to killing than dying. Her eyes, no longer bright with tears, were alight with malice. "But I can understand how when a man gets so aroused, he's got to do something about it or explode."

She came up on tiptoes and brushed a kiss across his lips. "I know the feeling, Lucky. Don't you think I want you, too? Don't you know that the only reason I'm saving myself is so our wedding night will be special? Don't you know how badly I want to make love to you right now?"

True, he had been mildly aroused when he left Susan after lunch the day before, but he had gotten hotter than that watching certain commercials on TV. His arousal then had been like a mild head cold when compared to the feverish delirium he'd experienced when he'd entered Dovey's giving body.

"Look, Susan," he said irritably, "all this talk about weddings—"

She laid her fingers against his lips. "Shh. I know we can't make an announcement until you get out of the mess you're in. Poor baby." She reached up with the intention of running her fingers through his hair. He snapped his head back and caught her hand before she could touch him.

"Announcement?"

"The announcement of our engagement, silly," she said, playfully tapping his chest. "And just so we can get this misunderstanding about the fire settled quickly, and to prove how much I love you, I'll say that you spent last night with me."

"*What?*"

"It's all over town that you woke up alone this morning and can't produce your alibi. So I'll say that I was with you. Mama and Daddy will have a fit, of course, but they'll accept our sleeping together as inevitable if I have an engagement ring on my finger. They'll be so happy we're finally making it official, they'll overlook our one night of sin."

She was either downright conniving or entertaining delusions. Either way, she was dangerous and had to be handled with kid gloves.

"What makes you think anyone will believe you if you come forward now and say I was with you last night?"

"I'll say that, at first, you wouldn't let me be your alibi because of what it would mean to my reputation. I insisted until you capitulated."

"Looks like you've got it figured from every angle."

"Ever since I heard you couldn't produce that *woman*, it's all I've thought about. I'll say I sneaked out after Mama and Daddy had gone to bed. Actually I did go out last night."

"What for?"

"I was so upset, I drove around looking for you, searching for your car at all the places you usually go. When I didn't find you, I came home. My parents never knew I went out. I could say that we met and spent the night together, passionately making love." She gave him an impish grin. "Which isn't a bad idea."

"That's not how you felt about it yesterday," he reminded her.

"A girl can change her mind."

She was as easy to see through as the Waterford vase on the mantel. She had turned him down yesterday, so he had slaked his lust with someone else. That was untenable to a conceited woman like Susan, especially when everybody in town knew about it. She had devised a way to save face and, at the same time, lasso him for good. Even though her lie would clear him, it was self-serving.

"You'd be willing to lie to save my hide? You'd do that for me?"

"And for me," she admitted. "I want you, Lucky Tyler. And I mean to have you, no matter what it takes."

Whether I want you or not, he thought.

"I'll call Sheriff Bush right now," she said suddenly, turning toward the phone.

Lucky's arm shot out. He caught her hand. "I can't let you do it, Susan."

Her bright smile dimmed. "Why not?"

"You could get in a lot of trouble by lying to federal investigators. I can't let you do that for me."

"I want to."

"And I appreciate it," he said with what he hoped sounded like sincerity. He could see, however, that she wasn't convinced. "Let me think about it. You know, Susan, perjury is a serious offense. I need to think it through before letting you do it."

Her smile returned, but there was a definite edge to her voice when she said, "Don't mull it over too long. I'm not sure how long my offer will stand."

What a conniving little bitch, he thought. Forcing himself to smile, he said, "You're something, you know that? When I first met you, I had no idea there was so much complexity beneath the surface."

"Whatever I want I go after. It's as simple as that."

God help the man she got her hooks into. Lucky silently vowed then and there that it wasn't going to be him. "Well, I've got a lot of thinking to do, Susan, so I'd better be going."

"Must you?" she whined.

"I must."

"Take this with you." She looped her arms around his neck, pulled his head down, and ground a wet, suggestive kiss upon his mouth. When she eventually pulled back, she whispered, "Maybe that'll make you think twice before going to another woman."

Lucky endured the kiss because he recognized the difference between feminine wiles and real treachery. Susan

Young exercised the latter. She would resort even to black-mail to get him to marry her.

As he went down her front walk, having made good a temporary escape, he wiped the remains of her kiss off his lips with the back of his hand.

It hadn't repelled him. It certainly hadn't stirred his ardor. It had left him feeling totally indifferent to it, some-thing that hadn't happened since he first discovered kissing under the tutelage of the preacher's daughter behind the choir loft of the First Baptist Church during vacation Bible school.

Between that first titillating mouth-to-mouth experi-mentation and Susan's ardent kiss, what had happened to immunize him against the effects?

A taste of Dovey, that's what.

The bartender groaned when he looked up and saw Lucky straddling one of the barstools. "I'd just as soon you take your business somewhere else tonight, Lucky, and give the place a rest."

"Shut up and draw me a beer. I'm not looking for trouble."

"As I recall," the bartender drawled, "that's what you said yesterday." He slid the beer in front of his customer.

Lucky sipped. "I'm in a jam."

"So I hear. It's all over town that you need an alibi for last night."

"Jeez, the grapevine around here is faster and more accurate than a fax machine."

The bartender's face split into a wide grin. "If you don't like the gossip, you shouldn't keep such a—what do they call it?—a high profile. Plain folks are fascinated by the activities of local celebrities."

Lucky cursed and took another sip of his drink. "You remember anything about that woman?"

"Not as much as you do, I'd bet," he chortled. His sappy grin faded beneath Lucky's warning glare. "Uh, well, let's see, natural redhead, wasn't she? And I don't mean anything lewd about that," he added hastily.

"Dark auburn hair, yeah."

" 'Bout so tall." He marked a spot near his shoulder, holding his hand parallel to the ground.

"I don't need a physical description," Lucky said impatiently. "Do you remember anything significant about her?"

"Significant?"

"Did you see her pull into the parking lot?"

The bartender searched his memory. "I think so. Came from the south, I believe."

"The south." Lucky assimilated that. "If you saw which direction she came from, you must've noticed her car."

"Sure did."

"What kind was it?"

"Red," he announced proudly, glad to be of service.

"I know it was red," Lucky growled. "But what kind?"

"Foreign, I think."

"Make?" The bartender shook his head. "Model?" Again Lucky received a negative answer.

"Great," he muttered, his highball glass at his lips.

"Well, you followed her, Lucky. If you didn't notice, how could you expect me to?"

"Don't worry about it. I just thought you might've. You know I don't recognize the make and model of any car manufactured after 1970. Like you, I just remember hers being compact and red. Maybe under hypnosis I could remember the license number, but I've been racking my brain all day, and can't come up with a single digit or letter of it."

"Uh-oh."

"What?" Lucky swiveled around on the stool, following the direction of the bartender's worried gaze. Coming through the door were Little Alvin and Jack Ed. They paused momentarily when they spotted Lucky. An expectant hush fell over the bar. Then the duo ambled toward a corner booth and sat down.

"Two beers each. Right now," Little Alvin bellowed to the bartender.

He uncapped four long necks and set them on a cork-lined tray. "I'll take it," Lucky offered congenially, sliding off his stool.

"Now, look, Lucky, I just got this place—"

"No trouble. Swear." Lucky gave the man his most

winning grin. Carrying the tray, he moved across the gritty hardwood floor toward the corner booth. Little Alvin and Jack Ed followed his progress with hooded eyes.

When he reached their booth, he set the tray on the table. "Drink up, boys."

Jack Ed sneered and suggested that Lucky do something to himself that was anatomically impossible.

Ignoring him, Lucky addressed Alvin. "Glad to see you can walk upright today."

Little Alvin glowered at him menacingly. "You'll get yours, you cocky bastard."

"Alvin, Alvin," Lucky said, shaking his head sorrowfully, "is that any way to talk to me after I've brought a peace offering?" He nodded down at the beer Alvin had almost guzzled in one swallow. "I put your drinks on my tab. Felt like it was the least I could do after our misunderstanding yesterday."

"You can't smooth-talk your way past me. Beat it."

The features of Lucky's face pulled taut. "Listen you—"

"Lucky!"

Chase's voice cut through the smoky, dense atmosphere. From the corner of his eye Lucky saw his brother weaving through the tables to join him at the end of Little Alvin's booth.

"Don't start anything else, for godsake," Chase warned him in a terse whisper.

"Well, if it ain't the rodeo star," Jack Ed said snidely, "come to save his little brother from another beatin'."

"That's not the way I heard it, Patterson."

Chase had been a bull rider in his youth. He'd won a considerable amount of prize money, and had made quite a name for himself on the rodeo circuit. But the danger associated with the sport had always worried his parents. They were greatly relieved when he became engaged to Tanya and retired from it with all his faculties and all his body parts still intact.

Chase didn't let Jack Ed provoke him. His unexpected appearance had had a calming effect on Lucky, who said now, "I just wanted to ask them some questions."

"I wouldn't mind asking them a few myself," Chase said.

Feeling expansive, Little Alvin propped his arms, which were as big around as pythons, along the back cushion of the booth. "About what?"

"About the fire last night in our garage," Chase said.

"About the woman who was in here yesterday," Lucky replied tightly.

Alvin responded to Lucky's question. "Heard she ran out on you," he said with a malicious grin. "Too bad. Always suspected that your success with the fairer sex was overrated." Jack Ed thought that was hilarious. His giggle was almost as high-pitched as a woman's.

"I don't believe for a minute you were playing cards with your brothers all night," Chase said.

"Did she ever give you her name?" Lucky asked, miraculously quelling the overwhelming impulse to wipe the gloating grin off Alvin's beefy face.

"You balled her and you don't even know her name?"

Lucky lunged toward the larger man. Chase grabbed him by the shoulders and pulled him back. "Let's get out of here."

"You son—"

"Let's go!" Chase dragged his younger brother backward across the lounge, with Lucky struggling every step of the way. His bootheels thumped along the floor as he dug them in, trying to get traction.

"Too bad you lost the one woman who could keep you out of jail, Tyler," Little Alvin taunted.

Lucky gnashed his teeth and let out a feral sound, straining to get loose from Chase. Chase, however, held tight. "Dammit, I'll knock you out cold myself if you don't settle down. What the hell's the matter with you?"

Once they had made it through the door, Chase slammed Lucky against the exterior wall of the building. Lucky threw off his brother's restraining hands. "You have to ask what the matter is?" he shouted. "They were right. I might go to jail."

"So what does that have to do with what went on in there?" Chase hitched his chin toward the tavern.

"I was looking for information about *her*."

"Why?"

"Why?"

"Yeah, why?" Chase settled his hands on his hips and confronted his short-tempered brother. "You've been acting just plain weird all day. I think locating this woman means more to you than providing yourself with an alibi."

"You're crazy."

"Don't call me crazy. I'm not the one picking fights with Little Alvin two days straight over the same broad."

Lucky was ready with a vehement denial that she was a "broad" when he caught himself. The protest would confirm Chase's suspicions. Belligerently he said, "Just leave me the hell alone and let me deal with this my way, okay?"

"Not okay. You're my brother. The Tylers stick together. If you're in trouble, we're all in trouble. And since you can't seem to stay out of it, you're stuck with me as your protector."

They looked away from each other, each trying to get hold of his temper. Lucky was the first to come around. "Oh hell, Chase, you know I'm glad you intervened. At least in hindsight I am. I couldn't afford to get my other eye pulverized."

Chase grinned and slapped him between the shoulder blades. "Follow me to our house. Mother's been so upset all day, Tanya offered to cook dinner for everybody."

"Her famous pot roast?" Lucky asked hopefully.

"That's right."

"Hmm," he sighed, smacking his lips. "Tell me—brother to brother—is she as good in the bedroom as she is in the kitchen?"

"You'll die wondering." He shoved Lucky in the direction

of his car. "And we'll both die at her hands if we spoil her dinner by being late."

Lucky was tailing Chase's car into town when it occurred to him that his return to the place had gained him nothing. He was no closer to locating Dovey than he'd been when he first woke up that morning, finding her side of their shared bed empty.

Chapter Seven

"Know what Susan Young is spreading all over town?"

In response to his sister's question, Lucky grunted with a lack of interest from behind his morning newspaper.

"That y'all are getting married." Sage popped a fat, juicy strawberry into her mouth and chewed with sybaritic enthusiasm. "I've gotta tell you that if you marry the snotty bitch, I'm disowning this family for good."

"Promises, promises." Lucky lowered the newspaper to take a sip of breakfast coffee. "You've been threatening to disown the family ever since Chase and I hid your first bra in the freezer. So far, we've had no such luck." He retreated from her glare by burying his head in the newspaper again.

Sage slathered cream cheese onto a slice of low-calorie whole-wheat toast. "Well, are you?" she mumbled around the first creamy bite.

"Am I what?"

"Marrying Susan Young."

Lucky laid aside the newspaper. "Get serious. While you're at it, get your older brother some more coffee."

"Haven't you ever heard of women's lib?" she asked crossly.

"Sure, I've heard of it."

Picking up his mug, he wagged it back and forth while smiling at her guilelessly. With a theatrical sigh she fetched the carafe from the coffee maker and refilled his mug.

"Thanks, brat."

"You're welcome." She slid back into her chair. "All kidding aside, Lucky, if Susan Young has got it in her head that you're her prospective groom, you'd better be shopping for a diamond ring. When she doesn't get her way, she causes trouble."

"What more can she do? I'm already in trouble up to my gills."

A week had passed since his fight with Little Alvin. It had been the longest week of Lucky's life. The area around his right eye had run the gamut of rainbow colors, and was still a sick, jaundiced yellow. The red line across his abdomen had faded to pink.

Together with Sheriff's Department deputies and insurance investigators, federal agents continued to sift through the debris left by the fire. Due to the unfavorable publicity, Tyler Drilling's client list had dropped drastically. The note payment was coming due in less than a month, and what little revenue had been trickling in had stopped altogether. Bankruptcy seemed unavoidable. There wasn't even a glimmer of light on the dark horizon.

"One good thing," Chase had optimistically remarked the evening before, "they haven't turned up any hard evidence against you. Without something that places you on the scene at the time of the fire, they haven't got a case. It's all circumstantial."

"That's a plus from the legal standpoint," Lucky had said. "But until the insurance company is satisfied that we were victims and not perpetrators, they aren't going to honor our claim. So, while I won't go to jail, we're still in hock."

They desperately needed verification of Lucky's whereabouts that night in order to eliminate him as an arson suspect. They desperately needed Dovey.

Thus far, however, his attempts to track her had led him nowhere except in circles. Daily he polled the patrons of the place, asking everyone who had witnessed the incident with Little Alvin and Jack Ed if he remembered anything about the elusive woman or her car. All the men remembered that she was a good-looking redhead. Beyond that, he had come up empty-handed.

A return trip to the motel to speak with the night clerk hadn't been productive either. The man remembered her, all right, but she had registered as Mary Smith, paid for one night with cash, and that was all he knew. The convenience-store clerk who had sold him the whiskey, steak, and aspirin had never seen him with Dovey.

"She couldn't have just vanished off the face of the earth!" Lucky had exclaimed to his family after his discouraging interview with the motel clerk. "She's somewhere, walking around, breathing, going about her business, eating, sleeping, having no idea of the havoc she's created in my life."

"Maybe not," Tanya had suggested.

He had stopped pacing and looked toward his sister-in-law. "What do you mean?"

"Maybe she's read about the fire in the newspaper and realizes she's your alibi, but hasn't come forward because she doesn't want to become involved."

"That's a possibility," Chase had said.

Because it irked Lucky to think so, he dismissed that worry. "It's only been in the local papers, and she said she wasn't from around here when Pat asked her. I think she was telling the truth when she gave Dallas as her address. She looked like a city girl."

But for the next several days he had logged a lot of miles on his Mustang, driving to neighboring communities and tracking down all the Mary Smiths on the lists of registered voters. He found several. One was eighty-two; one was middle-aged, blind, and living with her elderly parents; one was a coed. All were dead ends.

He considered combing Dallas, seeking out every Mary Smith, but he knew it would be a time-consuming chore and, in the end, an exercise in futility. Tongue-in-cheek, and very cleverly, she had used that fictitious name. Why? She hadn't known then that he would eventually be looking for her to serve as his alibi in a criminal investigation.

"Lucky, are you listening to me?"

Sage's impatient inquiry brought him back to the present. "Hmm? What? You were saying something about Susan?"

"I was saying that she's a spiteful bitch."

"How do you know so much about her? She was several classes ahead of you."

"But her legend lived on even after I got to high school."

"Legend?"

"Her meanness was legendary."

"Example?"

"She was so envious when one of her classmates was named Homecoming queen instead of her that she circulated the rumor that the girl had herpes."

Lucky gave a spontaneous burst of laughter.

"It's not funny!" Sage exclaimed. "The gossip ruined that girl's reputation and made the remainder of her days at high school pure hell. That's not all."

Propping her arm on the edge of the table, she leaned toward him. "Susan was named first alternate on the girls' varsity basketball team. The next morning, when the newly named team was suiting up for practice, a bank of lockers fell over on top of one of the girls and broke her arm. Susan was standing on the other side of the lockers."

"And it's believed that she pushed it over?"

"That's right."

"Sage, that's crazy. It's silly high school back-biting and nothing more."

She shook her head adamantly. "I don't think so. Some of my friends who have stayed in town and know Susan through clubs and such say she's a viper. If she wants to be the president of this or that, she'll do anything to get elected." Her eyes narrowed. "Now she's set her sights on you. She wants to be Mrs. Lucky Tyler."

"I wonder why?" he asked, honestly puzzled by Susan's fixation on him. They'd gone out steadily for the last few months, had shared a few laughs, smooched a little, but he'd never even breathed the word "marriage."

"That's easy," Sage replied to his rhetorically phrased question. "No other woman has had the distinction of marrying you. Those who keep notches on their bedposts prize the one you make. You're the local stud. It would be a feather in Susan's cap to break you."

"Local stud, huh?" he drawled, leaning far back in his chair.

"Will you stop with the conceit," Sage said with annoyance. "A man with gray chest hairs has nothing to be conceited about."

"Gray!" he exclaimed. He bent his head down to investigate the wedge of chest showing through his parted robe. "Those are blond."

"Susan's determination to have you, coupled with this nonsense about the fire, worries me."

"Those lighter hairs are blond, Sage."

"Will you forget the hairs! I was only kidding, for heaven's sake."

His sister's concern touched him, but he couldn't take her warnings about Susan seriously. Granted, the woman was a schemer. She was unquestionably selfish, and could have taught the green-eyed monster a thing or two about jealousy. But he hadn't exactly been born yesterday. Susan would have to practice some mighty refined chicanery to outsmart him.

Reaching across the table, he patted the top of Sage's unruly blond head. "Don't worry, brat. I wrote the book on how to take care of women."

"You don't—"

Her protest was cut short when a knock sounded on the back door. "That'll be Mother," she said, leaving her chair to open the door. "Oh, Pat!" she said with surprise. "We were expecting Mother back from an early trip to the produce stand down the highway."

"Mornin', Sage, Lucky." Pat stepped into the kitchen and removed his Stetson. "Got an extra cup of coffee?"

"Sure."

He thanked Sage for the cup of black coffee she poured him, blew on it, removed the matchstick from his mouth and sipped it, then stared into it for several silent moments. The coffee was a tactical delay.

If Pat had come in an official capacity to impart bad news, Lucky figured he would make it as easy on him as possible. "Why don't you tell us why you came out this morning, Pat?"

The family friend lowered himself into a chair across the table from Lucky. After glancing uncomfortably around the kitchen, he finally looked directly at the younger man. "Have you bought anything at Talbert's Hardware Store recently?"

"Talbert's Hardware?" he repeated with puzzlement. "Oh wait, yeah. I bought some railroad flares a few weeks back."

Pat Bush blew out a gust of air. "Where were you storing them?"

"In the—" Lucky refocused sharply on the sheriff. "In the garage that burned."

"They, uh, they've determined that the fire was caused by gasoline touched off by railroad flares. Nothing fancy. Simplest thing in the world."

Sage sank into the chair beside her brother and laid her hand on his shoulder. He plowed his fingers through his hair and held it back by settling his forehead in his palm. It was unnecessary for Pat to explain the significance of that find.

"I shouldn't be telling you this, Lucky," Pat said. "I'm here as a friend, not a law officer. Just thought I ought to warn you. They're preparing a case against you. Looks like now they might have enough probable cause to arrest you."

When the sheriff stood to go, Lucky roused himself. "Thanks, Pat. I know you're going out on a limb to tell me."

"When your daddy was dying, I promised him I'd look after Laurie and you kids. That pledge is more important to me than the oath I took when they pinned this badge on me." He moved toward the door. "Sage," he said, replacing his hat before stepping outside and pulling the door closed.

"Lucky," she said miserably, "what are you going to do?"

"Damned if I know."

In a fit of temper he hissed a vile word and banged his fist on the table. The blow rattled every piece of glass in the kitchen, even though it was somewhat cushioned by the newspaper he'd left lying open on the table.

His jaw grinding with aggravation, he stared down at the newsprint sightlessly, periodically spiking his enraged silence with a curse.

Suddenly his whole body tensed. He grabbed up the newspaper and held it close to his face. "I'll be damned," he whispered in awe. He laughed shortly. Then he laughed loudly.

In one motion he dropped the newspaper and stood up, sending his chair over backward and crashing to the floor. He left the kitchen at a run. By the time Sage caught up with him, he was taking the stairs two at a time.

"Lucky, what in the world . . . ?"

He disappeared at the top of the landing. She ran up the stairs after him and flung open the door to his bedroom. He was hiking a pair of jeans up over his hips.

"What's the matter? What are you doing? Where are you going?"

He pushed her aside on his way out of the room, wearing only his jeans, carrying a shirt and his boots with him.

She charged down the stairs after him. "Lucky, slow down! Tell me. What's going on?"

He was already vaulting into his open convertible when she bounded across the front porch after him. "Tell everybody I'll be back by nightfall!" he shouted over the roar of the Mustang's revving engine. "By then I'll be able to clear this whole thing up."

"Here's that reference material you wanted from the morgue." The gofer dumped a mountain of files on her desk.

Holding the last bite of her lunch sandwich between her teeth, she frowned at the extent of the research material and mumbled, "Thanks for nothing."

"Anything else?"

She bit into the sandwich, chewed, swallowed, then blotted her mouth with a paper napkin. "Coffee. From a fresh pot, please," she called after the young man as he dashed off. He was a college student who interned at the newspaper three afternoons a week. He hadn't been there long enough to become jaded. He was still starstruck and eager to please.

Her position as editorial columnist entitled her to a glass cubicle of an office, but the constant noise and hustle from the sprawling city room filtered into it. To anyone unaccustomed to newspaper offices, the incessant noise and motion would have been distracting. She didn't even notice.

That's why she wasn't attuned to the change in the climate that occurred when a man stepped off the elevator and asked for her.

His appearance had an immediate effect on the women in the room. It wasn't only that he was tall, slim-hipped, blond, blue-eyed, and handsome. It was the purposeful way he crossed the city room, as though it were a battlefield on which he'd just won the day and was about to collect the spoils of war. Even the most feminist among them secretly fantasized about being part of those spoils.

He also attracted the curiosity of the men, who, to a man, were glad they didn't have to tangle with him. It wasn't that he was of such an intimidating size, though his shoulders were broad and his chest wide. No, it was the expression on his face that was quelling. His jaw was set with inflexible resolve. His eyes were steady and unblinking; they could have been focused on a target caught in the crosshairs of a rifle sight.

He paused momentarily at the door of the small glass enclosure and stared in at the woman, who was bent over an open file on her desk, absorbed by its contents. A stillness had fallen over the city room. Computer keyboards stood silent. Ringing phones went unanswered.

The woman in the glass office seemed the only one unmindful of his presence as she absently dragged a pencil through her loose dark auburn hair. Without glancing up from her reading matter, she waved her hand to signal him inside.

"Just set it there on the desk," she said. "It needs to cool off anyway."

He moved forward to stand at the edge of her littered desk. She was aware of him, but it was several moments before she realized that he wasn't the college student in the Argyle socks there to deliver a cup of fresh coffee. Raising her head, she gazed up at him through the wide lenses of her eyeglasses.

She dropped the pencil. Her lips parted. She uttered a small gasp.

"My God."

"Not quite," he said. "Lucky Tyler."

Chapter Eight

She swallowed visibly, but said nothing.

"While we're on the subject of names," Lucky said, "what's yours? Dovey? Or Mary Smith? Or is it *Devon Haines?*"

He slapped a newspaper, open to her column, onto her desk.

Her eyes lowered to the page, then swung back up to him. "Ordinarily they don't print my picture with my by-line. I didn't know they were going to do it with this article, or I would have asked them not to." Her voice was little more than a hoarse croak.

"I'm glad they did. I've been looking for you ever since you skipped out on me. For the second time."

The initial shock of seeing him was wearing off; she was gradually regaining her composure. She assumed the haughty demeanor that set Lucky's teeth on edge. He recognized the expression she had worn while telling him off for interfering with her struggle with Little Alvin.

"If I had wanted you to know my name, I would have given it to you." She threw her shoulders back, shaking her hair off them. "Obviously I preferred to remain anonymous, Mr. Tyler, so if you would be so kind—"

" 'Kind' be damned," he interrupted. "If you want to talk here and let all the spectators in on it, fine." With a jerking motion of his head he indicated the city room behind him. "Or would you rather talk in private? Either way is okay with me . . . Dovey."

He deliberately slurred the last word, letting her know the extent of his anger, and that, if necessary, he had no qualms about discussing in front of an audience what had transpired in the motel room. Obviously she did. Her face paled.

"I suppose I could spare you a moment."

"Smart choice."

He took her arm the minute she rounded the desk and escorted her through the city room, where the onlookers made no pretense of subtlety. Speculative conversation resumed the instant Lucky and Devon cleared the doorway.

"Here are the elevators." She feebly pointed them out when he marched past them without even slowing down.

Propelling her toward the heavy fire door marked STAIRS, he took hold of the knob and pushed it open. "This'll do." He guided her through the doorway and followed closely behind.

She spun around to confront him. "I don't know what you're doing here, or what you expect to gain by—"

"You'll know in good time. First things first."

He shoved his fingers up through her hair and cupped her head. Tipping it back, he captured her surprised lips in a fiery kiss.

Inexorably moving forward, he backed her into the wall without decreasing the pressure of his lips on hers. She strangled on her protests and ground the heels of her hands against his shoulders, trying to push him off.

"Stop!" she managed to rasp out when he came up for air.

Lucky, however, had a week's worth of pent-up frustration to expend, a week's worth of lust to slake, and he couldn't have been budged by a Sherman tank.

"I'm not finished yet."

He sealed their mouths together again, employing the technique he'd begun developing with the preacher's daughter and over the years had mastered to an enviable expertise. The pads of his fingertips pressed into her scalp, while his thumbs met beneath her chin to stroke the smoothest expanse of skin he'd ever felt except for the insides of her thighs.

She never had a chance.

Her protests grew fainter, until they no longer qualified as gargled threats, but sounded more like whimpers of arousal. She stopped resisting the thrusts of his tongue as it hungrily plumbed her mouth again and again.

His first taste of her in more than a week reawakened an appetite that had been whetted but far from satisfied. He angled his body closer to hers, sent his tongue deeper into her mouth, and tilted his hips forward, nudging the cleft of her thighs, wanting, wanting, wanting. . . .

Suddenly coming to his senses, he raised his head and smiled down at her. Gently he flicked his tongue against the corner of her lips, savoring the flavor of her kiss, and whispered, "You're the one, all right. I'd know you anywhere."

"What are you doing?"

"Trying to figure out a convenient way into your blouse." He frowned at the back buttons. "Later."

She raised a hand to her lips and touched them gingerly. "You shouldn't have kissed me like that, Mr. Tyler."

"My mother tells me I've always been guilty of doing things I shouldn't do. My conscience doesn't have a very loud speaking voice. Sometimes I don't hear it." He smiled engagingly and ducked his head for another kiss.

Devon staved him off. "Please don't."

"Why not?"

"Because I don't want you to."

"Liar."

"How dare—"

"You want it as much as I do."

Her eyes flashed like summer lightning, the kind of hot white lightning that brings no rain. She slipped around him and made a beeline for the door leading back into the corridor. Before she could pull it open, he reached beyond her shoulder and flattened his hand against it.

She executed a stiff military about-face. "I don't know what you hoped to gain by finding me, Mr. Tyler, but you're in for a disappointment. What happened last week was a fluke."

"You'll have to be more specific. Are you talking about the barroom brawl or our night together?"

"Our . . . our night together," she repeated, all but choking on the words. "I want to forget it ever happened."

"Sorry. No can do, Dovey."

"Stop calling me Dovey! Now that you know it isn't my real name, it sounds ridiculous."

"Right. I can't believe I ever took you for a woman named something as whimsical as Dovey."

"If you persist in bothering me, I'll have to call—"

"Security? Great, call them. I'm sure they'd love to hear all about my business with you."

The ruse worked. He watched as she obviously considered several options and hastily discarded them all. Finally, crossing her arms over her middle, she looked up at him and demanded, "Well, what do you want?"

"If you're still in doubt, hug me real tight."

Her eyes skittered down the front of his body, then hastily came back up to meet his. "Besides the obvious," she said ungraciously, "what do you want?"

"To talk to you. But not here. Is there someplace we can go?"

"There's a sandwich shop across the street."

"Good. I haven't eaten lunch. Lead the way."

·   ·   ·

"What'll you have?" Lucky asked, consulting her from across the diner's turquoise tile table.

"Nothing."

To the waitress, he said, "One cheeseburger, cooked medium." He glanced down at Devon, looked pointedly at her mouth, and added, "Cut the onions. French fries, chocolate shake." Politely addressing Devon again, he asked, "Sure you don't want something?"

"I'm sure."

Handing the menus back to the waitress, he said, "Bring us two coffees, too."

"You don't take no for an answer, do you?" Devon asked, after the waitress had withdrawn.

"Rarely from a woman," he admitted.

"I thought as much."

"What makes you think so?"

"You're the overbearing, macho type."

To her irritation, he smiled. "That's me. Caveman Tyler."

Lucky was having the time of his life just looking at her. She was wearing a loose, soft blouse that buttoned down the back. It was primly styled and had full long sleeves, cuffed at her wrists. Beneath the sheer ivory fabric, he could see the outline of quality lingerie. She was wearing the blouse with a plain straight black skirt. For all its practicality and austerity, the outfit was as sexy as hell.

"I suppose sharing a motel bedroom with a stranger is nothing new to you," she remarked.

"It's happened."

"Not to me."

The waitress arrived with their coffees. Lucky watched Devon mindlessly raise hers to her lips and sip at it before she remembered that she had originally declined it. Coffee sloshed over the rim of the cup and into the saucer when she set it down emphatically.

"Now that we're alone, will you please tell me what we have to talk about?"

"What were you doing in the place?" he asked.

"That dive where we happened to meet?"

"Right."

"Did you read my story in this morning's paper?"

He cocked his head to one side, unsure what relevance her question had to his. "No. I didn't get past the picture of you."

"If you had read it, you would have realized I was in that tavern doing research."

He settled his cheek in the palm of his hand, propped his elbow on the table, and regarded her calmly as he silently invited her to elaborate. She took a deep breath.

"My column this week was on the rights still denied women, despite the strides we've taken in the past two decades toward achieving equality."

"You went into the place and bought a drink. What right were you denied?"

"My right to be left alone."

He grunted noncommittally.

She continued, "A woman still can't go into a bar alone without every man in there assuming that she's on the make, to pick up a man or be picked up. The thesis of my article was that there are still bastions of our society that women have yet to infiltrate, much less conquer.

"What took place in the bar proved my point. I did nothing to encourage the attention of those two rednecks. I sat quietly in my booth, drinking my beer, until they came over and started hassling me. It wasn't . . ." She paused and glared at him. "What are you laughing at?"

"I was just thinking that if you were missing a few teeth, and had acne and thick ankles, you probably could have drunk your beer in peace."

The waitress arrived with his food. Once she had set the platters in front of him, Devon picked up her argument.

"In other words, a woman who isn't particularly attractive is *safe* from male attention."

"You look mad," he said, all innocence. "I thought I was being complimentary."

"How much more sexist could you be than to judge a woman's worth—or a man's for that matter—strictly on the basis of looks?"

She brushed locks of her thick, lustrous hair off her shoulders. If she wanted him to judge her on the merits of her mind, Lucky thought, she should stop practicing feminine witchcraft like tossing around that mass of dark red hair and looking so damned seductive.

"Sorry, Devon, it's just not in my genes to think of you as anything but a beautiful, exciting woman."

"Is that spelled g-e-n-e-s or j-e-a-n-s?"

Casually he shook salt and pepper over the patty of the cheeseburger, then placed the top bun on it—all without ever taking his eyes off her. "Both. Better not ask which one makes the most convincing argument." He bit into the cheeseburger and derived satisfaction not only from its taste, but from her obvious discomfiture.

"Tell me, then," she said, making a stab at being composed, "if I had been missing teeth, et cetera, would you still have come to my rescue?"

He reached for the catsup. "Damn right I would have. But," he said, aiming his finger toward the ceiling to emphasize that he was about to make the most important point of his argument, "I probably wouldn't have followed you afterward. I wouldn't have stretched out on your bed." He lowered his voice and leaned across the table, bringing them nose to nose. "I wouldn't have wanted you to go on blowing on my belly forever, and I wouldn't have woken up later wanting to blow on yours."

For a moment she was too stunned to move. Then she grabbed her purse and scooted toward the opening of the booth. Lucky raised his booted foot beneath the table and propped it on the opposite bench, blocking her escape.

"Hey, you asked, remember? I was just being honest, Devon."

"Spare me your honesty from now on. I want to leave. Now."

"Uh-uh. We've still got a lot to talk about." In no apparent hurry, he took another bite of his cheeseburger and dunked a French fry into the blob of catsup he'd poured onto his plate. "Why'd you get mad when I intervened?"

"Because I wanted to handle the situation myself. Part of my research was to see how a woman could get out of a situation like that if forced into one. You took away my opportunity of seeing it through."

"I took away your opportunity of getting to know Little Alvin and Jack Ed better."

"Possibly," she admitted with chagrin. "They were a bit more than I bargained for. I had expected wolf whistles, perhaps a pass or two. I hadn't expected to be manhandled.

"And I'll tell you beforehand," she went on, "that you're mentioned in the article, too. Not by name, of course. You're referred to as a man with the White Knight syndrome."

"What's that?"

"He makes it his personal crusade to rescue damsels in distress."

"Hey, I like that." He sucked on the straw in his milk shake. "Why'd you use the phony name to check into the motel?"

Apparently she hadn't intended him to take the White

Knight reference as a compliment. Dropping her forehead into her hand, she began massaging her temples. "I don't know. Whim. Sometimes people recognize my name and want to take issue with one article or another. I didn't feel up to conversation that evening."

He polished off the milk shake and pushed aside the glass, along with his empty plate. The waitress passed with a carafe of fresh coffee and refilled their cups before taking his dishes away.

"You never thought it would matter what name you used," Lucky said softly.

She raised her head. "No. I never thought it would matter. I never expected to see you again."

"That's because you don't know me very well."

His simple statement caused a worried frown to appear between her brows. "What do you want? Why have you come here looking for me?"

"You know what I want, Devon." His eyes slowly moved from the top of her head, over her face and throat, to her breasts. When his eyes reconnected with hers, he said, "I want another night in bed with you. This time we'll both be naked. I'll be looking at you with two clear eyes. And I won't waste any time sleeping."

"That's impossible." Her voice was so husky it was barely audible. "I'm telling you now, so you'll know and won't waste my time or yours. It is impossible. If that's all you came for—"

"It isn't."

"Then what? Hush money? Do you plan to blackmail me now that you know my name means something in this city?"

He ground his teeth in an effort to control his temper. "Don't ever say anything like that to me again, Devon. My name means something in my own town. The Tylers don't need anything or anybody badly enough to resort to black-mail."

"I'm sorry I offended you and your family name."

She said it as if she meant it, as if it was out of character for her to deliver such a low blow unless she was terribly upset. Lucky believed she was. Her original anxiety over seeing him had returned. It showed on her lovely features and in the depth of her green eyes.

"Just please tell me what you want, so I can go back to work and you can leave."

"You weren't just another pickup, Devon."

"Am I supposed to be flattered by that?"

"I'd like for you to be."

She shook her head. "I can't accommodate you. Being a one-night stand made me feel cheap."

"You were more than a one-night stand. My night with you is very significant to my future."

"Oh please," she groaned. "Don't add insult to injury by feeding me juvenile lines like that."

"You are my alibi."

Chapter Nine

"Alibi? Like in a crime?"

"Exactly like in a crime."

Devon shook her head. "I don't understand."

Lucky told her about the fire. "Several pieces of large machinery were destroyed. The damage is estimated at close to seven figures. At this point Tyler Drilling is stuck with the loss."

As always, whenever he thought about it, he became frustrated. "It's crazy. If the local authorities were handling the investigation alone, we, my family and I, would never have fallen under suspicion. But with the feds in on it . . .

"See, apparently a lot of oilmen who are in financial straits are taking desperate measures. I'm sure fraud is rampant. So, the insurance companies are on the alert. Of course their suspicions are unfounded in this case, but we've got to prove them wrong. My brother can verify his whereabouts that night. I can't. Not without you."

She regarded him closely for several moments before averting her head to gaze through the window at the traffic moving along the congested downtown boulevard.

"So you want me to go on record as your alibi. You couldn't have been in Milton Point setting fire to the garage because you were in bed with me all night."

"That sums it up."

She swung her gaze back to him. "I can't do it."

Before he could react, she slid from the booth and headed for the door of the diner. "Hey, what the—" Standing, he worked his hand into the pocket of his jeans and tossed a ten-dollar bill onto the table. "Thanks!" he shouted to the waitress as he bolted through the door in pursuit of Devon Haines.

He caught up with her at the intersection where she was jaywalking. "What the hell do you mean you can't?" He took hold of her upper arm and halted her in the middle of the street. Horns began blaring around them. A beer truck swerved to avoid a collision.

Lucky ushered her to the curb. Once they had reached the sidewalk, he drew her out of the flow of pedestrian traffic and repeated his question. "This time I really can't take no for an answer, Devon."

"You'll have to. I can't vouch for your whereabouts that night."

"The hell you can't," he ground out. Pulling her against him, he lowered his head to within whispering distance of hers. "You know I was lying beside you all night. I fell asleep before you did. You were gone by the time I woke up the following morning. And if you've forgotten what happened in between, I'll be happy to refresh your memory."

She nervously dampened her lips with her tongue. "I don't need to be reminded, thank you."

"At least you're not denying it happened."

"No, it happened, but I wish it hadn't. I'm not proud of it. I'm certainly not going to confess it to the world." She wrested her arm free. "I'm sorry you're in trouble. Truly I am. But that fire has nothing to do with me."

"Maybe not, but you're the only thing standing between jail and me."

"Oh, I doubt that. A man like you always lands on his feet. I'm sure that before you're formally charged, you'll see a way out." She began backing away from him. "In any event I won't be able to help you."

She turned and entered the newspaper building through the revolving bronze doors. Lucky charged after her. By the time he was disgorged into the lobby by the rapidly turning doors, she was about to step onto the elevator. He raced for it.

Two uniformed guards lunged for him, catching him by the arms from behind. "Hey, buddy, you bothering Ms. Haines?" Apparently they'd been asked to intercept him.

"This won't help, Devon!" Lucky shouted to the closing elevator doors. She refused to meet his eyes as she punched the button for her floor.

He struggled with the security guards. "Let go of me.

I'm leaving, I'm leaving." They didn't take his word for it, but pushed him through the revolving doors.

"If you come back, we'll call the police!" one shouted after him.

Lucky yelled back an obscenity, then stood glaring at the front of the building while pedestrians eddied around him. "Now what?" he muttered. What the hell did she mean by "I can't"?

Using the transmitter, Devon lowered the automatic garage door, then let herself into the condo through the connecting kitchen door. Once inside, she ran through the dim, silent rooms until she reached the living room, where she watched the street through the shutters until she was satisfied that Lucky Tyler hadn't followed her home. She wouldn't put it past him to try something like that. She'd driven home with one eye on the road and the other on her rearview mirror.

The shock of seeing him standing at the edge of her desk this afternoon had affected her more than she wanted to admit. Usually adept at masking her feelings, she feared she hadn't been successful in hiding her reaction to his unexpected appearance. Several of her cohorts had noticed how rattled she was and had teased her about it when she returned to her office.

"Who's the hunk?"

"Nobody."

"*Nobody?*"

"Just a man I know."

"Someone out of your murky past, Devon?"

You could say it had been murky, she thought now. But the "past" had been as recent as last week. None of her coworkers would guess that.

Finally convinced he hadn't followed her home, she walked toward the back of her house, where the master suite was located. Shedding her skirt and blouse, she gazed longingly through the patio door toward the swimming pool. A swim would cool her off. She'd felt feverish ever since she'd looked up expecting to see the gofer's affable face, and instead had met Lucky Tyler's smoldering blue stare. Several strenuous laps would relax her. She was as jittery as a kitten, wondering when he would pop up next.

He would. She knew he would.

She stepped into a pair of skimpy swim trunks. After taking a towel from the Lucite rack in the bathroom, she slid open the patio door and stepped out into her secluded backyard, almost completely taken up by the pool itself.

There was very little lawn to maintain, only the shrubbery that grew along the cedar privacy fence which let her indulge in semi-nude swimming. On the deck she had a gas grill and numerous potted plants. Because her days were spent mostly indoors, she enjoyed spending the evenings on her deck, tending the plants, even reading research material for her articles. Swimming laps in the pool was also an excellent form of exercise, and about the only one she liked.

Dropping the towel onto a chaise, she dived into the deep end of the pool. The cooling waters closed over her. Serenely she glided along the bottom, swimming from one end to the other in one breath. Only her head cleared the surface in the shallow end, then, taking another deep breath, she executed a surface dive and went under again.

By the time she had swum several laps, her lungs, heart, and limbs felt exercised and were aching pleasurably from the exertion. Peeling her sodden hair back with both hands, she started up the steps in the shallow end. She walked across the deck, head down.

Not until she almost stepped on his boots did she notice him. Then her head snapped up.

Lucky was sprawled in the patio chair beside the chaise. He was half reclining on his spine, his hands folded over his belt buckle, his long legs stretched far out in front of him, ankles crossed. Her towel was draped over one of his thighs. Beneath a shelf of tawny brows, his eyes were riveted on her bare breasts.

Rousing himself, he lifted his gaze to hers. "Towel?" he asked, extending it to her.

She snatched it from him and wound it around her bare torso. "What are you doing here? How did you get in?" She distinctly remembered checking to make sure all the doors were locked and bolted.

"I climbed over the fence. How high is that damn thing anyway? I landed hard. Think I threw my knee out. Old football injury."

His insouciance infuriated her. He acted as though jumping her eight-foot privacy fence was something he did every day at dusk. "You followed me home," she accused him.

"How else would I find out where you live? Since you sicced the guards on me, nobody at the newspaper was going to give me your address. You aren't listed in the telephone directory. I checked.

"See, Devon, the first time I checked the directory, I was looking for Mary Smith. There're dozens of those. But I thought I'd give Devon Haines a try. Sure enough, you aren't there." He ran a glance down her. "Is it heated?"

In the lavender glow of twilight, his eyes shone like twin blue lanterns. They were unsettling. In fact, she hadn't had a coherent thought since he had showed up at her office. The possible effects his reappearance could have on her life filled her with dread. What a fool she had been to lull herself into believing that she could come away unscathed from her earth-shattering experience with him.

Realizing that he was waiting for an answer to a question she couldn't remember, she said, "Pardon?"

"The pool. Is it heated?"

"Why?"

"Because you've got goose bumps as big as mosquito bites, and your lips are turning blue."

She pulled the towel tighter around her. "The air is chilly."

"Then we'd better go inside."

"*I'm* going inside. You're leaving."

"I want a drink, and from the looks of it, you could use one."

He casually slid open the patio door. "After you," he said courteously, stepping aside. Because she was chilled to the bone and because she wanted to put on more clothes as quickly as possible, she swept past him and reentered her bedroom.

"Where's the kitchen?"

"I asked you to leave, Mr. Tyler."

"You don't want a drink?" He dropped into the upholstered easy chair in the corner and crossed an ankle over the opposite knee. "Okay. We'll dispense with the drinks and start our discussion here and now."

It was hard to maintain her dignity, much less her belligerent insistence that he leave, when her teeth were chattering and her hair was dripping icy rivulets of water onto her shoulders and chest. His eyes kept straying to her breasts. Devon was keenly aware that her rigid nipples were making impressions against the thick terry cloth.

"It's a small house," she said scornfully. "I'm sure you can find the kitchen on your own."

Smiling, he rolled out of the chair. Standing only inches from her, he cupped his hand around her shoulder and used his thumb to whisk drops of water off the slope of her breast. In a low, stirring voice he said, "I like you wet."

To demonstrate her immunity to him, she slammed the door in his wake. He would never know that because of his touch her knees were about to liquefy. She dropped the towel, peeled off the swim trunks, and vigorously toweled herself. She dressed in a two-piece velour lounger, because it was quick, convenient, and warm. It also covered her from neck to ankle. Not wanting to take the time to dry her hair, she fashioned a turban out of a towel.

The lamps in the living room had been turned on, and Lucky was surveying her compact-disc library. When he heard her come in, he turned his head.

Their gazes locked. Seconds ticked off ponderously while they continued to stare at each other as if mesmerized.

Devon could remember things about him, small things that only a lover would know, yet he was a complete stranger to her. Suddenly, and with a degree of desperation that shocked her, she realized she was greedy for information. She wanted to know every trivial detail of Lucky Tyler's life.

All she really knew about him was that he adhered to a code of chivalry that had almost disappeared in contemporary America, that he had a keen sense of humor and a pair of startling blue eyes, and that his touch could set her on fire. She couldn't easily dismiss from her mind what had passed between them on their night together . . . even though she had no choice but to try and forget it.

His expression told her that he was also finding it impossible to forget.

At last he said, "All I could find was beer." He was

drinking his from the bottle, but on the faux marble block she used as a coffee table, he'd set a cold beer and a glass. She acknowledged her drink with a thank you, but made no move toward it. "Don't you want it?"

"What I want, Mr. Tyler, is to know why you think you can so grossly invade my privacy." She complimented herself on sounding imperious and cool.

"Is that what I've done?"

"What else would you call it? You've harassed me at my office, and trespassed on my private property."

"So why haven't you called the police?"

He was also a cocky bastard, she decided. He knew why she hadn't called the police. His knowing smile grated on her. Forgetting to be cool, she raised her voice. "Why did you follow me home?"

"Because I'm not finished with you."

"Well, that's just too damn bad, Mr. Tyler, because I was finished with you the minute—"

"You left my bed?"

She fell silent.

He took advantage of her speechlessness. "Is that why you stayed with me that night? Were you that hard up for a man? Would any man have done?"

"No, no, and no!"

He responded as though she had said yes. "Then, in the morning, once I'd done stud duty for you, you figured it was all right to sneak out."

"You're wrong," she said, stubbornly shaking her head. "I won't even honor that with a denial."

He set his beer on a shelf in the bookcase and, in two strides, came even with her. His hands bracketed her shoulders, lifting her slightly up and forward. "What else am I supposed to think, huh? Why'd you hightail it out of that motel room?"

"Because I was disgusted."

He was taken aback by her answer. No woman had ever said that to him. "Disgusted? With me?"

"With myself," she lashed out. "With the situation. I didn't want to hash through it again. If you make a habit of sleeping with women you don't know, I'm sure you can understand morning-after awkwardness."

Gnawing on his inner cheek, he assimilated what she'd said and apparently agreed with her. Then, taking another tack, he asked, "Why did you pull that disappearing act this afternoon?"

"Because we had nothing more to talk about."

"Wrong."

"Right."

"Are you going to ask me to spend the night tonight?"

"No!" she said, aghast.

"Then we've got something more to talk about."

"I think that's what's really bothering you," she said heatedly. "You're certain that every woman you meet is panting to go to bed with you. Well, take a good look at the exception, Mr. Tyler. You're only hounding me because I walked out on you and not the other way around. Your ego has been stung."

"Maybe," he admitted grudgingly. "Partially."

"Nurse it someplace else, with someone else. I don't want to see you again. Haven't I made that plain enough?"

"Oh yeah. You've made it plain. But you haven't convinced me, Devon. You haven't even convinced yourself."

He drew her forward with such force that the towel slipped from her head and her hair tumbled out of it. His mouth was damp and demanding as it settled against her lips.

Far from resenting his aggressiveness, she responded to it, reveling in his potency and his blatant hunger for her. Instead of pulling away, as her mind dictated that she should, she treated herself to the heat and urgency of his kisses.

His hands slid beneath her top to splay open across her back and hold her closer to him. She loved his touch on her skin and longed to take the same kind of liberties with him. He was tough, all sinew and muscle. Her curves molded pliantly to his manliness. She loved the rasp of his stubble against her face, the taste of his mouth, the scent of his skin. She was starved for his masculinity.

When he raised the hem of her top, she felt the cold, exciting bite of his metal belt buckle against her bare midriff. Then his hands moved over her breasts—reshaping, stroking, teasing, then gratifying by drawing his thumbs across her nipples.

"Devon," he murmured roughly when he felt their beading reaction through the silk cup of her bra. "Why are you making this so hard?"

She yanked herself away from him, backing up as though he represented something terrifying, which he did. Oddly enough, he was smiling.

"I didn't mean that in a crude or lewd way. I meant 'hard' as in difficult."

"I know what you meant," she said breathlessly, unable to find her full voice. "It's not only difficult, it's impossible. I told you that earlier. Now, please go, and don't bother me again."

"You're bothered all right."

She followed his gaze down to her swollen breasts, defined so well against the soft cloth of her pullover. She would be lying to herself as well as to him to deny that she desired him. On a near-sob she said, "Please go."

"Devon, forget how and where we met. Think only about how it was when we woke up in bed together and turned to each other."

She closed her hands over her ears. "I can't."

"Why?" He forced her hands back down to her sides. "Why, when it was so damn good, won't you let yourself remember?"

"I don't owe you any explanations."

"The hell you don't," he said, his voice low and fierce. "The kiss you just gave me makes a lie out of everything you're saying. You're hungry for me. As hungry as I am for you. I believe that entitles me to an explanation."

His incisive arguments, combined with his sex appeal, were weakening her resolve. Pulling her hands free of his and lashing out defensively, she cried, "I can't see you anymore. Ever. Now, please go away."

Lucky switched tactics. Hooking his thumbs in his belt loops, he assumed a slouching stance, his body thrown slightly off-center. Arrogantly he tilted his head to one side.

"Okay, for the sake of argument, let's say that the kisses we've shared didn't leave us both damned near senseless. Let's say that your blood's not running hot and thick right now. Let's forget all that and focus our attention on my problem—besides the one I have with you, that is. Let's discuss how badly I need you for my alibi."

She was shaking her head long before he finished, first in denial of her physical reactions to him, then to the idea of her testifying to the authorities on his behalf.

"No one can know that I spent the night with you," she said adamantly. "No one. Is that understood? I certainly can't make it a matter of public record." Her previous chill, temporarily dispelled by their embrace, returned. She ran her hands up and down her arms as though to restore circulation.

"You can't just shrug off this arson rap as a frivolous misfortune of mine."

"I'm not. I'm terribly sorry that you're in trouble."

"More than just trouble, Devon. These federal guys are damned serious."

"What kind of case have they got against you?"

"Flimsy and circumstantial," he admitted. "I would never get convicted, but I don't expect we could raise bail. I do not cotton to the idea of going to jail for any length of time, especially for something I didn't do. I don't even like the idea of being charged with a felony. My family, our business, would be irreparably damaged by something like that." Gently he took her by the shoulders again. "Devon, be reasonable about this. You've got to help me."

"No I don't. You can't force me."

"I shouldn't have to. Why won't you just come forward like any decent person would?"

"I can't!"

"Tell me why."

"I *can't!*"

"*Why?*"

"Because I'm married!"

Chapter Ten

"She's married."

Lucky's two glum words echoed as dismally as a death knell. Seated at the bar in Tanya and Chase's small apartment kitchen, he stared forlornly into the cup of coffee his sister-in-law had brewed for him.

He had arrived at their apartment complex before dawn. Ignoring the early hour, he'd knocked on their door and got them out of bed, his unkempt hair and stubble of beard chasing away their annoyance at having been awakened so early.

Besides looking as though he needed a shave, a hot meal, and twelve hours of sleep, Lucky had hair windblown from driving all the way from Dallas, a distance of over a hundred miles, with the top of his convertible down, going at speeds they dared not guess and would rather not know. Strands of dark blond hair were radiating from his head like straw.

His family had been worried about him since yesterday morning. The last one to see him had been Sage. According to her, he had left the house half-dressed, at a dead run, and without a word of explanation.

Now several moments transpired before Chase repeated his brother's bleak report. "Married?"

"Married. You know, matrimony, holy wedlock."

Tanya, having poured her husband and herself another cup of coffee, sat down on one of the barstools. "How do you know, Lucky?"

"She told me." After a lengthy, deep, wet kiss, he thought bitterly.

"You finally tracked her down?"

"Yesterday."

"Where?"

"Dallas."

"What's her name?"

"Devon Haines."

"That sounds familiar."

"You've probably read her newspaper column."

"Sure!" Chase exclaimed, thumping the bar with his fist. "Devon Haines."

"I accidentally stumbled over her byline and picture in yesterday morning's paper."

Lucky recounted the rest of the story to them, leaving out the personal aspects of it and glossing over the tempestuous hours he'd spent in a bowling alley and batting barn—so he'd have something to hit legitimately—

after his meeting with her and until he decided to drive home.

"The lady did not want to be found," he said. "When I did find her, she refused to cooperate, said she wouldn't, *couldn't*, be my alibi. Now I know why." The coffee was scalding hot, but he tossed it back as though the mug were a shot glass full of whiskey. Tanya silently rose to get him a refill.

"Did you meet her husband?" Chase wanted to know.

"No."

"Was he there?"

"No."

"Where was he?"

"I don't know."

"What's his name?"

"I don't know."

"If she's married, what was she doing sleeping with you?"

"I don't know that either. Who the hell can figure out what goes on inside a woman's head?"

Angrily Lucky flung himself off the barstool and began to prowl the length of the galley kitchen. "This is one situation I've never run across. I don't have any experience, and I'm stumped." He stopped pacing to address his audience. "Don't get me wrong. I'm not claiming to be an angel. I confess to having done some pretty wild things with women."

"I don't think anyone could dispute that."

"We've done some pretty wild things together."

Chase cast an uncomfortable glance toward his wife. His love for Tanya McDaniel had tamed the former rodeo star considerably. "If it's all the same to you, I'd just as soon not discuss our escapades in front of Tanya."

"Those escapades aren't the point," Lucky said irritably. "Tanya knows you were a hell-raiser before she came along. My point is that for all my carousing, I have never slept with a married woman. I drew the line at that." Mindlessly he rubbed his stomach, as though the very thought of adultery made him queasy.

"I never would even go out with a divorcée until the final, final papers were *final*. So this broad," he said irreverently, aiming his index finger in the general direction of Dallas, "not only duped me with the phony name bit, but tricked me into doing something that, old-fashioned as it sounds, I believe is morally wrong."

He returned to his seat, dejectedly throwing himself onto the padded cushion. Eyes vacant and bleary, he contemplated near space.

"Lucky," Chase ventured after a lengthy period of silence, "what are you going to do?"

"Probably ten to twenty for arson."

"Don't say that!" Tanya cried. "You can't go to prison for something you didn't do."

"You know what I meant, Lucky," Chase said. "You can't let her off the hook that easily. She fooled around, so she can damn well pay the consequences."

"I used that argument."

"And?"

"It got me nowhere."

"Appeal to her basic human decency."

"I did that too. Didn't shake her a smidgen. If she would run around on her husband, I doubt she has a sense of decency. Although," he added on a mumble, "she seemed decent enough at first."

"Well, if worse comes to worst, Pat Bush could subpoena her."

"To appear before a federal grand jury." Lucky sighed and tiredly dug his fingertips into his eye sockets, which were shadowed by fatigue. "I was hoping it wouldn't have to go even that far. With business so bad . . ." He lowered his hands and looked at his brother. "I'm sorry, Chase. I really screwed up this time. And the worst of it is that I'm dragging Tyler Drilling, you, and everybody else down with me."

Chase rose from his barstool and affectionately slapped his younger brother between the shoulder blades. "Your hide is more valuable to me than the business. I'm worried about the guy who actually set the fire. What's the bastard planning to do next?" He consulted the wall clock. "Guess I'd better get on out there and baby-sit those investigators."

"I'll be along later."

"Uh-uh. You're taking the day off."

"Says who?"

"Says me."

"You're not my boss."

"Today I am."

They'd been playing that universal sibling game almost since they were old enough to talk. Lucky gave in much sooner than usual.

Chase said, "You look like hell. Stay home today. Get some sleep." Turning, he headed for the bedroom. "If you're gone by the time I get out of the shower, I'll be in touch later today."

After Chase had withdrawn, Tanya smiled at her brother-in-law. "What would you like for breakfast?"

"Nothing," he replied, getting to his feet. "Thanks, though." At the front door of the apartment, he pulled her into a hug. "I should take a cue from my big brother, find a woman like you, marry her, and quit screwing around for good. Problem is, since you've been taken, there aren't any good broads left."

Laughing, she shoved him away. "Lucky, I seriously doubt you'll sweep a woman off her feet by referring to her as a broad."

He smiled, but there was more chagrin than humor behind it. His blue eyes were tired and dull and puzzled. "Tanya, why would a married woman share a motel room with a total stranger in the first place, then let him make love to her?"

"It happens all the time, Lucky. Don't you read the statistics?"

"I know, but . . ." He gauged her worried frown. "I know you probably feel uncomfortable talking about this with me, but I feel like a jerk discussing it with another man, even Chase. Will you listen? Please?"

"Of course."

He hesitated, but only momentarily. "Devon just wasn't the type to pick up a stranger and go to bed with him. I've been with plenty of women who do it routinely, and she was different."

"How so?"

"In every way. Looks. Attitude. Actions." He shook his head in bafflement. "Why would she take a life-threatening risk like that? For all she knew, I was a psychopath, or had a venereal disease or God knows what else. She's married. She and her husband live well. She's got a successful career. Why would she risk all that? And if she's got the guts to do it, why get squeamish when it's time to 'fess up?"

"I don't know, Lucky," Tanya said, sounding genuinely sorry that she couldn't provide him with an answer. "I can't imagine being unfaithful to Chase. I can't imagine even being tempted."

He squinted his eyes with concentration. "I don't think she planned it to happen. It wasn't like she was on the make. In fact, she tried everything she could to avoid me. She's almost militant in her feminism, takes issue with sexual labels, things like that. Real defensive about it." He paused, carefully choosing words to describe Devon Haines to Tanya.

"She's put together well, you know? Dresses professionally. Seems to have every situation under control. I certainly couldn't call her flighty." He blew out a gust of air, indicative of the depth of his confusion.

"She's just not whimsical. And it's not like she seduced me, or even vice-versa. I mean, it just sorta happened. We were both half-asleep and kinda rolled toward each other, and I started touching her, kissing her, and she started responding, and before we knew it, we were . . . you know."

During his speech Tanya had been watching him closely. "Lucky," she asked softly, "which bothers you most? The fact that she declines to come forward and clear you? Or the fact that she's married?"

He abruptly pulled his chin back a notch. "What do you mean by that?"

"For the past week you've been obsessed with finding out who this woman is and where she lives."

"Because she's my alibi."

"Are you sure that's the only reason?"

"Yes. Hell yes." He reached for the doorknob and pulled the door open. "Listen, Tanya, I don't want you or anybody else to get any romantic notions about her."

"I see."

"I mean it."

"I understand."

"That's it. She's my alibi. Period." Standing silhouetted in the open doorway, he made an umpire's "safe" motion with his hands. When he did, he rapped his knuckles against the doorframe. "Ouch! Damn!" Sucking on an injured knuckle, he added, "Besides, as it turns out, she's married."

A few moments later Chase, rubbing dry his dark hair with a towel, wearing another around his middle, came to Tanya's side. She was standing in the doorway, watching Lucky's taillights disappear around the nearest corner.

"What was all the shouting about?" he asked.

"That was Lucky," she said, closing the door. "He was adamantly denying that this woman means anything more to him than an alibi."

"Does he think you're hard of hearing?"

She laughed. "No, but I think he is."

"Huh?"

"He's not listening to his heart."

"I don't get your meaning."

"You're not supposed to," she replied coyly. "You're a man."

"You know, that secret little smile of yours drives me crazy." He bent down to nuzzle her neck. "Makes me horny as hell."

"I know," she whispered back, moving against him seductively. "Why do you think I wear it so often?"

Chase dropped both the towels and carried her into their bedroom.

Half an hour later the covers were helplessly tangled around their naked bodies, but neither noticed or cared. They were sated. While Tanya lay on her back, eyes closed, Chase idly caressed her breasts, which bore the faint, rosy markings of recent lovemaking.

"I feel sorry for Lucky," she remarked dreamily.

"So do I. He's got himself in a real jam."

"I'm not talking strictly about the fire. One way or another, he'll be exonerated. This might represent a setback in his life, but that's all it'll be."

"Then why do you feel sorry for him?"

She opened her eyes and looked at her husband, reaching up to lovingly brush damp strands of hair off his forehead. "I think the encounter with this Haines woman has had more of an impact than he's willing to admit. And even if he does admit it, whether publicly or to himself, there's nothing he can do about it. It was finished before it started."

"Define 'it.' "

She shrugged. "A meaningful relationship, I suppose."

"A meaningful relationship? With a woman? My brother?" Laughing, Chase rolled onto his back.

Tanya propped herself up on one elbow. "You think the notion is that ridiculous?"

"As long as there's more than one living, breathing female alive on planet Earth, Lucky will never be faithful to just one."

"I think you're doing him an injustice. He's more sensitive than you think. And he can be very loyal."

"Oh, I agree. He can be very loyal to several women at one time." Laughter lurked beneath his serious words. "Did I ever tell you how Lucky got his nickname?"

"Come to think of it, no."

"You never wondered why a James Lawrence would be nicknamed Lucky?"

"I took it for granted. For as long as I've known you, that's what you and everyone else has called him."

Stacking both hands behind his head, Chase laughed softly. "I was in tenth grade. He was in ninth, about fourteen, I guess. There was this girl, a woman really, about twenty, who lived in Kilgore. To put it bluntly, she was a tramp. She worked at being a tramp. Real hot-looking. Dressed to display her endowments. She kept all the boys in several counties in a constant state of arousal, but never came across with the goods.

"So one night, me and some of my friends decided to take a car—we couldn't legally drive yet—and go to Kilgore for a look-see at this gal. Lucky begged to come along. We finally agreed after he threatened to squeal our plans to our parents.

"Off we went. After driving around Kilgore for an hour, we found her. She was strutting her stuff at one of the local bowling alleys. All of us ogled until our eyes were bugging out and our tongues were lolling. But Lucky was the only one who worked up the courage to speak to her. Damned if the rascal didn't end up smooth-talking his way into her car, then into her house.

"Positively awestruck, we followed them there. He stayed inside for two hours. The kid who'd sneaked out the family car was in a panic to get back to Milton Point before his folks discovered it missing. He finally started honking the horn. When Lucky came out from around back, he was pulling on his shirt and wearing this very smug grin on his face.

"It made me mad as hell that my little brother had succeeded in doing what so many others had tried to do and failed. I said, 'Quit grinning, you little bastard. You just lucked out, is all.' 'Call me Lucky,' he said, still wearing that complacent grin."

Tanya was trying to look horrified while suppressing a giggle. "You're both incorrigible. How did you explain his new nickname to your parents?"

"I forget now what explanation we came up with. Anyway, from that night forward, the name stuck. He's been Lucky to everybody."

Tanya sighed, resting her head on Chase's hairy chest and sadly recalling what had prompted the story. "I don't think he's feeling very lucky these days."

"No," Chase agreed. Folding his arms around her, he held her close. "But I am."

·   ·   ·

Devon had reams of research material to read, dozens of periodicals to peruse, and thousands of words to compose, but she couldn't concentrate on anything except her encounter with Lucky the evening before.

In her mind she continued to see his face as it had looked when she told him she was married. His expression had been a mix of incredulity and outrage. His eyes, initially blank with stupefaction, had grown frigid by degrees, until they achieved that hard, cold glare that she shivered beneath even in recollection.

Feeling restless, she left the enclosure of her office and took the long route through the city room to the alcove of vending machines. Desultorily she inserted the required coinage into the refrigerated box. The coins dropped into the concealed bin with a metallic echo that sounded as hollow as she felt. Coworkers spoke to her as she passed their desks on her way back. She pretended not to hear.

"Hey, Devon, what happened with the blond hunk yesterday?"

Ignoring that question, she closed her office door behind her to discourage interruption and returned to her desk, setting aside the cold drink. She hadn't really been thirsty. Getting the drink had merely been a diversion from her haunting thoughts.

"I'm married."

Bending her head over her desk and holding it between

her hands, she repeated the words. "I'm married. I'm married."

And yet she wasn't. The license was signed. The judge had pronounced her wed. It was official. As far as the sovereign state of Texas was concerned, she was married.

"But I'm not," she whispered with frustration.

It was a marriage she could easily get out of. She certainly had the grounds to seek an annulment. Anyone who heard her case would sympathize. No one acquainted with the facts would condemn her.

She, Devon Haines alone, was standing in the way of her own freedom from a marriage that amounted to no more than a piece of paper. But it was the right thing to do. She had walked into it with both eyes open. Whether or not it was a bad decision, she had to live with it.

Lucky Tyler didn't know the conditions of her marital status. He probably wouldn't care. He condemned her for being an unfaithful married woman who had duped him into sharing a night of sin and was now unwilling to pay the price. There was no way she could help him without jeopardizing herself and her husband.

She'd seen the contempt in Lucky's eyes. She could have dispelled it with a few simple sentences of explanation, but she had held her silence.

He hadn't realized the truth.

When he entered her, he had mistaken the reason for the sudden tensing of her body. He had obviously taken it for passion, not pain. He had misinterpreted her sharp, gasping breath. His previous kisses had prepared her to receive him too well. She was so moist, he hadn't noticed the snugness.

By the time he was buried deep inside her and moving within, it had been too late to consider the consequences of what she was doing. Like him, she had become oblivious to everything except the undulating, swelling sensations that had engulfed them.

She was glad the alarming truth had been obscured by eroticism. If he knew that she was a virgin, this cloudy situation could turn turbulent. Then again, she wished with all her heart that he knew.

Memories of their lovemaking caused a bittersweet ache in the center of her soul. She marveled over it, exulted in the pleasure, and lamented its brevity.

Her office door was suddenly flung open. "You asked to see this article when the copy editor was finished."

She raised her head and brushed the tears off her cheeks, reaching for the papers. "Oh yes, thanks," she told the gofer.

"Say, are you okay?"

"I'm fine."

"Sure?"

She gave him a watery smile and reassured him before he left. Self-pity was an emotion she refused to surrender to. She had welcomed Lucky's fierce, yet tender loving. Because on that night, above all other nights, she had so desperately needed loving.

But wasn't it poignantly ironic that in the arms of a stranger she had glimpsed what could be—should be—and wasn't?

"Lucky!"

He groaned and covered his tousled head with his pillow. It was immediately wrestled from his grasp. "Go away," he snarled.

"Will you please wake up and tell this woman to stop calling?"

He rolled to his back and blinked his disgruntled sister into focus. She was standing beside his bed, glaring down at him, her mood as tenuous as the narrow straps of her bikini.

"What woman?" he asked hopefully, reaching for the receiver of the telephone extension on his nightstand.

"Susan Young."

If the telephone had suddenly turned into a cobra ready to strike, he couldn't have snatched his hand back any quicker.

Sage, with supreme exasperation, plugged in the cord he had previously disconnected, lifted the receiver, and, without bothering to cover the mouthpiece, said, "She's been making a nuisance of herself by calling every hour on the hour for two whole days. Will you please talk to her so I can sunbathe in peace?"

She thrust the phone at him. He caught it, juggled it

against his bare chest, then mouthed "brat" as he raised it to his ear. "Susan," he said in a voice that would melt butter twenty yards away, "how are you? Thanks for calling. I was just thinking about you."

Sage poked her index finger into her open mouth, mimicking gagging herself, then sat down on the edge of the mattress, unabashedly eavesdropping on her brother's conversation.

His temperament was touchy at best, but she wasn't intimidated by his formidable frown. "What's been going on?" he said into the receiver.

He listened for a moment, but cut into Susan's diatribe. "I know I haven't been around and haven't called. I wanted to protect you from this mess."

"If she falls for that, she's not only devious, she's stupid."

Lucky shot his sister a threatening look. "Until this mess blows over, I didn't think we should see each other. I didn't want to involve you . . . Yeah, I know what you offered to tell them, but—" He listened for another while. "Susan, I can't let you do that. I think too much of you."

"Oh please." Sage groaned. "What's she offering to do? Bed the feds?"

Overriding his sister's sarcastic words, Lucky said, "Give me an hour. . . . Promise. I'll be there in an hour." Thoughtfully he replaced the receiver and continued to stare at it until Sage spoke.

"Well? What was that all about?"

"None of your business. Will you kindly haul yourself off my bed, so I can get up and get dressed?"

"How juvenile. I've seen you in skivvies before."

"For your information, Miss Sophistication, I came to bed straight from the shower, and am buck naked beneath this sheet. Now, unless you want to be educated, get the hell out of here. I told Susan I'd be at her house in an hour."

"Really!" said Sage, taking umbrage. "Do you think I've lived under a rock? Male nudity doesn't shock or offend me. I know what all the parts look like and how they work."

Lucky frowned as he took in her skimpy attire. "Listen here, young lady, I expect you to behave yourself in a manner becoming a lady when it comes to the opposite sex," he said sternly.

"Ha! You're a fine one to talk. Do you behave yourself like a gentleman?"

"Do you run around the wild young studs dressed like that?" he demanded, nodding down at her bikini.

"You gawk at women in bikinis."

"So? Male prerogative."

"Like hell!" Sage exclaimed. "That's a double standard."

A mental image of Devon emerging from the swimming pool, peeling back her wet hair with both hands;

buttocks and mound covered by triangles of bronze, metallic fabric; breasts bare, heavy, gleaming, beaded with sparkling drops of water.

Sage was right. He had gawked, and it was a double standard. But that didn't keep his body from reacting to the alluring mental picture.

"You gotta leave now," he said in a voice so low it sounded like a growl.

"Here lately, you're such a grouch." She left the bed and flounced toward the door. However, she pulled up short and turned back, her expression no longer irritable, but sympathetic.

"Chase came by at lunch to check on you. Mother and I told him you were sleeping. He said not to wake you up, that you needed the rest. He, uh, he told us about the Haines woman, Lucky. I'm sorry."

Despite his foul mood, he winked at her. "Thanks, brat. I appreciate your concern."

Once Sage had closed the door, he flung back the sheet and went to his bureau. It took him a long time to dress because he often found himself standing motionless staring into space, or forgetting what he'd gone to the closet for, or wondering why he was searching through a particular drawer. His mind kept straying back to Devon. Damn, he still wanted to see her.

Instead, he had to go see Susan. After avoiding her and her preposterous marriage proposal for more than a week, he acknowledged that he couldn't delay dealing with it any longer.

"Jeez, I dread this," he muttered to himself as he finally left his bedroom and loped down the stairs.

He didn't realize until later just how much his dread had been warranted.

Chapter Eleven

It was almost as though she had expected him.

Devon didn't react with as much surprise as he had anticipated. Her car rolled to a halt beside his where he was parked at the curb in front of her condo. She gazed at him for a moment, her expression revealing little, before she pulled into the driveway.

Lucky stepped out of his Mustang and moved toward the garage door that had opened automatically for Devon's car. They met in the driveway. Obviously she had just come from work. She was dressed in a suit, although she was carrying, not wearing, the jacket. Sunglasses held her hair away from her face. Her other hand held a large, flat pizza box.

"Hi," he said, his expression solemn.

"Hello."

"I, uh . . ." He shuffled and glanced up at the storm clouds darkening the sky. "Is your husband at home?"

"No."

"I don't want to make this any more difficult for you than it has to be."

"Then what are you doing here?"

"I've got to talk to you." He drew his lips tight and said through his teeth, "Dammit, you've got to help me, Devon."

She glanced around worriedly, as though prying eyes might be peeking at them from the other houses on the block. Finally she nodded curtly.

"Come on in." She led him through the garage, lowered the door by depressing the switch on the wall, and asked him to hold the pizza while she unlocked the kitchen door. He followed her inside and deposited the pizza on the white tile countertop.

She flicked another switch. Cold blue fluorescent lighting flickered on. "I'll be back in a minute."

She disappeared through a doorway. Lucky moved to the window overlooking her backyard. It had started to rain. Fat drops bounced on the water in the pool and splattered on the deck. They were such opulent drops, they bent down the leaves of her plants. A jagged streak of lightning divided the sky just above the horizon. Moments later it was followed by a drumroll of thunder.

"Are you hungry?"

He turned. She had come into the kitchen behind him, having changed into a pair of old jeans, a loose pullover, and a pair of soft leather moccasins. Her hair looked freshly brushed. Without the armor of her business suit she looked younger, more vulnerable.

"I guess. Hadn't thought about it."

"Do you like pepperoni pizza?"

"Sure."

"Give me a minute to make a salad."

Lucky was dumbfounded. Was she actually inviting him to stay for supper? He'd expected her to slam the door in his face—if she'd been the one to answer it. If he had encountered her husband on the other side of the threshold, he planned to ask directions or something equally as ludicrous.

When he hadn't gotten an answer after ringing her doorbell, he had decided to wait and see who turned up first and play it by ear from there. Being invited to dinner hadn't even crossed his mind as a possibility.

She had removed salad greens and tomatoes from the refrigerator and was calmly tearing lettuce into a bowl. He said, "You don't seem surprised to see me."

"I'm not."

He propped his hip against the counter. "How come?"

"You said you never take no for an answer from a woman." She lifted her eyes to his. "I believe you. Excuse me." She nudged him aside, reached into the refrigerator again and took out a bottle of salad dressing, and, to his further astonishment, a bottle of red wine. She passed it to him, along with a corkscrew, which she took from a drawer. "Would you please?"

Mystified by her composure, Lucky peeled the sealing material off the wine bottle and twisted the corkscrew into the cork. He watched her set the table with two place settings. She placed several slices of pizza in the microwave oven to warm.

"Glasses?"

"Beneath the cabinet."

He noticed then that two rows of wineglass stems were hanging upside down from a rack mounted on the underside of the cabinet. He slid out two and poured each of them a glass of wine. Devon lighted a candle, placed it in the center of the table, and motioned him into a chair.

Lucky approached the table, bringing with him the two glasses of wine, along with the bottle, and sat down in the chair she'd indicated. She sat down across from him and began serving his plate from the large salad bowl. Once both their plates were filled with salad and pizza, he reached across the table and caught her hand in the act of reaching for her wineglass.

"What gives with you?" he asked tautly.

"What do you mean?"

"What happens if your husband comes home and finds us sharing a cozy candlelight dinner?"

"Would that bother you?"

"A whole hell of a lot."

"He won't."

"You're sure?"

"I'm sure. He won't be home tonight." She pulled her hand back, reached for her glass, and sipped the wine.

The mingling, mouthwatering aromas of oregano and mozzarella had reminded Lucky that he hadn't eaten all day. He took a huge bite of pizza and washed it down with a swallow of wine. Wine wasn't his beverage of choice, but it seemed appropriate to drink when the woman he was sharing his meal with had hair the same deep red color.

"It's good," he said politely.

"Thank you."

"Do you do this often?"

She bit into a slice of pizza, pulling on the stringy cheese until it eventually broke off. "What? Bring pizza home for dinner?"

Lucky munched on his own chewy bite, swallowed, and said with a patience he didn't feel, "No, have men over for dinner when your husband is out of town."

"I didn't say he was out of town. I just said he wouldn't be home tonight."

Tired of her word games, he set his fists on either side of his plate and glared at her until she looked up at him. "Do you do this often?"

She held out for a few moments more before answering. Eventually her stubbornness surrendered to his. "You're the first man I've had to dinner in this house. Now, does that salve your ego, or whatever the hell it is that causes you to badger me about things that are none of your business?"

"Yeah, thanks."

"You're welcome."

"I'm flattered."

"Don't be. I just knew you wouldn't go away without first having your 'talk.' I was hungry." She shrugged, letting him draw his own conclusion. "It's certainly not a violation of the marriage vows for two adults to share a pizza."

"Unless those same two adults have shared a pillow."

Her eyes connected with his and reflected the glazed shock of a nocturnal animal caught in headlights bearing down on it.

To increase her astonishment even more, lightning struck nearby. Following a rending sound like the cracking of a bullwhip, all the lights went out except for the steadily burning flame of the candle.

"Are you all right?" Lucky asked, stunned by the sudden absence of the sterile fluorescent lighting.

"Of course. I'm fine." She didn't look fine. The hand that reached for her wineglass was trembling.

"Devon." Acting on instinct, he reached across the table to capture her hand. It was cold. He enfolded it in the warmth of his. After glancing over each of her chilled fingertips with his thumb, he settled it in the cup of her palm, stroking evocatively. "About that, Devon . . ."

"About what?"

"About us sharing a pillow, a bed. You don't have any-thing to worry about." Her head tilted quizzically. "I mean about birth control or anything. I took care of that. I didn't know if you were aware of—"

"Yes, yes, I was," she stammered. "Thank you. You behaved . . ." She faltered and swallowed with difficulty. "You were a perfect gentleman about that."

His crooked grin was self-deprecating. "If I'd been a perfect gentleman, I wouldn't have tracked you down, tricked my way into your room, and coerced you into let-ting me stay the night."

"You were injured. By the way, how's the knife wound?" She lowered her gaze to his midsection.

"It's okay. You can barely see it anymore."

"Oh."

He didn't know at exactly what point in the conversa-tion they had started whispering. It was silly, really, but somehow the topic, the setting, and the mood called for soft, confidential voices.

They simultaneously realized that their eyes seemed locked to each other and that he was still stroking her palm. Guiltily she pulled her hand from his grasp, though he was reluctant to let it go. Taking his cue from her, he resumed eating, but his appetite for food had deserted him, to be replaced by hunger for her.

The only sounds in the silent house were those of the rain pelting the windows and of cutlery against their plates. However, if sexual awareness and suppressed long-ings were capable of generating sound, the noise would have been as blaring as a brass band.

"More pizza?" she asked.

"No thanks."

"Salad?"

He shook his head. As she cleared the dishes from the table, he refilled both their wineglasses. When she returned to the table, he noticed their reflections in the window glass. It was a portrait of intimacy, a man and a woman sharing a candlelight dinner. Devon noticed it too.

"Appearances can be deceiving."

"Yes," she answered softly.

After a moment he said, "Devon, I'm going to shoot straight with you. You don't know me very well, but I assure you that shooting straight is not something I usually do with a woman."

"I don't find that at all hard to believe." She was smiling as she raised her wineglass to her lips.

"No, I guess not," he said ruefully. Leaning back in his chair, he contemplated the candle's flame through the ruby contents of his wineglass. "There's this girl in Milton Point that I've been seeing for a couple of months."

"Rest assured that I don't intend to make trouble between you and your girlfriend."

"That's not what this is about," he said crossly.

"Then why bring it up?"

"Because you need to know about her."

"What makes you think I'm interested in your romances?"

"This isn't about romance. Just hear me out, okay? Then you'll get your turn." She gave him a small nod of concession. "This girl's daddy is a big shot at the bank that's holding a loan on my business."

"Is that why you were dating her?"

He got the impression that she would be disappointed if he said yes. "No. I started seeing Susan because she was one of the few available women in town that I hadn't been to bed with yet."

She cast her eyes downward. "I see."

"I told you I was going to shoot straight, Devon."

"And I appreciate your honesty," she replied huskily. "Go on."

"Susan is spoiled rotten. Accustomed to winding her daddy and everybody else around her little finger. Selfish. Self-centered." He could go on and on, but felt that he had captured the essence of Susan's personality and didn't want to be accused of overkill. "Anyway, she's made up her mind that she wants to be Mrs. Lucky Tyler."

"Why?"

He shrugged. "My sister says because it would distinguish her."

"That's considered a distinction in Milton Point?"

"By some," he said testily.

"I take it you're not too keen on the idea of marrying her."

"There's no chance in hell that I'm going to marry her."

"Have you told her that?"

"Twice."

"Apparently she doesn't take no for an answer either."

His temper snapped. Scowling, he said, "I'm pouring out my guts here, trying to explain things to you, and all you can do is make these snide little remarks."

"Your romantic intrigues might be fascinating to some women, but I don't see what your problems with this Susan have to do with me."

"I'm getting to that."

"Please do."

"Last week Susan volunteered to lie to the authorities, saying that she had slept with me the night of the fire."

"In exchange for a wedding ring, I suppose."

"Bingo."

"To which you said . . . ?"

"Nothing. I didn't take it seriously. I thought maybe if I ignored her, she'd give up and go away."

"No such luck?"

"No such luck. Today she called and insisted on seeing me."

"What happened?"

"She's threatened to tell another lie. Only this time she

says she'll tell them that I outlined to her my plan to torch our garage and use the insurance money to pay off the bank note."

"They would never believe her."

"The hell they wouldn't. To their way of thinking, she would be making an ultimate sacrifice. She's willing to squander her reputation as a Goody Two Shoes by making it public that she's been sleeping with me."

"Has she?"

He could tell that she regretted asking the question almost before she'd completed it. That gave him a glimmer of hope. She cared enough to wonder about his other lovers. Could she also be a tad jealous?

"No, Devon. I've never slept with her. I swear." His eyes bore deeply into hers, trying to impress the truth into her mind. Her next question indicated that she had been persuaded.

"Then what have you got to worry about?"

"Plenty. Susan can be very convincing. Hell, this afternoon, I almost believed her myself when she began to cry and say that she couldn't hold in her ugly secret any longer.

" 'I can't go through the rest of my life with this on my conscience,' she said, or words to that effect. She was talking like it was fact, going on and on about how unhappy I'd made her by confiding my nefarious plan to her."

Devon's fingers absently trailed up and down the stem of her wineglass while she pondered what he'd told her.

"I presume that the only way Susan would be happy again is if you proposed marriage, in which case she would conveniently forget that you're an arsonist."

"That was the implication, yeah. If we were formally engaged, she would switch her stories to 'protect' me."

"At the same time protecting your business from bankruptcy."

He nodded grimly. "I dismissed her threats until today. This afternoon I saw just how destructive she could be."

"Hell hath no fury, et cetera."

"Especially since I was supposed to be having dinner with her when I was in bed with you."

Devon's lips parted, but remained speechless.

"When she found out about that, well, that really capped it. My sister, Sage, tried to warn me about Susan. I laughed off her warnings. I shouldn't have. Susan is devious and audacious, willing to go to any lengths to get what she's after.

"Damn my own hide, I made it easy for her to trap me, and at the same time bring down my whole family. Out of pure spite, she's not above making our lives hell. She can and will do it."

"Unless I tell the authorities where you really were the night of the fire," Devon said slowly.

"That's right." With emotional gruffness he added, "Unless you tell them that I was making love to you."

"Don't call it that!" Devon's words were a whisper, but an exclamation just the same. She left her chair so hurriedly that her thigh bumped the rim of the table and rocked the candle.

Lucky left his chair just as quickly. Devon was leaning into the countertop, her hands curled into fists on the tiles along the edge.

He stepped behind her and, for a split second, wrestled with his conscience. He shouldn't touch her. He shouldn't. Even knowing that, he placed one of his hands on the countertop beside hers and curved his other arm around her waist, flattening his hand on her stomach and burying his face in the nape of her neck. He luxuriated in the silky feel of her hair against his lips.

"That's what it was, Devon. Deny it with your dying breath if it soothes your conscience, but that won't ever change what it was."

"Leave me alone," she moaned. "Please."

"Listen to me," he said urgently. "That arson rap isn't the only reason I'm here. You know that. You knew it yesterday. I would have come looking for you whether or not I was in trouble. I had to see you again.

"You wanted to see me again just as badly. I don't care how many times you deny it, I know it's true. You're not only running from involvement in a criminal case and what effects it might have on your life. You're running from this." He lightly ground his hand over her belly, skimmed her mound, the top of her thigh.

"Don't! Don't touch me like that."

"Why?"

"Because . . . because . . ."

"Because it drives you as crazy as it does me."

"Stop."

"Only if you tell me I'm wrong about the way you feel. Tell me I'm wrong, Devon, then I'll stop."

"Please. Just leave me alone."

"I can't." He groaned. "I can't."

She turned her head toward her shoulder. He lowered his. Their mouths met in a greedy kiss. She turned into the circle of his arms, which pulled her against him. Resting his hands on her hips, guiding them, he positioned her against him.

As his passions burned hotter, he also got angrier because he knew she was forbidden to him. Despite his penchant to misbehave during Sunday school, some spiritual training had penetrated his young mind. That formal religious instruction, plus all the moral lessons drilled into him by his conscientious parents, declared that this was wrong, wrong, wrong.

Yet he couldn't deny himself her kisses, not when her mouth was warm and sweet and eager. He kept telling himself that the next kiss would be the last—forever. But one only made him hungry for more.

"Dammit, Devon, resist me. Stop this. Stop me." He was so obsessed with her, he was seized by a primal urge to fight for her. Pressing her head between his hands, he tilted her head back drastically. "Where is he? Where is the slob you're married to? Where was he when you were traveling around East Texas alone? Is he crazy to give you that kind of freedom? Is he blind? Why isn't the bastard here now, protecting you from me, protecting you from yourself?"

Lucky had posed the questions rhetorically. He didn't really expect answers. That's why he was shocked when she cried, "He's in prison!"

The lights suddenly came back on.

Chapter Twelve

Lucky blinked several times. Watching him, Devon realized it was from shock as much as from the sudden glare of the fluorescent tubes overhead. The stark light was offensive and unwelcome. It revealed too much. She edged out from between Lucky and the counter and switched it off. She was more comfortable with only the glow from the single candle on the table. It made her feel less exposed.

"Prison?" He remained in the same spot, as though his boots were nailed to the floor.

"The minimum-security federal prison in East Texas. It's only about fifty miles from—"

"I know where it is."

"I'd been there to see him and was on my way home when I decided to do some research for my article. I figured that a tavern in a less urban area would better prove my theory. As it turned out, I was right."

That was all the explanation he needed. At least, it was

all he was going to get. She wasn't going to provide him with a detailed account of her visit with her husband, which had left her terribly upset. It was none of his business to know how shattering that visit had been.

By pure chance Lucky Tyler had happened to be at the right place at the right time—or the wrong place and time, depending on one's point of view—to take advantage of her highly emotional state.

"What's he in the pen for?"

"Insider trading. SEC violations."

"Did he do it?"

"Of course not!" she lied. "Do you think I'd marry a criminal?" At least she'd believed in his innocence when she'd married him.

"How the hell do I know?" He moved then, bearing down on her angrily. "All I really know about you is that you cheat on your husband."

The accusation sounded ugly. Because she couldn't tell him the truth, she pretended to be angry and responded with a quick denial. "I do not!"

"That's not the way I remember it."

Moving to the door, she jerked it open. "You can leave the same way you came in—through the back door. I'll open the garage for you."

"Not that easy, Devon."

"Now that you understand the awkward position you've placed me in, I'm asking you to go."

"I don't understand anything!" he shouted, reaching beyond her shoulder to slam the door closed again. It created a waft of air that disturbed the candle and made it flicker, projecting wavering shadows of them onto the walls. "We're about to have our second night together."

"What are you talking about?"

"I'm not leaving until I have a full explanation from you."

"I don't owe you—"

"Is Haines your name or his?"

"Mine. His name is Shelby. Greg Shelby."

"How long have you been married?"

She was in no mood to be grilled, but he wasn't going to leave without the full picture, and, she admitted, she couldn't blame him. If their positions were reversed, she would be just as frustrated as he. He wouldn't have to know all of it. Just some of it. That would pacify him.

Or would it? When she fell victim to his compelling blue stare, as now, his eyes seemed to see straight through her. It was unsettling, even frightening. What if she accidentally let her guard down and by way of a look, a sigh, prompted him to guess or learn the single most important fact of that night that he didn't seem to remember?

To cover her uneasiness, she politely asked, "Would you like some coffee?"

"No."

"Something?"

"Answers."

"Let's go into the living room."

She cupped her hand behind the candle flame and blew it out. In darkness she navigated the hallway leading into the living room. There, she switched on only one lamp before taking a seat in the corner of an ivory upholstered sofa. Lucky dropped onto the hassock in front of the blue leather chair, spread his knees wide, and loosely clasped his hands between them.

"Shoot," he said.

She began without preamble. "When Greg's trial came up, I asked my editor's permission to do a feature story on him."

"You didn't know him before that?"

"No."

"What piqued your interest enough to want to write about him?"

"Most criminals, from serial killers to petty thieves, fit a particular profile," she said. "White-collar criminals are generally arrogant and condescending toward their prosecutors, whether they're proved guilty or not."

"Go on."

"Well, from what I'd read about Greg, he didn't fit that profile. He was pathetically earnest in his denials of any wrongdoing. That intrigued me. I sold my editor on the idea. He said to go for it. Next, I had to go through Greg's attorney and the D.A.'s Office to get their permission. This took several weeks.

"Greg's lawyer stipulated that he be present during the interviews, which I agreed to. The prosecutor stipulated that the articles would have to be read and approved by someone in the D.A.'s Office before publication. You see, they couldn't lean toward either guilt or innocence, but had to be completely unbiased." Lucky nodded. "When everyone was satisfied, I was finally granted my first interview with Greg."

"Love at first sight?"

"No, but I was attracted."

"Physically?"

"Among other things."

"A man in handcuffs can be a real turn-on."

She ignored his sarcasm. "He wasn't in jail at the time. He had posted bail."

Thinking back on that first meeting in his attorney's office, Devon recalled wondering how anyone could suspect Greg of being guilty of an outstanding parking ticket, much less a felony. He was impeccably dressed in a three-piece, very conservative charcoal-gray suit, white shirt, sedately striped tie. His reddish-brown hair had been carefully combed back from his high, smooth forehead. He could have given Emily Post lessons on courtesy.

"What did you get from that first meeting?" Lucky asked.

"A sense of his background."

"Which was?"

"He was reared in a Pennsylvania steel town by very strict and religious parents from whom he was—and is to this day—estranged."

"Why? I can't imagine willfully cutting myself off from my family."

Devon could have guessed that. Earlier he had expressed regret over causing his family their present difficulties. Apparently what affected one Tyler affected them all, and each took the others' problems to heart.

"Greg wasn't fortunate enough to have the family closeness that you enjoy, Mr. Tyler. Indeed, few people are," she said reflectively, sadly. "Greg's father had worked for the same steel company all his life. He couldn't grasp the concept of playing the stock market, and ridiculed Greg for not holding down a steady job."

"So you've never met his parents?"

"No."

"What about yours? What do they think of having a son-in-law in jail?"

"My parents are dead."

"Oh. I'm sorry. I know how it feels to lose a parent. My dad died a couple of years ago." She acknowledged that with a nod of her head. "How soon after that first meeting did you start dating Shelby?"

"We've never had an actual date." The statement drew a frown of disbelief from Lucky. "It's true. His attorney advised us against being seen together socially. It wouldn't be appropriate for a man on trial to be seen doing the town."

"So the courtship took place under the lawyer's watchful eye? Bet he got a kick out of that," Lucky commented scornfully.

"He isn't a voyeur. After the first couple of meetings he realized he could trust me, that I wasn't there to exploit his client, so he left us alone."

"How convenient."

"Actually it was," she snapped. "We had time to get to know each other."

"I'll bet."

"I realized just how falsely Greg had been accused. He knew that someone in his firm had leaked valuable information to certain clients. Whoever it was had been very clever. He left a trail of evidence pointing directly at Greg. Greg's defense was based solely on his lack of material gain. If he'd committed the crime for profit, where was the profit?"

"Hey," Lucky said, "I'm not the jury. They've already reached a verdict. I'm more interested in you . . . and Greg, of course."

"As time went on, Greg and I became more emotionally involved."

"Hmm."

"It was difficult to maintain an objective viewpoint."

"No doubt."

"I wanted to defend him myself, so I had to give up writing the articles. They created a conflict of interest that no credible journalist can afford. Greg was upset by that. He hadn't wanted our romance to interfere with my career."

"The free publicity couldn't have been all that bad either."

That comment struck a sore spot. "What's that supposed to mean?"

"Nothing, nothing," Lucky said tiredly, as though it didn't matter. "So when Shelby popped the question, you said yes?"

"That's right. He asked me to marry him as soon as the trial was over. But I wanted to get married right then."

"Why?"

Yes, why? What had she been out to prove? That she was smarter than his accusers, that she was right in her estimation of him when everyone else was wrong? Or had it gone back to her mother's death a few years earlier? Her mother's earnest claims of being ill still echoed inside her head. Had they overlapped with Greg's avowals of innocence?

"I'm in pain, Devon. Truly. I can't stand it. Please help me."

"I'm innocent, Devon. I swear it. You've got to help me."

She couldn't turn a deaf ear to a desperate person seeking help. Because of what had happened with her mother, her heart was compelled to believe Greg, even when the facts didn't bear out his claims of innocence.

Only later had she realized she'd been duped. She had bought his entire act, swallowed the bait whole, played right into his hands. It was almost as though Greg had crawled inside her head and heard her mother's feeble voice saying the words that haunted Devon. He had known exactly how to manipulate her to pity.

To admit that to Lucky Tyler was unthinkable, however.

She continued to defend Greg adamantly, because there was no graceful way out. Besides, he *was*, legally, her husband. Marriage carried with it responsibilities one didn't just turn one's back on.

In answer to Lucky's question, she perpetuated the myth she had created, even though she knew it to be a justification for her gullibility. "I married him to demonstrate my confidence in his innocence. We were married in a civil ceremony in his lawyer's office."

"So how long between the nuptials and his conviction?"

"Two days. Greg was the only witness his defense attorney called to the stand," she explained. "He was eloquent and sincere. I couldn't believe my ears when the jury returned a guilty verdict."

She closed her eyes. "I can still see the bailiffs moving toward him to take him into custody. Greg looked stricken."

And furious, she thought. His failure to sway the jurors had enraged him. Those twelve people hadn't been convinced of his sincerity. She was the only one who had been fooled.

"How long ago was that?"

"Eleven months."

"What was his sentence?"

"Two years in prison. Ten years probation. His lawyer says he'll probably serve less than half that."

"So he could be paroled soon."

"He comes up for review in a few weeks."

Lucky stood up and put his back to her. He slid his

hands, palms out, into the hip pockets of his jeans. There was a palpable tension in the way he held his shoulders. When he came back around, his expression was fierce and angry.

"How many times in the last eleven months have you cheated on him?"

"None of your business."

"The hell it's not!" Grabbing her hand, he pulled her to her feet. "I don't know if I'm one of dozens, one of an elite few, or the one and only. Frankly I don't know which I prefer, but I damn sure want to know."

"It doesn't make any difference."

"It does to me."

Tears threatened. She wanted to shout the truth at him. *You're the only one. Ever.* Instead, her voice cracking, she whispered, "You're the only one."

His shoulders relaxed marginally, and some of the ferocity in his eyes dimmed. "Guess I'll have to take your word for that."

"Whether you do or not, it's the truth."

"Do you love him?"

"He's my husband."

"That's not what I asked."

"I'm not going to discuss my relationship with my husband with you."

"Why not?"

"Because you have no right to know."

"You shared your body, but you won't share a few facts?"

"I didn't *share* anything." She protested verbally, but the words didn't originate in her heart. "What happened just . . . evolved. It started with a few kisses and went from there. You caught me unaware."

"You were unaware of my tongue on your nipple?"

No, she inwardly groaned. She remembered every touch in vivid detail, but desperately wished she didn't. "I was half-asleep. I merely responded to the stimuli."

He took a menacing step forward. "If you tell me you were pretending that I was your husband, I'll strangle you."

"No," she said tearfully, "I wasn't pretending that."

Unable to meet his stare, she lowered her eyes. The silence in the house pressed in on her suffocatingly. His sheer physicality overwhelmed her.

To put essential space between them, she began to wander restlessly around the room, restacking magazines on the end table, looking for any task that would keep her hands occupied and her eyes off him.

"They used to stone women for doing what you did."

Fluffing the sofa pillows, she sprang erect. "What *we* did, Mr. Tyler. You were in that bed too."

"I remember," he said tightly. "I'm willing to take my share of the responsibility for what happened. You're not."

Placing her hands on her hips, she confronted him belligerently. "What would you suggest I do? Go through the city passing out rocks to everyone? Or start wearing a red letter *A* on my chest? In some cultures, they behead adulterers. Do you think justice would be served then? If so, are you willing to place your head on the same chopping block? Because it sure as hell was on the same pillow."

That reminder abruptly ended the shouting match. She turned her back on him.

"I had a lapse of judgment and made a mistake," she said. "Believe me, my conscience has been punishing me ever since."

He moved in behind her and spoke her name, his voice soft and consoling now. Taking her by the shoulders, he turned her around to face him and tilted her head up with a finger beneath her chin.

"I don't want to punish you. Whether you believe it or not, I blame myself a whole lot more than I blame you. I could confess ten sins to every one of yours, I'm sure. Adultery has *never* been one of them before, but . . ."

As their gazes moved together and locked, his voice dwindled to nothingness.

"Never?" she said hoarsely.

"Never."

"If you had known I was married . . ."

He pondered his answer for several seconds before saying, "I'm not sure it would have mattered."

Then, not only did their stares merge, but their recollections as well. Each remembered the smell and touch and taste of the other. Each had actively participated in what happened in that motel-room bed. Each had to accept his share of the blame, take responsibility for it.

"I have to vouch for you," she whispered. "I really don't have a choice, do I?"

"Yes, you do," he replied, surprising her. "I won't force you to, Devon."

"But if I don't, it'll mean so much more hardship on you and your family. I can't let that happen. Ever since you told me yesterday about the fire, I've known I would eventually have to come forward as your alibi. It's the right thing to do." She gave a wistful little smile. "I guess I was hoping for a miracle that would make it unnecessary."

He touched the corner of her smile with his fingertip. "Your husband will never have to know. We'll keep your identity a secret. I haven't been officially charged. I'm just a prime suspect. Once you've told them that I was with you from dusk to dawn that night, I'll be cleared, and you'll be free to go. It'll never become a matter of public record."

Situations of this magnitude were rarely resolved that easily, she knew. Still, she didn't want to throw a cloak of pessimism over his expectations. "I'll take tomorrow off and come to Milton Point. I want to get it over with as soon as possible."

"I would appreciate that too," he said. "The sooner I'm off the hook, the better."

His mouth split into the same sort of grin he'd first given her from the end of her booth in the bar. It made him dashingly, piratically handsome.

Since the night she had spent with him, she had asked herself a million times how she could have done such a foolhardy thing. The more time she spent with him, the more reasonable the explanations became. What woman, no matter how level-headed and self-reliant, could resist that smile?

Even though she was still suffering the consequences of submitting to it, she felt her body once again growing warm and fluid as a result of it. "Where should I go when I get to Milton Point?" she asked, forcing herself to think pragmatically.

"Why don't you come to the house around noon? I'll call Pat and have him bring out the investigators to take your deposition or whatever they need."

"Who's Pat?"

"The sheriff, Pat Bush. You met him, remember? It's a good thing, too, because he can positively identify you as the woman I picked up in the place."

"You didn't exactly pick me up."

"Figure of speech. No call to get riled."

"Well, I am riled. I've agreed to do what you want, so please leave now." She marched to the front door and pulled it open.

"Don't you need directions to my house?"

"I'll look up the address in the phone book."

"Suit yourself."

"I always do," she retorted, unwilling to let him have the last word.

He got it anyway. Before he stepped across the threshold, his hand shot out and curved around the nape of her neck. He hauled her mouth up to his for a scorching kiss. " 'Night, Dovey," he whispered before releasing her and ambling down the sidewalk.

Chapter Thirteen

She was still miffed when he greeted her at his front door at noon the following day. He had known the goodnight kiss would make her mad. That's why he'd done it. He took mischievous pleasure in provoking her simply because she was so easily and delightfully provoked. He was challenged to see how many different ways he could do it.

Besides, he had wanted to kiss her.

He wanted to now too. But that didn't seem a very good idea, not when she took care not even to let her clothes brush against him as she entered the hallway of his home.

She was dressed for business in a pale yellow linen suit with a straight skirt, the hemline just at her knees, and a tailored jacket decorated with a silver lapel pin. Her matching silver earrings showed up well in her ears, because she had pulled her hair back into a no-nonsense bun. Her expression was just shy of combative.

"Hello," she said coolly.

"Hi." He gave her the cocky grin he knew she found aggravating.

"You failed to mention that you lived outside the city limits in the country."

"I offered to give directions, remember? You wouldn't let me. Did you get lost?"

"I'm here, aren't I?"

"Yeah, you're here, looking more like the preacher's wife come calling than an overnight alibi. Who's gonna believe I tumbled you?" The devil in him was kicking up his heels, goading him to say things he knew damn well would rub her the wrong way. But he felt he was justified in being ornery. He didn't particularly like her attitude either.

"What did you expect me to wear? A negligee?"

"I—"

"Lucky, has our guest arrived?"

Laurie Tyler entered the hallway through an arched opening. "Hello," she said pleasantly, extending her hand to Devon. "I'm Laurie Tyler, Lucky's mother."

"I'm Devon Haines."

"Come in, Ms. Haines. Everybody's out in the kitchen. I don't know why we have so many extra rooms in this house. I think we'd have been better off just building one enormous kitchen. Seems like that's where everybody always ends up."

"Are the investigators here already?" Devon asked with uncertainty, glancing over her shoulder at the cars parked in the semicircular driveway.

"Not yet. Those belong to family," Laurie told her.

"Curious onlookers," Lucky said sardonically. "You've drawn a crowd."

He received a reproving look from his mother before she took Devon by the forearm and led the way. "Lunch is a casual meal around here. Chicken salad is on the menu today. I thought that sounded good since the weather is so muggy. You're hungry, I hope?"

"Well, I, yes, I suppose. I hadn't counted on eating lunch."

Lucky observed the two women as he followed them through the formal dining room, which was reserved for holidays, birthdays, and special parties. His mother's unqualified friendliness had flustered Devon. Laurie often had that effect on strangers. Until given grounds to change her mind, she was always accepting of people, and had a knack for putting them at ease.

She propelled Devon into the kitchen and announced her to the rest as though she *were* a new preacher's wife come calling. "Everybody, this is Devon Haines, who has so unselfishly agreed to help Lucky out of this trouble he's in. Devon, that's Tanya, my daughter-in-law; Sage, my youngest child; and Chase, Lucky's older brother."

They regarded her with unabashed curiosity, but murmured polite hellos, knowing that Laurie would tolerate nothing less.

"Sage, scoot your chair over and let Devon sit there between you and Lucky. Devon, would you like iced tea or lemonade?"

"Uh, iced tea, please."

"Fine, I'll get it. Sugar and lemon are on the table. Lucky, hand her that plate out of the refrigerator. And you can start on your lunch now that she's here." As she passed the glass of iced tea to Devon she added, "He was too nervous to eat before you arrived."

"I wasn't nervous," he remarked crossly. He set the prefilled plates on the table and threw his leg over the seat of his chair, straddling it. "I was afraid she wouldn't show."

Devon reacted as though she'd been goosed. "I said I would, didn't I?"

"Yeah, but you've been known to skip without giving prior notice."

"Well, she's here and that's the important thing," Chase said, intervening when Tanya gouged him in the ribs with her elbow. "We're all very glad that you agreed to clear Lucky, Ms. Haines. At no small expense to yourself."

"Because you're married and all." Sage, who had remained blessedly silent, could restrain herself no longer. "You sure don't look like what I thought one of Lucky's pickups would."

"Sage!"

"I didn't mean to be rude, Mother. I know you're as surprised as I am that she's not wearing dragon-green eyeshadow and fishnet stockings. I like your suit, by the way," she said, smiling at Devon guilelessly.

"Th-thank you," Devon stammered.

Having wanted to agitate Devon himself a few moments

ago, Lucky now wanted to throttle his little sister for being so rude. Devon's cheeks were flushed and her eyes abnormally bright, but her lips looked pale beneath her pearly beige lipstick.

Tanya threw her a lifeline. "How long have you been a journalist, Ms. Haines?"

"Going on five years," Devon replied, giving Tanya a grateful smile. "Ever since I graduated from college. I started out writing obits and fillers for a smaller newspaper in South Texas before getting the job in Dallas."

"I read your columns faithfully. They're very interesting."

"Tactfully put," she said with a soft laugh. "Sometimes my readers take issue with me."

"I don't always agree with your opinion," Tanya admitted with a smile, "but you always give me food for thought."

"I'm glad to hear that."

"Do you write at home, or do you go to the newspaper offices every day?" Sage wanted to know.

"Where do you get your ideas?" Chase asked.

"Y'all hush and let Ms. Haines eat her lunch," Laurie said, then disobeyed her own order and asked, "Do you use one of those word processors?"

Devon laughed. "I don't mind the questions. Really. I enjoy talking about my work."

She answered their questions in turn. Lucky was interested in her answers himself, but tried not to let his interest show as he ate chicken salad that he didn't even taste.

His family was treating her like the Queen of Sheba. Hell, he was the one in trouble, not her. Why weren't they giving her the third degree about sleeping with strangers the way they'd given him?

Even as he posed these disgruntled questions to himself, he knew that if any of them breathed a disparaging word to her, he'd jump right down their throats in her defense.

"Who called Pat?" Laurie asked. She had parted the curtains and was looking through the window over the sink at the approaching patrol car.

"I didn't," Lucky said. "I thought we were going to wait until after lunch, Chase."

"So did I. I didn't call him."

Chase left his chair and moved to stand beside his mother at the window. "He's alone. The agents aren't with him." He had the back door opened before Pat even reached it. The sheriff stepped into the kitchen and removed his hat and sunglasses.

"Hi, everybody." Nodding down at the table, he added, "Sorry to interrupt your lunch."

"Please join us, Pat," Laurie said. "There's plenty."

"I can't, but thanks."

"Something to drink?"

"Nothing, thanks."

So far Pat had avoided looking at any of them directly

and was uneasily shifting his weight from one foot to the other while restlessly moving his fingers around the brim of his hat—dead giveaways that this wasn't a social call.

Lucky pushed aside his unfinished plate and stood up. "What is it, Pat?"

Pat Bush looked at him with a beleaguered expression. He removed a folded document from the breast pocket of his uniform shirt. "I have a warrant for your arrest."

Sage and Tanya gasped. Laurie raised a hand to her chest as though someone had just wounded her. Devon's pale lips parted in surprise. Chase's reaction was volatile. He exclaimed, "What the hell?"

Lucky snatched the document from the sheriff, scanned it, then tossed it down onto the table. He muttered words his mother wouldn't normally have allowed spoken in her house. "I have an alibi," he told Pat, pointing down at Devon.

"So I see. Ma'am." After acknowledging her, Pat looked back at Lucky. "Once a warrant has been issued, I haven't got a choice. You'll have to come with me now. Chase can bring the lady in when they start to question you. It'll all be cleared up soon."

"Does he have to be placed under arrest?" Laurie asked.

"I'm sorry about it, Laurie, but, yeah, he does. He can finish his lunch though. I'm in no hurry to get back to town."

"Well, I'm in a hurry to get this mess over with. Let's go." Lucky stamped toward the door.

Pat caught his arm. "We've got to do this by the book. I've got to Mirandize you."

"Fine," Lucky said tautly. "But can we go outside? I don't want my mother to have to listen."

"Don't patronize me, James Lawrence," she said sharply. "I'm not a shrinking violet who needs protection from anything unpleasant. I fought your daddy's cancer for two years before losing him to it. I'm unwilling to give up another member of my family just now, so if they want a fight, they'll get one," she said staunchly.

"Way to go, Mother," said Sage, looking just as determined as Laurie.

Lucky winked at his mother. "Fix something good for supper, because I'll be home way before then." He went through the back door. Pat doffed his hat to the ladies and followed him out.

Pat read him his rights. "Hate like hell having to do this," he mumbled as he clamped the handcuffs around Lucky's wrists.

"Just do it and stop apologizing for it. I understand. It's your duty."

"I'm doubly glad you've got the woman."

"Why?" Lucky asked as he ducked his head and climbed into the backseat of the patrol car. Pat's grim tone of voice sounded discouraging and made him uneasy.

" 'Cause they've got Susan Young, and she, my friend, is saying you did it."

. . .

One had to admire Devon's composure as she entered the interrogation room. The two federal agents smoked like chimneys, so the small room was filled with smoke. She was like a breath of fresh air as she entered with Pat.

He directed her to a chair; she sat down without compromising her straight, proud posture. Lucky tried to catch her eye and give her an encouraging nod, but she didn't even glance in his direction. Instead, she gave the agent her undivided attention.

Once the pleasantries were out of the way, he got down to business. "Mr. Tyler claims that he was with you the night his building burned to the ground."

Her green stare was cool and steady. "That's right. He was."

Pat sat down on a corner of the table in front of her. In a far less intimidating voice he said, "Tell us how and when you two met."

"As you know, Sheriff Bush, we met that same afternoon in a lounge on Highway Two Seventy-seven." A frown wrinkled her brow. "I'm not sure about the name."

"It doesn't have a name," Pat said.

"Oh. Then I guess that's why I don't remember it."

"Just tell us what happened," one of the agents interjected impatiently as he lit another cigarette.

Calmly Devon told them about going into the place to do research on her article on sexism. She admitted that it wasn't wise. "However, I was being as unobtrusive as possible. With absolutely no encouragement from me, two men approached my table and offered to buy me a drink. They refused to take no for an answer."

Her eyes suddenly connected with Lucky's. Inadvertently she had used the phrase that they had frequently batted back and forth. He figured that everybody in the room could hear the sizzle of the current that arced between them. Devon quickly averted her head.

She told the rest of the story, perfectly corroborating Pat's and his own account. She verbally led the investigators into the motel room.

"I opened my door to Mr. Tyler because he was hurt." That was a slight distortion of fact, but only he could testify otherwise, and he wasn't going to. "I tended to his wounds," she said. "He was in no condition to drive, so he . . . he stayed there with me all night, and was there when I left the following morning, which was around six o'clock."

Lucky looked up at his two accusers and gave them a gloating smile. "Now, can we cut the rest of this crap?"

They ignored him. One motioned Pat off the corner of the table and assumed that position directly in front of Devon. "Are you a licensed physician, Ms. Haines?"

"What the—"

Devon overrode Lucky's angry exclamation. "Of course not."

"But you felt qualified to take care of a knife wound and

a black eye that, by all accounts, came close to blinding him?"

"On the contrary, I didn't feel qualified at all. I advised Mr. Tyler to go to a hospital, but he refused."

"How come?"

"You'll have to ask him."

"I did," the agent replied, frowning. "He, in turn, asked me, given the choice, would I rather spend the night in a hospital emergency room or with you."

Through the pall of tobacco smoke, she gave Lucky an injured, inquisitive, incredulous look. "It was a joke, Devon. A joke."

Paler than she had been only moments before, she turned back to the agent. "I was only concerned about Mr. Tyler's injuries," she said quietly. "He'd received those injuries while protecting me, so I felt somewhat responsible. When he refused to get medical help, I did the best I could to take care of him. I thought that was the least I could do to repay him for coming to my defense."

"Did you sleep with him, too, to pay him back for coming to your defense?"

Lucky was out of his chair before his next heartbeat. "Now just a damn minute. She—" Pat's hand fell heavily on his shoulder and spun him around.

"Sit down and shut up."

Pat looked ready to kill him, but Lucky realized that Pat was acting in his best interests. He flung himself back into his chair, glaring balefully at the agent.

"Well, Ms. Haines?"

"Mr. Tyler appeared to be exhausted. I believe he'd had quite a lot to drink. He certainly shouldn't have been driving. When he asked me to let him stay, I let him stay. He hinted at internal injuries."

The two agents looked at each other and shared an arrogant, just-between-us-boys laugh. "And you believed him?" one asked.

"I'll have to remember to use that line myself," the other chimed in.

Lucky didn't have a chance to come out of his chair this time. The sheriff's hand was on his shoulder, anchoring him in his seat. But he snarled at the two agents who were making this as difficult for Devon as they possibly could. They seemed to enjoy her embarrassment.

"I didn't know if he had internal injuries or not," she said sharply. "And neither do you." Her chin went up a notch. "His eye was battered. He could have had a concussion or any number of head injuries too. I did what I thought was best."

"And you're to be commended for your charity," one drawled, winking at the other. "You said he was there in the morning when you left around six o'clock."

"That's right," she replied curtly. Her contempt for them was plain. Knowing how she felt about sexism, Lucky realized that their taunts were intolerable to her. Under the circumstances she was holding up well.

"He was still sleeping when you left?"

"Yes. Soundly."

"He'd been that way all night?"

She faltered, but finally answered, "Yes."

"How do you know?"

"I know."

The agent stood up and slid his hands into his pockets. "Couldn't he have slipped out, driven back to town, set a torch to the garage where they kept all that heavily insured equipment, then returned to the room without you ever knowing he was gone?"

"No."

"It wouldn't have taken him more than, hmm, say two hours."

"He didn't leave."

"You're sure?"

"Positive."

"You sound so definite."

"I am."

"There's a fair amount of space in a motel room to move around, Ms. Haines. Couldn't he have—"

"We were sharing not only the room, but the bed," she stated, her eyes flashing. "If you wanted me to admit that, why weren't you man enough to come right out and ask instead of pussyfooting around?"

"Amen," Lucky intoned.

"Mr. Tyler and I were sleeping in the same bed," Devon continued. "A double bed. Very close to each other, out of necessity. And if Mr. Tyler had gotten up and left the room, he would have awakened me. I'm not that sound a sleeper."

God, she was terrific. Lucky wanted to give her a standing ovation. Or a kiss. Or both. She'd cut the s.o.b.'s down to size. But they weren't giving up entirely.

"Did you sleep without waking up through the night?"

Lucky recognized the trap and hoped that Devon did. If she said yes, they could claim that he had sneaked out and returned without her knowledge, planning all along to use her as his alibi. Her alternative was to admit that she had been intimate with a stranger.

"No." At greater risk to herself, she had opted for the latter choice. Lucky admired her spunk, but suffered for her pride. "I woke up once."

"What for?"

Despite Pat's restraint, Lucky shot from the seat of the chair. "What the hell difference does it make?"

Pat shoved him back down, stepped in front of him, and used his own body as a shield between Lucky and the agents, whom Lucky was prepared to tear apart with his bare hands.

With Lucky temporarily quelled, Pat appealed to the agents. "Look, you two, Ms. Haines has volunteered to come here. You know she's married and that this is uncomfortable for her. Take it easy, okay?"

They ignored him. "Answer the question, Ms. Haines."

She glared at the agent, cast Lucky a swift glance, then

lowered her head to address her damp, clenched hands lying in her lap. "During the night, Mr. Tyler and I . . . were physically intimate."

"Can you prove it?"

Her head snapped up. "Can you prove we weren't?"

"No," the agent retorted, "but I've got another woman in another room claiming virtually the same thing, except she says that he bragged to her about setting a fire to collect insurance money."

"She's lying."

"Is she?"

"Yes."

"How do we know?"

"Because he was with me all night."

"Screwing?"

It would have taken more than Pat Bush's substantial bulk to stop Lucky then. Roaring like a pouncing lion, he launched himself across the room toward the agent who had practically spat the nasty word in Devon's face.

He threw the agent off balance and into the table, sending it crashing to the floor. Cheap wood splintered. Devon gave a surprised cry, sprang from her chair, and backed toward the door out of harm's way.

But then Chase pulled open the door and came barreling through, nearly mowing her down. He'd been waiting in the squad room, but at the first hint of trouble had come charging in to offer assistance to his younger brother.

The second agent, the one not being pummeled by Lucky's flying fists, charged forward to help his cohort. He was grabbed from behind. "Not so fast, buddy," Chase growled into the agent's ear as he restrained him.

Pat, recovering from his dismay, dodged Lucky's fists, grabbed him by the collar, and pulled him to his feet. "What the hell's the matter with you?" he shouted. "This isn't going to help."

He slammed the younger man against the wall and pinned him there by splaying one hand open over Lucky's chest. With his other hand he assisted the agent to his feet.

Lucky's torso was heaving from exertion and fury. He aimed his index finger at the agent. "You son of a bitch. Don't you ever talk to her—"

"I'm filing assault charges against you!" the agent shouted. He took a folded white handkerchief from his pocket and tried to stanch the flow of bright red blood from his cut lip.

"You'll do nothing of the sort," Pat declared in a loud voice. "If you do, I'll go to your superiors and lodge a formal complaint against you for the way you've conducted this interrogation. You intentionally badgered and humiliated Ms. Haines, who was doing her best to cooperate with your investigation."

"He's right," Chase said through gritted teeth. He had the agent's hands up between his shoulder blades. He pushed them higher. The man groaned. "Isn't he right?

Before you answer, maybe you should know that half a dozen deputies and I were listening through the door to every word said in this room."

"Maybe," the agent gasped, "maybe he did get a little out of hand."

"Chase," Pat barked, "let him go. His eyes are bugging out."

Lucky was virtually unaware of what was going on around him. He had tasted blood and wanted more. Glaring at the agent malevolently, he threatened, "I'm gonna nail you—"

"Lucky, shut up!" Pat called forward a deputy from among those congregated in the doorway. "Take him upstairs and lock him up."

"Huh?" The sobering thought of a jail cell snapped Lucky out of his murderous mood. "What for?"

"Suspected arson, remember?" Pat said calmly, nodding the deputy toward Lucky.

"But I'm innocent!"

"That's how you can plead before the judge later this afternoon. In the meantime I recommend you teach your mouth some manners and cool off your temper."

Lucky was too dumbfounded to resist the deputy's manhandling. Besides, this deputy had played on the same regional championship baseball team with Lucky and had been a friend for years. He looked at Devon. "Take her home, Chase."

"Right," his brother said. "Stay the hell out of trouble, will you?"

"See you in court," Lucky quipped as he was escorted through the door. His smile vanished, however, when the crowd of deputies, clerks, and dispatchers parted for him, and he noticed a spot of color in the otherwise monochromatic gray squad room.

Susan Young was standing against the far wall, twirling a strand of hair around her finger and smiling complacently.

Chapter Fourteen

"That was a damn stupid thing to do."

The pickup truck with Tyler Drilling Co. stenciled onto the doors jounced over a chuckhole. Chase downshifted, giving his brother a fulminating glance across the truck's interior. The upholstery's color was no longer distinguishable. It bore layers of grime from scores of drilling sites.

"Don't you know the penalty for assaulting a federal agent?"

"No, do you?" Lucky shot back.

"You know what I mean."

"Well, I wasn't penalized, so leave me alone, okay?" Lucky slumped lower in his seat as Chase herded the pickup through the twilight evening toward their family home. Then, feeling bad for acting surly toward his brother, he added, "Thanks for posting my bail."

"Thank Tanya. The money came out of her house fund."

"Her what?"

"Her house fund. She wants to buy a house, and has been saving money for a down payment."

Lucky shoved back his dark blond hair. "Jeez. I feel terrible."

"Not as terrible as you'd feel spending the time before your trial in jail. And not as terrible as you'd feel if the judge had listened to the prosecutor and placed your bail higher than we could afford."

The federal agents had convinced the prosecutor that they had enough evidence against James Lawrence Tyler to arraign him on an arson charge. They contended that if one woman would lie on his behalf, another would. Why should they believe Devon over Susan? It would be left to the court to decide the veracity of each woman and determine Lucky's guilt or innocence.

Everyone on Lucky's side believed that the agents were acting out of pique now more than conviction of his guilt, but unfortunately there was nothing they could do about it at this point.

Lucky's attorney had pleaded with the judge to reduce the amount of bail recommended by the prosecutor. He cited how well known Lucky was in the community, and guaranteed that his client had every intention of appearing in court to deny the allegations and clear his name. The judge had known the Tyler boys all their lives. They were rowdy, but hardly criminals. He'd been lenient.

"How's Devon?" Lucky asked now.

"Pretty shaken up. Mother took her under her wing."

"Is there any way we can keep her name out of the newspapers? At least until the actual trial?"

"So far, nobody but the people in that interrogation room know who your alibi is. I doubt the feds will tell anybody. They don't want anyone to know that one of them was overpowered and damn near beat to a pulp." Chase cast his brother another glance of reprimand. "Dumb move, Lucky. If Pat hadn't been there to smooth things over, you'd be in a world of hurt."

Lucky, however, was only interested in Devon's opinion of him. "She probably thinks I'm a hothead."

"You *are* a hothead."

"And you're not?"

"I've got better sense than to attack a federal agent."

"One of them never talked to your woman like that agent did."

"Oh, so now she's 'your woman'?" Chase asked.

"Just an expression."

"Or a Freudian slip."

Lucky stared glumly through the bug-splattered windshield. "Who ever would have thought a fistfight at the place would result in a mess like this?"

Chase offered no reply, but the question had been rhetorical anyway. Broodily Lucky contemplated the scenery that whizzed past. "Anybody seen or heard from Little Alvin and Jack Ed lately?"

"Nope. They're keeping a low profile."

"If you ask me, the feds would do better to lay off us and Devon and go after those two."

"Yeah, but nobody asked you." Chase wheeled the truck into the lane leading to the house, from which mellow golden light was pouring through the windows. "Don't entertain any notions about going after them yourself," Chase warned. "We don't need another assault charge against you."

"Devon's still here."

Lucky was heartened by the sight of her red compact in the driveway. Chase parked the truck beside it. Once out of the pickup, Lucky jogged up the steps and through the front door.

"Hey, everybody, the jailbird is free!"

"That's not funny," Laurie admonished as he entered the living room where she was sitting with Devon, Sage, and Tanya. Chase had phoned ahead and reported the outcome of the arraignment.

"Neither is jail," Lucky said in an appropriately solemn tone. Crossing to where Devon was seated on the sofa, he dropped down beside her and, without compunction, covered her knee with his hand. "You okay?"

"I'm fine."

"Did those bastards give you any grief after I was taken away?"

"No. They allowed me to leave. Chase drove me here." She gave Laurie, Sage, and Tanya smiles. "I've been well looked after, although all the fuss was unnecessary."

"After the dreadful way you were treated?" Laurie stood up. "Of course it was necessary, and then some. My family owes you a debt of gratitude, Devon." She moved toward the arched opening. "Boys, wash up. We've been holding dinner for you."

"I'd like a chance to speak to Devon alone, Mother," Lucky said.

"After dinner. I'm sure she's famished. Chase, stop that smooching and usher everybody into the dining room, please."

Chase reluctantly released Tanya, whose neck he'd been nibbling. Laughing, he remarked, "We should have had Mother in that interrogation room with us today. They wouldn't have dared cross her."

Laurie had heeded Lucky's earlier request and cooked a sumptuous country dinner of fried chicken, mashed potatoes, gravy, corn on the cob, and black-eyed peas. She'd made his favorite banana pudding for dessert. Despite the events of the afternoon, the mood at the dinner table was jolly.

As they were finishing their dessert and coffee, Tanya clinked her fork against her drinking glass. Everyone fell silent and looked at her, surprised because she so rarely called attention to herself.

"I think this family needs a piece of good news." Reaching for her husband's hand, she smiled into his eyes and proclaimed, "There's a new Tyler on the way. I'm pregnant."

Laurie clasped her hands beneath her chin, her eyes immediately growing misty. "Oh, how wonderful!"

Sage gave a raucous, unladylike hoot.

Lucky guffawed. "Don't look now, big brother, but you just dropped a gooey bite of pudding into your lap."

Chase, gaping at his wife, lowered his empty spoon back into his dessert plate. "You . . . you mean it? You're sure?"

Gleefully Tanya bobbed her head up and down. "You're going to be a daddy."

Having reached the white wooden fence that enclosed the peach orchard, Devon rested her forearms on the top rung and took a deep, cleansing breath. Lucky stood beside her. It was the first moment they'd had alone since Chase had brought him back from town. Following Tanya's announcement, everybody had started firing questions at once, which she fielded with poise.

No, she wasn't very far along, but the pregnancy had been positively confirmed.

Yes, she was feeling quite well, thank you.

No, she hadn't had any morning sickness yet.

Yes, she was due around the first of the year.

No, the doctor didn't expect any difficulties.

Discussion of the baby had prolonged dinner. Finally Laurie had stood to clear the table, shooing Devon and Lucky out. The evening was close and warm, the air heavy with humidity and the heady, fertile scents of spring.

Turning her head toward Lucky, Devon asked, "Did you know?"

"What? About Tanya?" He shook his head. "No. But it didn't really surprise me. They've made no secret of wanting kids. It was just a matter of time. I'm glad she chose tonight to announce it."

The top railing of the fence caught him in the middle of his back as he leaned against it and turned to face her. There was a soft breeze blowing, lifting strands of burnished hair out of her restrictive bun. Sage had loaned her some clothes. She had traded her business suit for a casual, long-skirted jumper worn over a T-shirt. She was making it tough on him to decide which way he liked her best. Whether soft or sophisticated, she always looked terrific.

"Your mother is really something," she was saying. "She's strong and yet compassionate. A rare combination."

"Thanks. I think she's special too. I was afraid you'd think the Tylers are all a little crazy. Picking fights one minute. Crying over a coming baby the next."

She plucked a leaf off the nearest peach tree and began to pull it through her fingers. "No, it's nice, the closeness you share."

"You didn't have a close family?"

"Not really. Just my parents and me. No brothers or sisters."

Lucky couldn't imagine such a thing and said so. "Chase and I used to fight like cats and dogs. Still do sometimes.

But we're best friends, too, and would do anything for each other."

"That's obvious. I remember the look on his face when he came charging through the door of that interrogation room."

Enough time had elapsed that they could smile about it now. Lucky was the first to turn serious again. "I thought the family bonds might weaken after Dad died. Instead, they're stronger than ever. Mother's held us together admirably."

"Tell me about him."

"My dad? He was strict, but fair. All us kids knew we were loved. He spoiled us and spanked us equally, I guess you could say. To him there were no gray areas where honesty and integrity are concerned. We knew he loved God, his country, and our mother. He was openly affectionate with her, and always respectful."

"So it stands to reason that his son would leap to the defense of a woman in distress."

He gave her a self-deprecating grin and a slight shrug. "Conditioned reflex." Reaching out, he caught a loose strand of her hair and rubbed it between his fingers. "What was life like for Devon Haines when she was a little girl?"

"Lonely at times." Her expression became introspective. "Unlike your father, mine wasn't a very warm and giving person. In fact, he was demanding. My mother fetched and carried for him from the moment she said 'I do' until the day he died. Their roles were rigidly defined. He was the domineering breadwinner; she was the obedient good little wife. She spent her days keeping his castle spotless, and her evenings waiting on him hand and foot."

"Hmm. Is that why their little girl turned out to be such a militant feminist?"

"I'm not militant."

Lucky raised his hands in surrender. "I'm unarmed."

"I'm sorry," she said with chagrin. "Maybe I am a trifle defensive."

"That's okay." Then, bending down closer to her, he whispered, "If your eyes keep flashing green fire like that, I'm gonna have to kiss you." He said it teasingly, but his eyes conveyed the message that he meant it.

Devon looked away to stare down the neat, straight row of carefully cultivated peach trees. Their branches were already burdened with unripened fruit.

"My mother's whole life revolved around my father. When he died, she was left with nothing to live for."

"What about you?"

"I guess I didn't really count."

"That rejection must have hurt."

"It did." She sighed. "Two miserable years after my father's death, she died too."

"How?"

The ground beneath them held her attention for a moment. When she began speaking, her voice was thick. "For as long as I can remember, my mother was a hypochondriac. She constantly complained of minor aches and pains. They kept her from attending functions throughout my schooling. I couldn't have friends over because she felt bad. That kind of thing."

Lucky muttered something unflattering about the late Mrs. Haines, but Devon shook her head. "I guess the hypochondria was her only means of getting attention from my father. Anyway, I learned early on to dismiss mother's 'illnesses.'

"After my father died, they increased in frequency and severity. Because her life had been so wrapped up in his, she had nothing to occupy her mind except her own body and its many failings. I was just out of college, scrambling to find a job that would subsidize her pension. Frankly, hearing about each stabbing pain and dull ache drove me crazy. I tuned her out as much as possible." She pinched off a piece of the leaf and tossed it into the wind.

"She began to claim that the pains were getting worse. The more she complained about her discomfort, the more stubbornly I ignored her. I thought that honoring the hypochondria would only encourage it."

She rolled her lips inward and pressed on them so hard that the rims turned white. Lucky saw the tears collecting in her eyes. He took her hand and interlaced her fingers with his.

"One day Mother said she was having difficulty in swallowing. She couldn't eat. Everything I gave her came right back up. I . . . I relented and took her to see the doctor."

Unable to go on, she pulled her hand from his and covered her face with both hands.

He rubbed her between the shoulder blades. "What happened, Devon?" Instinctively he knew that she had never talked about this with anyone. He was flattered, but it hurt him to see her in such emotional distress.

She pulled in a choppy breath and lowered her hands. "She was dead within two weeks. Inoperable stomach cancer."

"Oh, damn."

She took a clean tissue from the pocket of the jumper and blotted her eyes and nose. Her pretty features were etched with misery and guilt.

"You couldn't have known," he said softly.

"I should have."

"Not based on your past experience."

"I should have listened to her. I should have done something."

"The result would probably have been the same, Devon." His father had died of cancer after fighting it for months.

"Yes, probably," Devon said. "But if I hadn't disregarded her, she wouldn't have suffered. I turned my back on her at a time when she needed someone to believe her."

"From what you said, she had turned her back on you first."

She dusted her hands of the leaf she had shredded. "We weren't tuned in to each other the way you Tylers are. So I can't relate to the camaraderie your family shares, but I think the way you rally together is enviable."

He sensed that the topic of her mother's death was now closed. He wouldn't press. She had opened up to him. It had been too brief a glimpse into Devon's psyche, but he coveted information about her.

He matched her more lighthearted tone. "You don't think we're loud, boisterous, and overwhelming?"

She laughed softly. "A little, perhaps."

"Yeah, we can get pretty rambunctious."

"But it must be nice, knowing you have someone you can count on to stand up for you, no matter what."

"You don't?" He caught her beneath the chin with his fingertip and turned her head to face him. "What about your husband?"

"He's not in a position to rally to my aid now, is he?"

"What if he were in a position to? Would he?"

She lifted her chin off the perch of his finger and turned away again. Lucky dropped his arm to his side. The emotional turmoil on her face was plain. He hated to think he was the one responsible for it.

"You'll have to tell him about us now, won't you?" he asked softly.

"Yes."

"I'm sorry, Devon. I had hoped to prevent that." If he had hoped it badly enough, he would have left her alone, he thought wryly. He wouldn't have asked her to come to Milton Point and counter Susan's lie with the truth. But thinking primarily of himself, he had coerced her to come. He was confident of acquittal; Devon, however, would suffer permanent consequences. "When will you see him?"

"Tomorrow. I don't want him to hear about it from someone else before I've had a chance to explain. That's why I accepted your mother's invitation to spend the night here. Since I'm this close to the prison, it would be silly to drive back to Dallas, only to have to return to East Texas in the morning."

Lucky wasn't as interested in the logistics of travel as he was in what form her explanation would take. "What are you going to say to him?"

Ruefully she shook her head. "I don't know yet."

"What are you going to tell him about me?"

"As little as possible."

"Are you going to tell him how we met?"

"I suppose that'll be a start."

"About Little Alvin, Jack Ed, the fight?"

"I suppose."

"You'll explain why you were in the place."

"He'll understand that part."

"But not the rest. What'll you tell him about the motel?"

"I don't know," she admitted with increasing impatience.

"Well, you'd better think of something."

She turned on him with agitation. "Tell me, Lucky, what should I say? What *can* I say? What words could possibly make this situation easier for him to accept, hmm? Put yourself in his place. He's in prison. How would you react if your roles were reversed? How would you feel if I were your wife and had slept with another man?"

He reached for her and pulled her against him, snarling, "If you were my wife, you wouldn't have slept with another man."

She deflected his kiss. "Don't." He could tell by her tone that she wasn't being coy. He gazed into her eyes. "Don't," she repeated firmly. "Let me go."

He relaxed his embrace; she stepped out of it. "For reasons I can't comprehend, your family has been cordial to me when all I deserve from them is scorn and contempt. I expected to be shunned like a woman of the streets. Instead, they've been inordinately kind. I won't betray their consideration by playing your tramp."

His body was pulled taut, as though he were held back by an invisible leash. "You're not a tramp," he said meaningfully. "I never thought of you that way. I never treated you that way. Didn't I nearly throttle someone today for suggesting that you were?"

Suddenly she ducked her head, and he thought it might be because of the tears that had filled her eyes. "So far," she said in a low, stirring voice, "I've got only one sin to confess to my husband. Please don't make it any worse, Lucky."

"That's the first time you've called me by name," he murmured, taking a step nearer. "That's a beginning."

She raised her head. Their eyes met and held. Eventually she moistened her lips, pulled the lower one through her teeth, and whispered, "We aren't allowed a beginning."

Having said that, she turned and headed for the house.

"My, my. Wonders never cease."

At the sound of his sister's voice, Lucky angrily spun around. "What the hell are you doing out here?"

Sage stepped from behind one of the peach trees. "There's actually a woman who can say no to Lucky Tyler. My faith in womankind has been restored."

"Shut up, brat," he grumbled. "How long have you been there?"

"Long enough to set my heart to palpitating."

"Why were you spying on us?"

"I wasn't. Mother sent me out to tell you that Chase and Tanya are leaving. She thought you'd want to say congratulations one more time. I sensed the nature of your conversation, and decided it would be imprudent to interrupt."

"So you eavesdropped."

Unfazed, she fell into step beside her brother as he stamped toward the house. "Poor Lucky," she sighed theatrically. "He finally finds a woman he really wants, and she turns out to have the loathsome three."

"Loathsome three?"

"A brain, a conscience, and a husband."

Lucky glowered at her. "You know, the day Mother and Dad brought you home from the hospital, Chase and I considered tying you up in a gunnysack and tossing it into the stock pond. Too bad we didn't."

"Lucky looked ready to kill Sage when they came in," Tanya remarked.

Chase and she were driving home in their car. He'd left the truck at the house, unwilling to subject his wife to its rankness, rattles, and rough ride.

"Sage has always been a pain," he said, but with a grudgingly affectionate smile. "She must've said something to him about their houseguest."

"I like her."

"Sage?"

"No." Tanya corrected him indulgently, knowing he had intentionally misunderstood her. "Their houseguest."

"Hmm. She's okay, I guess. She pulled through for us today. Didn't crack under pressure, and stayed as cool as a cucumber. I believed every word she said. A jury will, too."

"Do you think she's attractive?"

Hearing the uncertainty in his wife's voice, Chase parked in their designated space at the apartment complex and turned to face her. "I think *you* are attractive," he avowed softly, stretching across the seat to gently kiss her forehead.

"But Devon's so smart and sophisticated."

"And you're so pregnant with my baby." Working his

way inside her clothing, Chase laid his hand on her bare abdomen. "When did you first suspect?"

"Last week. My period was more than two weeks late. I took a home pregnancy test yesterday, but didn't want to trust it entirely, no matter how reliable the guarantee on the box claimed it was. So I called the doctor and made an appointment for this morning. He confirmed it."

"You don't feel any different," he whispered as he caressed her.

Laughing, she ran her fingers through his hair. "I hope not. Not yet."

His caresses increased in intensity. Their kisses became prolonged. Finally Tanya pushed him away. "Maybe we had better go inside."

"Maybe we'd better," he agreed on a suggestive growl.

As soon as they had cleared the door to their apartment, he pulled her toward the living-room sofa. "Chase," she protested, "it's only a few more steps to the bedroom."

"That's too many."

He had already stripped off his shirt. Easing his zipper over his swollen sex, he pulled off his pants and underwear. Impatiently he removed Tanya's clothes, too. It wasn't until he was poised between her thighs that reason penetrated his passion.

"I won't hurt you, will I?"

"No."

"You'll tell me, won't you?"

"Yes, Chase."

"Promise?"

"Promise," she groaned, urging him forward and receiving him fully.

"God, I love you," he whispered into her hair several minutes later as they held each other in the sultry afterglow of their lovemaking.

"I love you too." Snuggling closer to him, she pressed her mouth against his chest. "I feel sorry for anybody who isn't as happy as we are. Especially Devon and Lucky."

Tanya didn't have an envious bone in her body. She was unselfish and generous to a fault. However, she harbored insecurities the same as any other human being. Hers stemmed from her background.

She came from a large, hardworking, but always poor farming family. Schooling beyond high school graduation had been out of the question, and she regarded anyone who had earned a college degree with disproportionate admiration.

It had been Tanya's sweet nature and unpretentiousness that had first attracted Chase. He recognized her insecurities and found them endearing, though he never discussed them with her. It was characteristic of her nature that while being awed by Devon Haines's panache, she could still feel sorry for her.

He said, "You link their names as though they're a pair."

"I think they would be if they could be," she said softly.

"Tanya," he said gruffly, smoothing back her fair hair, "you're going to make a wonderful mother."

"What makes you think so?"

"Because you have such a huge capacity for loving."

Her eyes grew misty as her fingers glided over the strong features of his face. "What a lovely thing to say, Chase."

"It's true."

Before they became too maudlin, she smiled. "You know, one thing that has limited capacity is this apartment. I spoke with a realtor a few weeks ago, before Lucky's troubles started. She said when we were ready to start looking for a house to contact her."

"She?"

"An old friend of yours. Marcie Johns."

"Goosey Johns!" he exclaimed on a laugh.

"Goosey?"

"That's what we used to call her."

"How awful."

"Naw. It was all in fun."

"She's very nice."

"Oh, I know that," he agreed. "She always was. We just goaded her because she was tall and skinny, wore glasses and braces, and studied all the time."

"Apparently she's getting the last laugh. She's a very successful businesswoman."

"So I've heard. She's got her own realty company now, doesn't she?"

"Mm-hmm. And even after robbing the kitty to pay Lucky's bail, I believe we'll have enough for a down payment. Know what?" Tanya said, propping herself up to look down at him. "I think Marcie had a crush on you when you were in school."

"Really?" No longer listening, he cupped one of her breasts and fanned the crest with his thumb. "Lord, that's beautiful."

"She asked a lot of questions about you, was curious to know how you were, that kind of thing."

"Goosey Johns was interested in books, not boys. Especially horny boys like me," he added, pulling Tanya astride his middle. Her body sheathed his hardness again. Breathlessly he asked, "Now can we talk about something else?"

They didn't talk about anything at all.

Chapter Fifteen

It had a tennis court, a nine-hole golf course, a weight room, a jogging track, a library stocked with current best-sellers. For all its amenities, however, it was still a prison.

Using her telephone credit card, Devon had called the warden's office from the Tylers' home the day before and scheduled a meeting with her husband for 9:00 A.M.

She had got up early, dressed, and gone downstairs. Laurie had insisted that she drink a cup of coffee before leaving. Sage was still asleep. She was told, without having asked, that Lucky had left early to return the company truck to headquarters in case it was needed.

A morning drive through the East Texas countryside in early summer should have been a pleasurable experience. Wildflowers dotted the pastures in which dairy and beef cattle grazed. She'd driven with the car windows rolled down. The south wind carried the scent of pine and honey-suckle. The peaceful hour it had taken to arrive at those iron gates should have calmed her nerves and prepared her for the dreaded forthcoming visit with her husband.

It hadn't.

Her palms were slick with perspiration as she was led into the room where inmates were allowed to greet their visitors. It was a large, airy room, having unadorned windows that overlooked the flower and vegetable gardens tended by the inmates themselves. The easy chairs and sofas were functional but comfortable. Current magazines were scattered around the various accent tables. There was a coffee maker with a freshly brewed carafe and, this morning, a box of doughnuts nearby.

"He'll be right here," she was told by the prison guard. "Help yourself to coffee and doughnuts while you wait."

"Thank you."

She wanted neither. Her stomach was roiling. Resting her purse on one of the chairs, she clasped her damp hands together and moved toward the windows.

What to say?

Greg, I've had an affair.

It hadn't been an affair. It had been a single night.

Greg, I had a one-night stand.

No, that sounded worse.

Greg, I was swept up in the passion of the moment.

Passion?

Passion.

Whatever else it had been, it had been passionate. How else could it have happened? Reason hadn't entered into it.

Not even romance. Common sense had played no part. Morality hadn't been considered. She'd been governed strictly by her passions.

And it had been glorious.

Ever since her night with Lucky, that traitorous thought had been throwing itself against the doors of her consciousness like a deranged beast trying to break down the barriers and get out to celebrate the event.

That's why she felt compelled to confess it to Greg. Whether he was likely to find out or not, she would have eventually told him. If her emotions hadn't gotten as tangled up as the sheets of the bed she had shared with Lucky Tyler, she might have kept the secret for the rest of her life, never divulging it to anyone.

But her emotions had become involved. Because they were, her conscience was. She felt guilty about it; therefore, she had to discuss it with Greg.

Her marriage to Greg was certainly unorthodox, but the legal document still decreed them husband and wife. She'd freely recited the vows to him, and just as freely she had broken those vows.

What Greg had done or hadn't done, whether or not he was innocent or guilty, whether or not he had used her and her newspaper column—none of that mattered. She was an adulterous wife.

Perhaps if he had given her a wedding night as she had wanted and expected him to . . .

Perhaps if her body hadn't been so starved for the loving attention he had withheld . . .

Perhaps if he hadn't declined his conjugal visits . . .

That had been the crushing blow. Only hours before she had met Lucky, she had discovered that Greg had been refusing conjugal visits with her. When asked why, he couldn't give her a satisfactory answer.

"Why, Greg, why?" He provided no answers, and only became angry when she persisted.

More than her father's self-absorption, more than her mother's neglect, more than anything in her life, that had been the ultimate rejection. Her self-confidence had been shattered, her self-esteem crushed. Was she so undesirable that even her prisoner husband wouldn't avail himself of her?

While she was in that frame of mind, fate maliciously matched her with Lucky Tyler. He had revived her dying spirit.

Still, no one had forced her at gunpoint to make love with him. Sure, she had needs; everyone had needs. But society would be plunged into chaos if people went around incontinently gratifying their needs.

Down the hallway she heard approaching footsteps and murmured conversation. Turning from the window, she lowered her hands to her sides, but reflexively clasped them together again. She moistened her lips, wondering if she should be smiling when he walked in. She wasn't sure she could even form a smile. Her features felt wooden.

Laurie Tyler had graciously pressed her suit for her. Devon always took special pains with her appearance when she came to see Greg, wanting her visits to be as pleasurable for him as possible. This morning, however, even the quality cosmetics Sage had loaned her didn't conceal the dark circles beneath her eyes, which hours of sleeplessness had left there.

The footsteps became more pronounced and the voices louder. Devon's heart began to thud painfully inside her chest. She swallowed with difficulty, though her mouth was so dry her saliva glands seemed to have been dammed. She tried to hold her lips still, but they quivered around a tentative smile.

Greg and the guard appeared in the doorway. "Have a good visit," the official said before withdrawing.

Greg looked trim and fit. He had told her that he played a lot of tennis during free time. His tanned skin always came as a mild surprise to her. He spent more time out-of-doors now than he had during the days of his trial, when he'd had a pallor.

The inmates here didn't wear prison garb, but their own clothing. Greg was always immaculately dressed, though his three-piece suits had been replaced by casual clothes and his Italian leather loafers by sneakers.

He moved further into the room. The confinement was beginning to tell on him, she noted. It caused a strain on all the inmates of this facility. To a man, they complained of the boredom. Accustomed to being movers and shakers in big business, they found it difficult to adjust to the forced idleness. Worse yet was that they no longer had the privilege of making their own decisions.

Instinctively Devon knew that he wouldn't welcome a broad smile and a cheerful "Good morning," and, fortunately, a subdued greeting coincided with her mood. So she stood stoic and silent in front of the windows as he crossed the room.

He didn't stop until they were within touching distance. It wasn't until then that she noticed he was carrying a newspaper. She glanced down at it curiously, then back up at him. His face was taut with rage. So unexpectedly that it caused her to jump, he slapped the newspaper onto the windowsill, then turned on his heels and strode from the room.

Her arid mouth opened, but she couldn't utter a single sound. She waited until he had cleared the doorway and turned down the hall before retrieving the newspaper.

It had been folded once. She opened it and noted that it was a Dallas paper, a competitor of the one she worked for. Greg had gratuitously underlined in red the pertinent headline.

She slumped against the armrest of the nearest chair and skimmed the incriminating article. For long moments afterward she sat there, clutching the newspaper to her chest, eyes closed, heart tripping, head throbbing.

She had so carefully outlined what she was going to say

to him, when, as it turned out, it hadn't been necessary to say anything. The newspaper account was disgustingly accurate.

"Promise me you won't fly off the handle and do something stupid." Chase, casting a tall, dark shadow across the office floor, filled the doorway.

Lucky was angled back in the swivel desk chair their grandfather and father had broken in for them. His boots were resting on the corner of the desk, another relic of oil-boom days. A telephone was cradled between his shoulder and ear. He waved his brother into the room.

"Yeah, we can send a crew out tomorrow to start setting up." He winked at his brother, and made the okay sign with his thumb and fingers. "We didn't lose all that much in the fire, so we're set to go. Just give me directions, and our boys'll be there by daybreak."

Bringing the chair erect, he reached for a pad and pencil and scribbled down the directions. "Route Four, you say? Uh-huh, two miles past the windmill. Got it. Right. Glad to be doing business with you again, Virgil."

He hung up the phone, sprang out of the chair, and gave an Indian whoop. "A contract! A biggie! Remember ol' Virgil Daboe over in Louisiana? He's got four good prospects for wells, and wants us to do the drilling. How 'bout that, big brother? Is that good news or what? Four new wells and a baby on the way! How can you stand that much good news in a twelve-hour period?"

On his way to the coffee maker, he walloped Chase between the shoulder blades. Pouring himself a cup of coffee, he said, "I'll call all the boys and tell them to get their gear—" He broke off as he raised the mug of coffee to his lips and realized that his brother wasn't sharing his jubilation. "What's the matter?"

"It's great about the contract," Chase said.

"Well, you sure as hell can't tell it by looking at you." Lucky set down his coffee. "What's wrong with you? I thought you'd be dancing on the ceiling about this."

"I probably would be, if I wasn't afraid I might have to hog-tie you to keep you out of more trouble."

"What are you talking about?"

"Somebody squealed, Lucky."

"Squealed?"

Chase had folded the front page of the newspaper lengthwise four times so he could slide it into the hip pocket of his jeans. Reluctantly he removed it and passed it to Lucky.

He read the story. The first words out of his mouth were vile. Subsequent words were even viler. Chase watched his brother warily, unsure of what he might do.

Lucky threw himself back into the desk chair. It went rolling back on its creaky casters. Bending at the waist, he plowed all ten fingers through his hair and recited a litany of oaths. When he finally ran out, he straightened up and asked, "Has Devon seen this yet?"

"Mother doesn't think so. She left early for the prison. They had coffee together, but Mother didn't open the paper until after she left."

"Just what the hell does this mean?" Lucky demanded, referring to the copy in the article. " 'According to an unnamed source.' "

"It means that whoever leaked the story is scared of what you might do to him if you ever find out who he is."

"He damned sure better be," Lucky said viciously. "And I'll find out who the bastard is. 'Agents were injured in the fracas that broke out when Tyler's mistress was allegedly insulted,' " he read.

" 'Fracas'? What the hell kind of word is 'fracas'? Devon wasn't 'allegedly insulted,' she *was* insulted. And calling her my mistress!" he shouted. "We were together once. *Once,* dammit."

Lucky flung himself from the chair and began pacing the office in long strides. "This is what I wanted to prevent," he said as he ground his fist into his opposite palm. "I wanted Devon to be protected from scandal."

"She would have lost her anonymity during the trial," Chase reasonably pointed out.

"I figured the case would never go to trial. I counted on something happening first. I thought maybe Susan would—" He stopped his pacing and rounded on Chase. "That's it." As heated and agitated as he'd been only seconds earlier, he was now remarkably calm. The switch was as sudden as closing a door against a fierce storm. "Susan."

"She leaked the story?"

"I'd bet Virgil's contract on it." He told Chase about seeing the banker's daughter in the squad room.

"Yeah, I saw her there too," Chase said. "She was grinning like the Cheshire cat. But would she risk having her name attached to this mess?"

"She lied to those agents, didn't she?" Lucky headed for the door.

Chase, well aware of Lucky's volatile temper, followed him outside. "Where are you going?"

"To see Miss Young."

"Lucky—"

"Hopefully between here and there I'll come up with an alternative to murder."

Clara, the Youngs' housekeeper, demurred when he asked to see Susan. Lucky was persistent, and eventually wore her down. She led him through the house to the backyard, where Susan was enjoying a late breakfast on the stone terrace. Like a hothouse orchid, she was surrounded by giant ferns and flowering plants.

He pinched a sprig of lilac from the fresh flower arrangement on the foyer table and carried it outside with him. As he crossed the lichen-covered stone terrace, he could hear Susan humming beneath her breath while liberally spreading orange marmalade over an English muffin. Lying on the table in front of her was the front page of the Dallas paper.

"You sure do make a pretty picture sitting there, Susan."

At the familiar sound of his voice she dropped her knife. It landed with a clatter on the china plate. She sprang from her chair and rounded it, placing it between them, as though filigree wrought iron could prevent him from snapping her in two.

"Lucky."

Her voice was feeble and airless. There was little color remaining in her face. The fingers gripping the back of her chair were bloodless. She backed up a step as he moved inexorably forward.

When he reached her, he raised his hand. She flinched.

Then her terrified eyes focused on the flower he was extending to her. "Good morning," he whispered, bending down and planting a light kiss on her cheek. She gaped at him wordlessly as he pulled back, then automatically accepted the flower.

"I didn't expect you," she croaked.

"Sorry I'm here so early," he said, nonchalantly pinching off a bite of her English muffin and popping it into his mouth, "but it's been days since I've seen you, and I just couldn't wait any longer. I hope—"

He stopped, made a point of noticing the newspaper, and muttered a curse. The look he gave her then was a mix of sheepishness and exasperation.

"Damn! I wanted to get over here before you saw that."
He gestured down to the article. "Susan, honey, I'm sorry."

She stared at him with speechless dismay.

Feigning disgust, he expelled a deep breath. "Some
loudmouthed snoop found out who I was with the night of
the fire and leaked that story about the Haines woman."
Appearing to be supremely exasperated, he plopped down
into one of the wrought iron chairs and hung his head.

"One mistake. One lousy mistake," he mumbled in self-
castigation. "How was I to know she was married? And to
a convict. Jeez!" He swore. "Of course, now you'll have to
tell the authorities that you lied to them about being with
me the night of the fire."

"I . . . I will?" Her voice had gone from low and faint to
high and thin.

"Of course, honey." He rose and took her shoulders between his hands. "I can't let you stick your neck out any
further than you already have. Yesterday, when I saw you
in that ugly squad room, I nearly died."

He touched her hair, smoothed it away from her neck. "I
knew the kind of questions they had put to you. Personal
things about us. Lord, how embarrassing that must have
been for you. How do you think I felt, knowing you were
making that sacrifice for me?"

He laid his hand over his heart. "And then do you know
what the bastards told me to throw me off balance? They
said that you claimed I had bragged to you about setting

that fire. Can you believe that? Sure, you joked with me about it the other night, but you weren't serious, right?"

"Uh, uh, right."

"Don't worry. I didn't fall for the ploy. I knew they were bluffing, trying to trap me into admitting something. You'd never betray me like that. Not when we were planning to get married. The last thing I ever wanted was for you to be dragged into this mess." He pulled her close and spoke into her hair. Astonishment had made her body limp.

"I appreciate everything you did to try and save me from prosecution, but I can't let you do any more. I can't let you be called into that courtroom to perjure yourself."

"Perjure myself?"

"Sure," he said, angling away from her. "If you testify under oath that I was with you the night of the fire, then the Haines woman says under oath that I was with her, I'll have to testify under oath that she's telling the truth. You'll be caught in your lie, sweetheart," he said gently. "That is, unless you recant your story immediately. The sooner, the better."

She pushed away from him, staring up at him whey-faced, on the verge of panic. "I never thought of that."

"I know you didn't. All you thought about was me, us, our marriage. Which, of course," he added regretfully, "can never be."

"Why not?"

He spread his arms at his sides in a gesture of helplessness. "Do you believe your mama and daddy would let you

marry me now, a guy who would sleep with a con's wife?
Think about it, sweetheart. They wouldn't stand for it.
Your daddy would probably cut you out of his will and
leave all his money to charity. They'd rather see you dead
than married to me. And, frankly, so would I." His voice
was laced with so much earnestness that she didn't hear the
irony underlying it.

Clasping her against him again, he hugged her tight for
several seconds before releasing her abruptly. "Good-bye,
Susan. Since all this has come out in the open, I can't ever
see you again."

Before she could speak another word, he left her, choosing to take the gravel path around the house rather than
going through its sepulchral hallway to reach the front. At
the corner of the house he turned and looked back.

"Save yourself while you can, Susan. Don't even give
yourself time to think about it. Call Pat."

"Yes, yes. I'll do that today. Right now."

"I can't tell you how much better that'll make me feel."
He blew her a kiss. "Good-bye."

Hanging his head, he walked with the measured gait of a
self-sacrificing patriot on his way to the guillotine. But he
was laughing up his sleeve and felt like kicking up his heels.

Chapter Sixteen

Devon was waiting for him the following morning when he arrived at Tyler Drilling headquarters. Sitting in a straight chair as prim and proper as a finishing-school student, she was talking to Chase and cradling one of their chipped, stained coffee mugs between her hands.

They shared a long stare across a shaft of sunlight in which dust motes danced as crazily as Lucky's pulse was racing at the sight of her.

Chase was the first to break the thick silence. "Devon showed up a few minutes ago," he explained awkwardly. He, too, was evidently at a loss as to why she was there. "We were just having some coffee. Want some, Lucky?"

"No thanks." He hadn't taken his eyes off Devon. Nor had hers strayed from him.

"The, uh, the crew has already left for Louisiana."

"That's good." .

Chase's futile attempts at conversation only emphasized

the teeming silence. Uneasily he cleared his throa
well, I need to be, uh, doing some things outside. S
later." As Chase went past Lucky on his way out, h
him with his elbow. It was a silent brotherly comr
that said, "Snap out of it."

Once Chase had closed the door behind himsel
remarked, "I'm surprised to see you here."

Her smile was swift and unsure. "I surprised r
coming."

He sat down in a ladder-back chair, his eyes ro
grily over her face.

"I've been trying to call you since yesterday a
Devon."

"I took my phone off the hook."

"I gathered that. Why?"

"After reading yesterday's newspaper, everyl
world was trying to call me, it seemed."

Lucky frowned. "I hate like hell that the stor
I wanted to keep you anonymous for as long
Please believe that."

"I know you had nothing to do with it. W
think was responsible?"

He told her about Susan. "She looked guilty
I confronted her. I'm convinced she made it he
find out who you were and, out of spite, spilled
a reporter."

"Well, it doesn't really matter now how
out. The damage is done."

He studied her a moment, noticing that her face was drawn and pale. The last twenty-four hours must have been pure hell for her. She was gripping the coffee mug as though it were a buoy in a turbulent lake.

"Do you really want that coffee?" he asked. Shaking her head, she passed the mug to him. He took it and set it on the desk, then turned back to her. The question uppermost in his mind couldn't be avoided any longer.

"How did things go with your husband yesterday?"

A small shudder went through her, though it was uncomfortably warm in the office. "By the time I arrived, Greg had read the story," she said softly. "He merely dropped the newspaper and walked out."

"Without a word?"

"Words would have been superfluous, wouldn't they?"

"I guess so," Lucky murmured.

He was thinking that if he had a wife whom he loved as much as any husband should love his wife, he would have given her the benefit of the doubt and asked a few questions. He wouldn't have reacted until she either denied or confirmed the newspaper story.

If she had denied it, he would have comforted her, then immediately set out to get a retraction. If she had confirmed it, he probably would have gone nuts and carried on something terrible.

A furious outburst, tears, anguish, teeth-gnashing, threats of retaliation. Those would be the expected jealous reactions.

They denoted feeling, passion. Simply stalking out was an almost inhuman response that made Greg Shelby sound cold,
unfeeling.

"What did you do?" Lucky wanted to know.

"I read the story through. At first I just sat there, stunned.
My character suffered in the translation. Somehow, once
they were written down, the facts sounded ugly and shameful. So tawdry." She shivered again.

Lucky reached beyond the back of his chair to take one
of her hands. "It wasn't, Devon."

"Wasn't it?" she asked, her eyes brimming.

"No."

The stare they exchanged then was so powerful, she pru-
dently withdrew her hand and used her tears as the excuse.
She brushed the back of her hand across her eyes.

"I had the prison guard try to get Greg to see me again,
but he refused. Once I returned to Dallas, I called the warden and got permission to speak to him by telephone. I
wanted desperately to explain." She shook her head mournfully. "He wouldn't even accept my call."

Lucky mentally called Greg Shelby every dirty name he
could think of. "So what now? Do you want me to go with
you to see him?"

"No!" Leaving her chair, she began roaming the office
restlessly. "I don't believe he'd be willing to see either of us
right now. After thinking it over and discussing it with
Greg's attorney—who isn't at all pleased with me either—

I think it's best to leave him alone for several days. He needs time to cool off and clear his head, so that when we do see each other again, he'll be able to listen calmly to my explanation."

"I don't know, Devon," he said doubtfully. "Given time to think about it, I would just get madder."

"Greg isn't as volatile as you."

"You're right about that." Lucky's concession wasn't intended as a compliment to Greg. "If you were my wife and some guy had messed with you, I'd've busted down the walls of that prison by now and be on my way to tear out his throat."

"Greg's not that . . . physical."

"Do you really think he'll eventually forgive and forget?"

"I hope so. Yes, in time, I believe he will."

The answer didn't cheer Lucky as it should have. Her husband sounded like a sanctimonious creep who could hold a grudge forever. Lucky hated to think of Devon being tied to Shelby for the rest of her life.

Somewhat querulously he asked, "Did you come all the way from Dallas to tell me this?"

"No. There was another reason." She returned to her seat. "This whole thing has blown up in my face. Since I went into that lounge and ordered a beer, I've had nothing but trouble. It's out now that I'm your alibi in an arson case. Until the trial is over, and God only knows when that will be, my life is going to be a three-ring circus. I can't have that. I *won't* have it."

"I don't like the prospect of being a notorious public figure any better than you. But what can we do about it?"

"We can clear you with the investigators."

"We tried, remember? It only got me into deeper Dutch. You too."

"But we didn't present them with the real arsonist."

For the space of several seconds Lucky gave her a blank stare. Then he began to laugh. "You want to play detective?"

"Look, the sooner we get you cleared, the sooner this thing will blow over and we can get on with our lives. It's not going to be easy to make amends to Greg, but it would be a start if he knew we wouldn't be going through a trial together, and that I wouldn't constantly be in your company. I'm sure he would enjoy hearing that I never had to see you again."

She was batting a thousand on dismal thoughts this morning, but since he didn't have a viable alternative, he remained silent.

"I've cleared my calendar," she said. "I told my editor that I'm taking a week's vacation and plan to devote the time to tracking down the arsonist. When I get back, I promised him a terrific story, as well as an article on how interrogators can and do intimidate witnesses. I think— What are you grinning about so idiotically, Mr. Tyler?"

"You."

"You find me amusing?"

"You like having control over things, don't you? Even police matters."

"So far the police haven't done anything to help you. I can't do any worse than they have."

"Granted."

"I don't trust other people to do things for me."

"Um-huh," he said. "You're what we used to call a smarty britches."

Still grinning, he stood up and stretched. He was feeling a million times better than he had been an hour ago. He had been concerned because he hadn't spoken with Devon since the story of her involvement had been leaked. He'd also been dreading an entire day of not seeing her.

Then, lo and behold, she'd showed up and planned to stay for a while. Damn, he was lucky! The dreary reminder of her convict husband was pushed aside. Greg Shelby was a loser, a jerk, and, if Lucky was any judge of women at all—and he considered himself an expert on the fair sex—not that great in the sack.

If Shelby had been the man Devon deserved, no amount of persuasion could have gotten her into bed with another man. He hadn't even had to persuade. Something about her marriage to this Shelby character wasn't right. Lucky respected her for not discussing her marital troubles with an outsider; on the other hand he wanted to know why she was married to a man who had made her so unhappy. Apparently he was being granted the time and opportunity to find out.

The only thing that clouded his sunny mood was that he wouldn't be able to touch her. They would be spending a lot of time together, but she was still off-limits. That was going to kill him, because wanting her had become his chief occupation. More than worrying about his failing business, more than worrying about the fabricated arson charge against him, his desire for Devon was all-consuming.

But seeing her under adverse circumstances was better than not seeing her at all.

"I always enjoyed playing cops and robbers," he said. "Where do we start?"

"First, I'd better check into a room. Where's the best place to stay?"

"My house."

"I can't, Lucky," she said, shaking her head adamantly. "The reasons should be obvious."

"My mother would skin me alive if I let you check into a motel. Anybody who knows her knows she isn't going to let any extramarital hanky-panky go on beneath her roof. So you're staying with us, and that's settled," he said with finality.

"But—"

"Devon," he said sternly, staving off her protests by holding up both hands, palms out. "No arguments."

She capitulated, but didn't seem too pleased about it. "First, I think we should find out exactly how the fire started."

"Gasoline and railroad flares," he said. "Pat already told

me. I had bought some flares recently. That confirmed their suspicions."

"Can we review the official crime report?"

"I don't know. I don't imagine it's a matter of public record."

"I wasn't talking about publicly. Privately. Couldn't your friend Sheriff Bush sneak us a copy?"

Lucky whistled through his teeth. "I'll ask him."

She turned and reached for the phone on the desk.

Lucky snatched the receiver from her hand. "*I'll* ask him. Maybe he'll show us a copy of the report after business hours."

"In the meantime I'd like to see the site of the fire."

"That's easy. It's only half a mile down the road from here." He surveyed her up and down, taking in her dress, high heels, and pale stockings. "The location is only suitable for roughnecks and raccoons. You can't go dressed like that."

"I'll change."

Lucky retrieved her suitcase from her car. She went into the cubicle in the office that was home to a commode and sink. While she was in there, Chase returned. He glanced around and found only Lucky seated behind the desk, speaking into the telephone.

"Where's Devon?"

Lucky cupped his hand over the mouthpiece. "In there," he said, indicating the bathroom door, "taking off her clothes."

When the bathroom door opened, Chase swiveled his head around so fast, his neck popped. Devon emerged, fully dressed in jeans. She was rolling up the sleeves of a casual shirt.

"What's going on?" Chase demanded.

Lucky shushed him and spoke into the phone. "Come on, Pat. I know I acted like a bad boy. Yes, I deserve to be horsewhipped. Now that I've contritely admitted the error of my ways, will you do it or not?"

He listened for a moment while his eyes appreciated the slender shapeliness of Devon's legs and the soft curves of her breasts. "Great. Ten-thirty. Hell no, we won't tell anybody."

"What's going on?" Chase repeated as Lucky hung up the phone.

"Pat's making the crime report available to Devon and me tonight."

"You just promised not to tell anybody," she cried, placing her hands on her hips.

"Chase isn't *anybody*. Pat would expect me to tell him."

"I still don't know what's going on," Chase reminded them.

"We're going to try to find out who set the fire, so I can be cleared of the charge."

"And I can be reconciled with my husband," Devon added.

Lucky declined to comment on her statement. Chase divided his incredulous glance between the two of them. He said, "Devon, would you please give me a minute alone with my brother?"

"I'll wait for you outside, Lucky."

"Be right there."

As soon as she was out of earshot, Chase encircled Lucky's biceps in a death grip. His face close, he said, "Have you lost your friggin' mind? You can't tamper with something like this. Who the hell do you two think you are, Kojak and Nancy Drew?"

"I'm a whole lot better looking than Kojak," Lucky replied cockily.

"I'm not joking," Chase said angrily.

"Neither am I."

"Aren't you?"

Lucky's blue eyes narrowed. "What do you mean by that crack?"

"Isn't this all just a game to you? A game that will keep you in close contact with a woman you have no business being around?"

"Stay out of this," Lucky said tightly, his humor vanishing. "What I do with Devon—"

"You'd better do *nothing* with Devon. She's married."

Lucky, resenting his brother's sermon, though it echoed the one he'd been preaching to himself, jerked his arm free. "I'm a grown-up. I don't need you for a conscience any more, big brother."

"I'm not trying to be your conscience." Chase sighed with chagrin. "Okay, maybe I am. But I'm more worried about her than I am you. She's the real victim here, Lucky. Her life has been turned upside down, and it's your fault."

"I don't need you to remind me of that, either."

"When you're done playing your games, what's she going to be left with, huh? A broken marriage and a broken heart?"

"You're wrong, Chase."

"Am I?"

"Yes! This time it isn't just a game."

Chase stared at him long and hard before stating softly, "That's what really worries me."

All that was left of the machinery garage was a dark area on the ground, covered by ashes that had been sifted through so many times they resembled gray face powder. The remains of the machinery had already been hauled away. What little that could be salvaged had been sold as scrap metal. The revenue from that sale had barely covered the crew's expenses to Louisiana.

Devon sighed as she kicked up a cloud of ashen dust with the toe of her sneaker. "Not much here to look at, is there?"

"I told you." Lucky was squatting; he scooped up handfuls of the ash and let it filter through his fingers.

"The fire was meant to be destructive, not just to serve as a warning of some sort," she observed aloud.

"The agents said that from the beginning. That's one of

the reasons they pointed accusing fingers at me. They said it burned quick and hot. The fire trucks never had a chance in hell of putting the thing out. The best they could do was save the woods surrounding it."

Devon moved to an area of green just beyond the perimeter of scorched ground. She sat down on the trunk of a fallen tree. Lucky joined her. They silently contemplated the charred area.

"This is just one of several company buildings, right?" she asked.

"Right. But this is where we kept most of our heavy equipment. This was definitely the place to set the costliest fire and make it look like I did it."

Tilting her head, she looked at him curiously. "Why do you automatically assume that the revenge was directed at you?"

He shrugged. "Who else? Mother? She's got more friends than she can count. Sage? She's just a kid."

"Jealous boyfriend?"

He dismissed that possibility with a curt shake of his head. "She hasn't ever been that seriously involved with any one guy. She scares off even the most determined. Chase has probably cultivated a few enemies, but I feel it here," he said, flattening his palm against his stomach, "in my gut, that it was aimed at me."

"Why?"

Setting her hands behind her, she braced herself up on

her arms. The pose drew her shirt tight across her breasts. Lucky had to concentrate on the caterpillar creeping along the tree trunk in order to keep himself from staring at them.

"I'm the one who's always getting into trouble." He lifted his eyes to hers. "Seems I have a knack for getting myself into tight places."

Spiders spinning webs between branches of the nearby trees were making more racket than Lucky and Devon while they peered deeply into one another's eyes. The breeze lifted their hair and flirted with their clothing, but they remained motionless, unblinking, thoroughly absorbed.

After a long moment, Devon roused herself. "Who have you been in trouble with?"

"Why are you curious?"

"Everyone's a suspect."

"Or are you just nosy?" he teased.

She blushed slightly. "Maybe. It's a habit. See, when I do a story on someone, I talk to everyone close to the subject. I gather bits of information from here and there until I can piece together the entire personality of the individual. Sometimes the least likely interview produces the most valuable tidbit, the single element that makes all the other elements click into place."

"Fascinating."

What he found most fascinating wasn't the topic, but her animated way of explaining how she worked. Her eyes weren't one pure hue, but myriad shades of green that sparkled when she was angry or excited about the subject under discussion.

They could also look as deep as wells when she became introspective or sad, as they had done that night in the orchard when she had talked about her parents. He doubted she knew how expressive her eyes were. If she did, she would train them not to give away so much.

Drawing himself back into the discussion, he asked, "But what has your work method got to do with me?"

"To get to the culprit, I have to go through you. So I'll approach it the same investigative way as if I were writing a story on you. I want to talk to a variety of people with whom Lucky Tyler has had contact. Tell me about everybody you've had trouble with in say, hmm, the last six months."

He laughed. "That'll take all afternoon."

"We've got all afternoon."

"Oh yeah. Right. Chase did say he had that drilling in Louisiana under way, didn't he? Well, let's see." Absently he scratched his neck. "Of course, most recently there was Little Alvin and Jack Ed."

"For the time being, let's set them aside. We'll come back to them. They're almost too obvious to be suspects."

"Okay, for starters, there was this guy in Longview. Owned a club over there."

"A club? Health club? Country club?"

"No, a, uh, you know."

"A nightclub?"

"Yeah. It's a . . . the kind of place where guys hang out. It's got girls. They hustle drinks and, you know, dance a little."

"A topless bar?"

"Sorta like that. Sure. I guess you could call it that."

Rolling her eyes, she said, "Don't spare my sensibilities, Lucky. We'll save time. What about this guy?"

"He accused me of coming on to one of his girls."

"Did you?"

"I bought her a few drinks."

"And for that he got upset?"

"Not exactly," he said, shifting uncomfortably.

"What? Exactly."

"I flirted with her. She read more into it than I intended. When I lost interest and stopped going there, she got depressed."

"How do you know?"

"This guy calls and starts bawling me out. Said she cried all the time, wouldn't work. Said I was bad for his business, 'cause she was a favorite with his customers. He told me to stay away from his club and his girls, this one in particular. I think he had the hots for her and was just jealous."

"Jealous enough to burn down your building?"

"I doubt it."

Devon took a deep breath. "Bears looking into. Who else?"

"There was a farmer."

"Let me guess," she said drolly. "He had a daughter."

"No. He had a cow."

After a moment's wary hesitance she shook her head. "I don't think I want to hear about this one."

Frowning at her lack of faith in him, he explained, "I was driving one of our trucks through a pasture on my way to a drilling site when a cow decided to play chicken with it."

"With what?"

"The truck."

"In other words, you ran over a cow."

"It was an accident! I swear, the dumb animal ran straight for my hood ornament. Anyway, she died."

"Surely you paid the farmer for the cow?"

"Hell, yes. We paid him more than she was worth. But he pitched a conniption fit and threatened to sue us for further damages."

"What happened?"

"Nothing. We never heard from him again, and assumed he had decided he'd come out ahead."

"Maybe not. Although I doubt a poor old farmer would have the moxie to set a fire."

"Poor old farmer, my foot. He was straight out of Texas A&M. You should have heard some of the names he called me."

"Okay, he's a possibility. Remember his name, and we'll check to see if he's bought any flares lately. Who else have you tussled with?"

He squinted into the sunlight. "Hmm. Oh yeah, the Irvings."

"Plural?"

"There's a clan of them over in Van Zandt County."

"Swell. That narrows it down," she muttered. "What did you do to them?"

"Nothing!"

"What did they accuse you of doing?"

He reached for her hands and sandwiched them between his own. "Swear to God, Devon, it wasn't me."

"Who did what?"

"Got Ella Doreen pregnant."

She stared at him in stupefaction for several seconds, then she began to laugh. "Is this a joke?"

"Hardly. You wouldn't have thought it was funny either if an army of shotgun-toting rednecks in overalls had come after you. They surrounded the office one day, demanding I make an honest woman of Ella Doreen and acknowledge her kid as mine."

"Was there any possibility that you were the, uh, donor?"

He shot her a retiring look. "She's just a kid, younger than Sage. I didn't even remember who she was until one of her kinfolk produced her from the back of a flatbed truck. Uncle Somebody shoved her forward to accuse me face-to-face."

"You recognized her then?"

"Sure. We had met a couple of weeks earlier in an office

building in Henderson. I was there to see a client. As I was crossing the lobby, I noticed this girl sitting there fanning herself, looking ready to throw up or faint or both. I asked if she needed any help. She told me she'd gotten dizzy and hot. And it *was* hotter than hell in there.

"So I helped her to her feet, escorted her outside, and offered to buy her a can of cola, which I did from one of the vending machines at the nearest filling station. We walked there. I was never even alone with her. The only thing I touched was her elbow.

"During our conversation she asked me what I did for a living, and seemed impressed by the business card I gave her. I remember her running her fingers over the engraving. That's it. After she assured me that she could call someone to come pick her up, I left her there, sitting on a stack of retreads, sipping her coke.

"As it turns out, she had been in Henderson to see a doctor in that building, and was already about four months pregnant. I couldn't possibly have fathered her chid. I was just a convenient scapegoat. Eventually she broke down and admitted it."

By the time he finished telling the tale, Devon was shaking her head with amazement. "You attract trouble like a lightning rod."

"Not intentionally."

"And it always centers around women. Even the cow." She looked away from him, adding softly, "And now me."

Laying his palm along her cheek, he turned her face toward him. "You look so sad."

"I am."

"Why? Was it terrible yesterday?"

"Yes. It was awful having to face my husband, both of us knowing that I had betrayed him. Physically. With you."

"And knowing you want to again."

She sucked in a quick little breath. Her eyes widened, and her lips parted. "I didn't say that, Lucky."

"You didn't have to." He brushed his thumb across her lower lip. She whimpered quietly. Glancing down at the peaked centers of her breasts, which were making impressions against her blouse, he whispered, "Just like before, your body says it for you."

Chapter Seventeen

Pat Bush was sitting on a picnic table in Dogwood Park, drinking from a longneck bottle of beer. It was against the rules to be drinking in uniform, but it was against the rules to hand over official crime reports to civilians, too, so he figured he might just as well be hanged for a sinner as a saint.

Devon scanned the top sheet of the stack of documents. One of the park's halogen security lamps provided her with enough light to read by. She had slipped on her glasses. "What's a trailer?"

"A trail of fuel leading back to the building," Pat explained. "There were several radiating out from the garage like spokes on a wheel. They set the flares to them."

"Then ran like hell," Lucky contributed from the adjacent playground, where he was sitting in a swing.

"Whoever did it was smart," said Pat, playing devil's advocate. "Apparently the perp shut off the ventilation system in the building first. The gasoline fumes collected like air inside a balloon. One spark introduced into those compressed fumes, and *ka-blooy.* You've got yourself an explosion hot enough to melt metal."

"Maybe we'll see something when we've gone over the material more carefully." Devon tried to inject some optimism into her voice, but Lucky knew that her hopes were as faint as his own. He rued the day he'd bought those flares, which the roughnecks sometimes used at night to mark the route to an out-of-the-way drilling site.

Pat finished his beer and conscientiously placed the empty bottle in the trash barrel. "Guess I'd better get home. It's late. If y'all turn up anything, let me know. But for the love of God keep your investigation covert. Don't do anything conspicuous."

"Don't worry, Pat. If we're caught, your name would never enter into an explanation of how we got the crime report."

"You didn't have to tell me that," the older man said to Lucky. He doffed the brim of his hat to Devon and ambled off through the park toward his squad car.

"Ready?" Lucky asked.

Devon pocketed her glasses, picked up the stack of documents, and allowed him to hold her hand as they moved in the opposite direction from Pat, toward Lucky's Mustang.

The house was dark when they arrived. Laurie had already gone to bed. A light shone from beneath Sage's door, and she had a radio on, but for all practical purposes she had retired to her room for the night, too.

At the door of the guest bedroom, which Laurie had hospitably prepared for her, Devon turned to Lucky. "Tomorrow we'll begin again, asking questions about anybody who might be harboring a grudge against you. One by one we'll eliminate them."

"Okay."

"Let me know if you think of anyone else, and I'll add him to my list."

"Okay."

"Are you listening?"

"Of course." Actually he wasn't. "You sleepy?"

"A little."

"I'm not. I've never been so keyed up."

"I started out this morning with a hundred-mile drive, remember?"

He nodded, but his eyes were fastened on her neck with the single-mindedness of a vampire. "Is, uh, is the bedroom okay?" he asked, reluctant to leave her. "Is the bed comfy?"

"I haven't tried it yet, but I'm sure it will be fine."

"Is the room hot?"

"Not at all."

"Too cool?"

"It's just right, Lucky."

"Got everything you need?"

"Yes."

"Towels?"

"Yes."

"Soap?"

"Yes."

"Toilet paper?"

She smiled. "Your mother is a thorough and gracious hostess. I even have a candy dish stocked with little candy bars."

"Oh well, then I guess you've got everything."

"Mm-hmm."

"But if you need anything else . . ."

"I won't."

" . . . like extra blankets, pillows . . ." He bent his head and brushed his mouth across hers. "Me."

He kissed her, fluidly, first touching the tip of his tongue to hers, then melding their mouths together. Groaning, he placed his arms around her and drew her against his body, which was full and feverish with a desire he'd studiously kept at bay until now, when he couldn't restrain himself any longer.

Just one taste of her. Only one. Then he might survive the night. But, by the second, his mouth became more possessive, his tongue more intimate, his hands more seductive. She ground protesting fists against his chest. He moaned her name when he finally surrendered and raised his head.

"We can't, Lucky."

"It's just a kiss."

"No it isn't."

"Just one kiss."

"It's wrong."

"I know, I know."

"Then let me go. Please."

He released her but didn't move away. Their eyes met and locked in a searing gaze. It gratified him to hear that she was as breathless as he, and that her protests were without conviction.

She slipped through the guest-room door and closed it behind her, but not before he saw in her eyes pinpoints of confusion and passion that matched those burning in his.

He hardly slept a wink that night, knowing she was only two doors away but unable to do a damn thing about it.

After three days of that he was on the verge of going stark staring mad. One by one the names on their list of possible suspects had fallen through the cracks of logic, reason, and fact. No one who had a recent grievance against him could have set the fire.

His mood was foul, his disposition sour, his language vulgar, his patience depleted, and all because he was desperate for Devon.

Her fourth morning in Milton Point she told him over coffee, "The farmer was our last chance, and he was in Arkansas buying cattle. It seems that the only people in town that night were those who love you. I don't know what else to do."

"Is that right?" He sneered. "I was under the impression that you knew everything. I thought you had a bag of tricks. Don't tell me you've run out."

Furiously she scraped back her chair and stood up, heading for the kitchen door. As she sailed past his chair he put out his arm, encircled her waist, drew her between his wide-spread thighs, and ground his forehead against her stomach.

"I'm sorry, I'm sorry." He butted his head against the soft heaviness of her breasts and rubbed his face in the fabric of her blouse, breathing in her fresh, clean scent. "I know I'm acting like a jerk, but I'm slowly dying, Devon. I'm going to explode if—"

"Somebody's coming."

She backed out of his reach only seconds before Laurie entered the kitchen, followed by Sage. If Laurie noticed the steamy atmosphere and their rosy, guilt-ridden faces, she didn't acknowledge them. Sage, however, split her knowing look between the two of them and winked saucily.

"Well, hello. We're not interrupting anything, are we?"

Lucky snarled at her.

"What's on your agenda today?" Laurie asked.

"Actually we hadn't decided on anything specific," Devon said feebly.

"Well, if you ask me, which I realize you haven't, you're overlooking the obvious."

"What's that, Mother?"

Lucky glanced up at her, curious in spite of his longing to thrash his impudent kid sister. He welcomed his mother's opinion—anything, in fact, that would momentarily distract him from his physical discomfort.

"That Cagney oaf and his unsavory friend."

"Little Alvin and Jack Ed Patterson?"

Laurie gave a delicate shudder at the very mention of their names. "Detestable people, especially Jack Ed. And those Cagney children were hellions from birth."

"But they're *so* obvious," Lucky argued.

"Maybe they figure that's what everyone is thinking and are using it to their benefit."

Devon and Lucky's eyes met as they considered the possibility. "She's got a point," Devon said. "They certainly were peeved at you."

"But they've got ironclad alibis."

"Lies," Sage retorted succinctly. "They've terrorized people into lying for them."

Lucky gnawed his lower lip as he thought it through. "It wouldn't be too smart to confront them. We promised Pat there would be no more trouble. Besides," he said with a grin, "I might not come out alive if I have another fight with Little Alvin."

"So, what are you thinking?" Devon asked.

"Little Alvin is as strong as an ox and meaner than Satan, but he's no mental giant."

"I agree. Jack Ed would have masterminded the fire."

"So let's use Little Alvin's cerebral weakness to our advantage."

"How?" she asked.

Lucky leaned back in his chair and slapped his thighs with satisfaction. "With the thing I do best. A con."

. . .

As they pulled up in front of the rusty mobile home, Devon nervously wet her lips and asked, "How do I look?"

"Plumb mouthwatering." Lucky switched off the Mustang's motor.

She tipped up the lenses of her dark glasses. "With this?" Sage had done an excellent job of painting on a black eye, using her vast array of eye shadows and shading crayons.

"Even with that." He was tempted to lean across the car's console and kiss her. But glancing at the windows of the mobile home, he realized Little Alvin could be watching them.

"You'll have to open your own door." He vaulted over the driver's door and headed for the trailer without giving her a backward glance. He knocked loudly on the front door of the trailer, then bawled over his shoulder at her. "Hurry up, will you?"

She moved into place beside him and muttered out the side of her mouth. "Macho pig."

The whispered words were barely out of her mouth when the front door was opened with such impetus, the entire building rocked on its concrete-block platform.

"What the hell do you want, Tyler?"

With admirable aplomb, Lucky stood his ground and growled back. "First off, I want to be invited inside."

"What for?"

"I'll tell you when I get inside."

"When boar hogs grow teats. Get the hell off my porch."

Little Alvin tried to slam the door in their faces, but Lucky caught it before it closed. "We either come in now alone, or come back later with Sheriff Bush. Then the decision won't be left to you."

Alvin regarded Lucky suspiciously, then gave Devon a lecherous leer. "Would the little lady like to come in by herself?"

"The little lady would not," said Lucky, grinding his teeth.

Alvin cursed, then turned inside and indicated with his head that they should follow. Lucky was about to step aside and let Devon go first, when she gave him a slight shove as a reminder that he was supposed to be portraying the role of a heel.

The place was a pigsty. It was furnished cheaply and littered with the debris of numerous meals and a collection of empty liquor bottles and beer cans. The only decorations were centerfolds that had been cut out of the crudest men's magazines and taped to the walls.

One look at those and Lucky felt Devon stiffen beside him. Just to be ornery, he walked over to one and studied it at length, murmuring an "hmm" of approval. He didn't wait for an invitation to sit down, but sprawled on a sofa. Taking Devon's hand, he dragged her down beside him and threw an arrogantly possessive arm around her.

"Whaddaya want?" their host asked.

"A cold beer would be nice. One for me and one for her," Lucky replied, jerking his head down toward Devon.

Scowling, Little Alvin lumbered into the adjacent kitchen and returned several moments later with three beers. After handing them theirs, he sat down across from them in what was apparently "his chair." There was a greasy spot on the headrest and worn spots in the upholstery where his behind fit into the seat and on the cushion where his feet rested when it reclined.

"Well?" he asked belligerently, after taking a sucking swig from his can of beer.

"Pat Bush gave me twenty minutes to make a deal with you."

Little Alvin barked a laugh. "You gotta be crazy, Tyler. I ain't making no deal with you about anything."

"I told you he wouldn't do it," Devon muttered.

"And I told you to keep your mouth shut and let me handle this," Lucky snapped, shooting her a threatening glance. "He may be dumb, but he's not stupid."

"Now just a damn—"

Lucky interrupted. "You want to hear this or not? Because every minute that you sit here shooting off your fat mouth is one minute you come closer to spending time in federal prison."

"For what?"

Devon laughed. Lucky frowned with impatience. "For

what?" he repeated scornfully. "Look, Alvin, cut the crap, all right? They've got enough evidence on you guys to send you to jail . . . even without a trial."

They saw a chasm open up then in his armor of insolence. His smug grin faltered. "What do you mean? What evidence?"

"Evidence, okay? There's not enough time to detail it all."

"When are you going to tell him about the paper?" Devon whined.

Lucky cursed, acting as if she had distracted him. "Will you put a lid on it and give me time to get this other business over with first?"

At the prearranged signal Devon removed her sunglasses and revealed her black eye. "I don't care about that stupid fire. You said—"

"What about the evidence the sheriff's got?" Little Alvin asked anxiously, cutting into their lovers' spat.

"Let me handle *my* business with the man first, okay? Then we'll get to yours." Lucky turned back to Alvin and lowered his voice. "She looked so damn good in the place, you know? Now . . ." He flung up his hands in exasperation. "Might have ended up better for everybody if you'd got her that night instead of me. Anyway, where was I?"

"The evidence they've got on me," Alvin squealed.

"Oh yeah, well, they're keeping the files officially closed. All I know is that Pat promised to pick up Jack Ed first, but who knows how long that might take? He could arrive any minute now." For good measure he glanced over his shoulder through the ratty curtains at the window.

"They're picking up Jack Ed?" Sweat popped out on Little Alvin's porcine face.

"As we speak. You know what a weasel that little s.o.b. is. He'd rat on his own mother. Lord only knows what he's gonna tell them about you. Probably that the fire was all your doing."

Little Alvin Cagney made a whimpering sound like a toddler who'd momentarily lost sight of his mother, and lunged for the door. Anticipating that, Lucky was right behind him, catching him by the collar and hauling him back.

"We're here to help you, Alvin."

"You think I was born yesterday, Tyler?"

"If you turn state's evidence, you'll get a lighter sentence. Otherwise, you're history."

"Liar." Little Alvin twisted and turned, trying to work himself free. Lucky hung on tenaciously. "Why would you come to warn me, Tyler?"

"I wouldn't. But Pat would. He needs one more piece of evidence to nail Jack Ed. Since he knew we were coming to see you on this other matter, he asked me to offer you a deal. Real decent of him, wasn't it? See, everybody knows that Jack Ed was the brains behind the arson, but they can't prove it."

"Th-that's right," Little Alvin stammered. "Hell, I

wasn't even thinking straight that night. You had kicked my nuts up to the back of my throat. But Jack Ed said—"

"Save it," Lucky hissed. "Give all the details to Pat when he gets here, things like where Jack Ed got those flares."

"His sister's garage," he babbled. "Her husband works for the highway department. Jack Ed said they'd think you did it because you carried flares—"

"I said save it. I'm not interested. When they find the flares, they're sure to find the gas cans, too."

"Yeah. We got them out of his brother-in-law's gar—"

"I said save it for Pat." He pushed Little Alvin back into his chair. The football lineman was quivering, a hairy blob of perspiring ectoplasm.

"Now that that's out of the way, will you see to my business?" Devon asked in a petulant tone.

Lucky blew out a breath. "Sure, sure. Get him something to write with."

"Write? Write what?" Alvin's eyes darted warily between Devon and Lucky.

"Did you read in the newspaper about her old man being in prison?"

Dumbly, Alvin nodded.

"Well, he accused her of taking up with me long before the night of the fire. He claims we'd been seeing each other even before he went to the pen. If the prison guards hadn't restrained him . . ."

Gesturing toward her black eye, Lucky trailed off ominously. "Anyway, could you just jot down a statement that I picked her up in the place? That it was just an accidental meeting."

"Sure, sure. I can do that."

"Good. I don't give a damn what her old man thinks, but she kept nagging me about it. You know how women are." Devon handed Alvin a piece of paper and a pencil. "While you're doing that, I'll call Pat on his mobile phone. I hope we're not too late. I'll tell him you're ready to talk. Right?"

"Right, right," Little Alvin agreed eagerly. "My folks warned me not to trust Jack Ed."

"They were right," Lucky said sagely. "When it comes to brains, you can't even compare you two." He clapped Alvin on the shoulder as though they were old friends. "His brother-in-law's garage, huh? I don't even want to know where he lives."

"Off Route Four. By that big grain silo."

Lucky looked at Devon over the top of Alvin's head and smiled.

Chapter Eighteen

They laughed so hard that tears streamed down their faces and they kept collapsing against each other. "By the time Pat got there, Little Alvin was blubbering like a baby about the atrocities inflicted on celebrities like him in prison. I always suspected that underneath his meanness he was nothing but a chicken-livered coward. Now I know it's true."

The Tylers were gathered in the living room. Chase, Tanya, Laurie, and Sage were the enthralled audience.

"I actually started feeling sorry for him," Devon said.

"Is that why you brewed him a cup of tea?"

"Tea?" Chase hooted. "Little Alvin sipping tea?"

"She borrowed a tea bag from one of his neighbors in the trailer park, brewed him a cup, and insisted he drink it while Pat and a deputy were waiting for Alvin's attorney to get there so they could take his deposition."

"Well, I think that was a lovely gesture," Laurie said, coming to Devon's defense. "But I can't say that I feel sorry for Alvin. Those Cagney kids were allowed to run roughshod over everybody without any parental supervision. It's a wonder to me they're not all behind bars by now."

"What about Jack Ed?" Chase wanted to know once he had contained his laughter.

"They've got an arrest warrant out for him. Since he thinks he's in the clear, he shouldn't be too hard to find."

"Oh, I'm so glad you're off the hook," Tanya said.

"Hopefully things will get back to normal now," Sage said. "By the way, Lucky, I went into town this morning and saw Susan Young at the dry cleaners. She kept her eyes to the floor. That's the first time since I've known her that she hasn't looked down her nose at me."

"Her dirty, rotten trick almost backfired this time," Chase said. "It put the fear of God into her."

"Or the fear of Lucky," Sage said, grinning at her brother.

Chase stood and extended a hand down to assist Tanya up. "I'm going to the office and call the insurance company. Now that we've been cleared of any criminal charges, they can process our claim."

"What will we do with the money?" Lucky asked him. "Pay back the bank in full, or replace the equipment we lost in the fire?"

"We need to discuss how to allocate it," Chase said.

"Not right now, you don't," Laurie said. "I don't want talk about business to spoil the mood." She took Tanya's arm as she walked with her to the door. "How's the house-hunting? Find anything yet?"

"This morning," Tanya reported with a smile. "Marcie took me to see one I really liked. I want Chase to see it."

"Soon," he promised.

"How are you feeling?" Laurie inquired.

"Fit as a fiddle. A little indigestion in the evenings."

They said their good-byes and left. Celebrating his brother's liberation, Chase honked his car horn as they sped down the lane toward the main road.

"Know what I feel like?" Lucky said. "A good, galloping ride. Who's game?"

"Sage and I have to pass," Laurie said. "We've got dental appointments in town."

"Oh, Mother—"

"I won't cancel it again, Sage. I've canceled three times already."

After an exchange that Sage was destined to lose, she reluctantly followed her mother out the back of the house where Laurie always parked her car. Lucky turned to Devon.

"That leaves you."

"I really should be getting back to Dallas."

"Mother obviously expects you to stay another night."

"How do you know?"

"She didn't say good-bye."

"She did so."

"That? That wasn't one of her formal good-byes. Her

formal good-byes take forever. Lots of hugs and Kleenex and stuff."

"There's nothing to keep me here any longer, Lucky."

"Surely you can spare an hour for a horseback ride," he said cajolingly. "Besides, you can't leave the family without first going through the rite of a formal good-bye."

His smile was so disarming, she capitulated after offering only a few more token excuses. "Give me time to wash off my black eye and change clothes," she said, heading for the stairs.

"Meet you in the stable."

Devon reined in behind Lucky, choking on the dust his mount had kicked up. "No fair," she shouted. "You cheated!"

"Naturally," he admitted breezily as he swung his leg over his saddle and dismounted. "How else could I be guaranteed to win?"

Devon slid from her saddle and jumped to the ground. "Then Lucky is a misnomer. You win by cheating."

Laughing, he took the reins from her and walked both horses into the stable. Its shadows were cool and refreshing in comparison to the sunny heat of the afternoon.

"I've had my share of luck, too," he told her. Skillfully he removed the saddles from the horses, then began walking them up and down the center aisle of the stable to cool them off. Devon walked alongside him.

"Is that how you got your nickname?"

"Sort of."

"Who gave it to you?"

His tanned face broke into a wide grin. "Chase."

"Why?"

"Well, he and some of his buddies . . ." He paused and glanced down at her. "Sure you want to hear this?"

"I'm sure."

"Okay. Just remember you asked."

"It sounds sordid."

"It is. One night when I was about fourteen, I black-mailed Chase and some of his friends into including me when they took out one of the boys' family car. We ended up over in Kilgore at a bowling alley. They'd gone there looking for a woman."

"Just any ol' woman?"

"No. A particular woman."

"Dare I ask why? Here, let me help." She scooped grain into a feed bucket while Lucky rubbed down the gelding she'd been riding. "Tell me about the woman."

His hands, one holding a currycomb, worked efficiently and smoothly over the animal's flesh. "She had a stupefying body, and showed it off to the yokels like us. Got her kicks wearing tight sweaters without a bra. That kind of thing."

They moved to the next stall and began working to-gether on the horse Lucky had been riding. "What hap-pened?" Devon asked as she positioned the feed bucket where the animal could reach it.

"I guess I wanted to prove that I was as much a stud as the rest of them even though I was younger. So I approached her and struck up a conversation."

"About what?"

"My father, who had been falsely accused of being a spy and was imprisoned somewhere behind the Iron Curtain."

Devon's hands fell still. She laughed with disbelief. "And she bought it?"

"I guess so. I never knew. Maybe she was just tired of the bowling alley. Anyway, when I told her I was collecting aluminum cans to recycle so I could raise the money to buy his way out of a Communist country, she invited me to her house and said I could have all the cans I could find."

Devon followed him to a deep utility sink at the back of the building where they washed their hands, sharing a bar of soap. "Meanwhile, Chase and his friends don't know what you're telling her," Devon said as she shook water off her hands before pulling a towel from the rack.

"Right. They thought she was taking me to her house for prurient purposes." He bobbed his eyebrows. "Behind her back, I was giving them the high sign, fanning my face, stuff like that, which would indicate that she was hot for me and vice versa."

"I've got the picture."

"So I rode with her to her house. I felt like a damn fool fishing soda cans out of her trash and placing them in the grocery sack she had provided. Although the scenery was good."

"Scenery?"

"The body."

"Oh yes, the body."

"She was an adolescent boy's dream. From an adult point of view—my taste has been considerably refined," he said, raking his eyes down Devon's slender shapeliness, "I realize she was a little overblown. Back then, though, I thought she was something.

"So, with my eyes glued to her bosom, I'm rifling through her garbage looking for cans, and she's chattering about how admirable it is of me to undertake this dangerous mission and how terrible it must be to be imprisoned in a foreign land. She had a ten-plus body, but a single-digit IQ."

"The type who causes the feminist movement to nose-dive."

"Exactly. She was a prototype."

He led Devon into a small room at the back of the stable. In it were a couple of chairs, a double bed with an iron headboard, which at some point in its long life had been painted china blue, and a compact refrigerator.

He pulled the string dangling from the ceiling fan, and it began to hum as it circulated the warm, still air. He took two canned drinks from the refrigerator and handed one to Devon, opening the other for himself.

"She never made a move on you?"

He shook his head with chagrin. "In retrospect I scolded

myself for laying it on so thick. I finally worked up enough nerve to embrace her, and she *comforted* me! Saying things like 'Poor baby.'

"In her eyes I was too damn noble to be corruptible, much less horny. When it came time for me to go—when there were no more cans in the house—I told her I'd go out the back. See, I knew Chase and the others would have followed us and were watching her house.

"With this rattling sack of cans in my arms, I went out her back door and hid in the bushes. It was an hour longer before the other guys started honking the car horn for me. I had taken off my shirt, given myself a few scratches across the chest and belly, messed up my hair, all to give the general impression that I'd just been laid by a she-cat."

Devon's expression was a mix of incredulity and hilarity. Groping behind her for the edge of the bed, she sat down. The ancient springs creaked. "I can't believe this. Proving your manhood was that important to you?"

"At that point in time I guess it was. Anyhow, the guys fell for it. By the time I got finished with my breathless, lurid account, they thought she'd taken me to bed and that I had experienced what they'd only dreamed about. That's when they started calling me Lucky. To this day, they don't know any different."

"Not even Chase?"

"No." His brows steepled. "You're not going to tell him, are you?"

Laughing, she flung her arms behind her head and fell back onto the bed. "And spoil the masculine myth? I wouldn't dream of it."

"Good." He sat on the edge of the bed and smiled down at her. "The point would be moot anyway, because it wasn't long after that night that I really became a man with a girl in my algebra class."

Devon's smile faltered; she averted her eyes. "Women have always been easy conquests for you, haven't they?"

She started to sit up, but Lucky slid his palms against hers and exerted enough pressure to keep the backs of her hands lying supine on the cheap bedspread beneath her.

"All but one, Devon. Nothing with you has been easy."

"Let me up."

"Not yet."

"I want to get up."

"So do I," he whispered hoarsely before covering her lips with his.

Their mouths came together hungrily and clung. He thrust his tongue between her lips, between her teeth, into her mouth. Their fingers interlocked as he moved his body above hers and used his knee to separate hers.

He released her hands and drove his up through her loose hair. They held her head still while his mouth gently ate hers. All resistance gone, she closed her arms around his torso, hugging him to her tightly. Her hands ran up and down his back, gripping the firm musculature.

Overhead the fan droned, fanning their bodies, which

burned hotter by the second. From the stable came an occasional snuffling sound made by horses. But the throaty sounds of want and need were all that echoed through their heads.

He tore his mouth from hers and peered deeply into her eyes. "I want you, Devon. Damn, but I want you . . ."

He kissed her again, ravenously, while he grappled with the buttons on her plain white shirt. When they were undone, he pushed the fabric aside. The front clasp of her bra fell open at a flick of his fingertips. He caressed her. His eyes adored her. His mouth drew in her sweet flesh and sucked it tenderly.

"Lucky," she breathed, half in anguish, half in ecstasy. Her fingers tunneled through his hair and clasped his head to her chest. Her thighs parted. He nestled his middle in her cleft, moved against it, rubbed it.

He kissed her breasts again and again, using his tongue to excite them. When she thought she couldn't be drawn any tighter, any higher, he brushed her nipples with rapid flicking motions of his tongue until they were tingling.

For weeks he had tried convincing himself that he wanted Devon Haines merely because he couldn't have her. He had told himself that his imagination had run rampant and that their one time together hadn't been as unique as his memory had made it out to be.

One taste of her, however, had shot that theory all to hell. He wanted her. He wanted her right now, and later today, and tomorrow, and the day after that, forever. He wanted the sight and sound and smell of her, the taste and the textures of her.

He wanted her laughter and her temper. He'd grown fond of her feminist defensiveness, her clever, analytical mind, and the delightful and annoying little surprises she constantly pulled on him. He wanted everything and all that Devon comprised.

As his lips kissed their way down her smooth belly, he unfastened her jeans and worked them past her waist. The open wedge fascinated him and he continued to explore it until he felt the softest hair against his lips.

"Devon," he murmured with longing. "Devon."

Pressing deeper, he parted his lips and kissed her earnestly. There was moisture and heat and need, which he wanted to probe.

"No!" Suddenly she shoved him off, rolled away, and drew herself into a ball. "It's wrong. I can't. I can't."

Lucky stared down at her, gasping for breath, trying to clear his head and make sense of a senseless situation. He saw her tears, but even before then he knew this wasn't some trick. She was suffering spiritual torment and emotional hell, and he couldn't bear it.

"It's okay, Devon," he said with soft gruffness, laying a hand on her shoulder. He made ineffectual attempts to draw her blouse together over her breasts, the tips of which were still rosy and moist from his caresses. "I'd never want you to do anything that would make you feel bad about yourself or about me. Never."

She turned her head and gazed up at him through eyes shimmering with tears. "I'm married, Lucky." Her voice trembled with desperation. "I'm married."

"I know."

The ancient bed rocked when he flung himself off it and stamped through the door. He paced the length of the stable a couple of times, cursing fate, gnashing his teeth in an effort to cool his passions and his temper.

However, when Devon appeared, his temper dissipated. Her despair killed it as nothing else could have. There were still tears in her eyes. Her lips, which were swollen from fervent kissing, made her look like a victim. What did that make him? The culprit?

Yes.

"I'll walk you back to the house now," he said gently. She didn't take the hand he extended to her, but fell into step beside him as they moved from the stable to the house.

As soon as they entered, she said, "It won't take me long to pack." Before he could stop her, she ran upstairs.

He wished his mother allowed liquor in the house. If he'd ever needed a whiskey, it was now. The longest ten minutes of his life was spent roaming the rooms of the house, knowing that Devon was upstairs, preparing to walk out of his life forever.

She had reached the bottom stair before he heard her tread and rushed to confront her there. At her side, she was carrying her packed suitcase.

"Devon—"

"Good-bye, Lucky. I'm glad everything worked out well for you. Of course, there was never any doubt in my mind that you would be cleared of the charges. Thank your mother for her hospitality, and say my good-byes to everyone. They're all so kind, so . . ." When her voice cracked, she sidestepped him and headed for the front door.

He caught her arm and spun her around. "You can't just leave like this."

"I have to."

"But you don't want to, Devon. Dammit, I know you don't."

"I'm married."

"To a guy you don't love."

"How do you know?"

He took a step closer. It was time to play hardball. Their futures were at stake. "Because if you did, you wouldn't have let me make love to you that first time. You weren't that sleepy. And you wouldn't have let what just happened, when you were wide awake, go so far.

"Know what else? I don't think he loves you either. If he did, he wouldn't have acted like he did when you went to explain things. He'd be gut-sick, or outraged, or determined to castrate and kill me, but he wouldn't act like a kid whose favorite toy had been damaged."

Her momentary defiance evaporated, and she lowered her head. "Whatever Greg says or does isn't the issue. It's what *we* do that counts. I'm leaving, Lucky. Talking about it won't change my mind."

"I can't let you just go."

"You don't have a choice. Neither do I."

Again she maneuvered around him. He delayed her again. "If you did have a choice—"

"But I don't."

"If you *did*," he repeated stubbornly, "would you want to stay with me?" She did something then that she had avoided doing since coming downstairs—she looked at him directly.

The yearning in her eyes mirrored his own. He exulted in it. Raising his hand, he stroked her cheek. "If you had a choice, would you let me love you like I want to?" he asked in a stirring voice.

The physical and emotional tug-of-war between them was almost palpable. Her eyes cried, *yes, yes!* But aloud she said nothing. Instead, she turned toward the door. "Good-bye, Lucky."

Abysmally dejected, he dropped down onto the bottom stair and listened to her light footsteps cross the porch and crunch in the gravel driveway. He heard her car door being opened, then closed, and the growl of the engine as she turned it on. He sat there long after the motor could no longer be heard and she had had time to put miles between them.

He listened very closely to something else—his own being. He lusted after this woman's body more than all the other bodies he'd ever known put together. His single sexual experience with her stood out above all the rest. He'd had many that were lustier, crazier, faster, slower, but none as heart-piercingly sweet, none that still haunted his mind.

His heart was saying that his craving for her wasn't entirely physical, however. He could no longer even imagine a life without Devon in it. There would be nothing to look forward to. Days would be dreaded rather than anticipated. Years. Decades.

His head was telling him that the situation was hopeless and that he'd known that from the time she had informed him she was married. Their worst enemy wasn't Greg Shelby; it was their own consciences. Neither could engage in an unscrupulous affair, and if they could, they wouldn't be attracted. They would be two different people. What a brutal irony, that the morals they respected in each other made their being together impossible.

But James Lawrence Tyler wasn't only lucky, he was eternally optimistic.

Nothing was impossible. He simply wouldn't accept this situation. Fate couldn't play a bad joke on him like this and get away with it. It couldn't end this way, with Devon just quitting his life and both of them being miserable about it. No way. He wouldn't allow it.

Hell no.

Chapter Nineteen

"Visits are limited to fifteen minutes."

Lucky was shown into the room where, a week earlier, Devon had met briefly with her husband. "I understand," he said to the official. "Thank you for arranging this meeting on such short notice."

During the bleak hours of the night before, it had occurred to Lucky that the manly thing to do would be to confront Devon's husband.

He wasn't yet sure what he was going to say to Greg Shelby. Was he supposed to say that he was sorry for making love to Devon? What an appalling thought. He wasn't sorry for it in the slightest. To say so would be a lie. He supposed he would just come right out and tell the man that he was in love with his wife.

That, too, had occurred to him during the bleak hours of the night.

For all his philandering, he'd always figured that one

day there would be a woman who would make sexual fidelity not only an obligation but a pleasure. Devon Haines was that woman. She had made monogamy the only form of sexual activity he wanted to engage in.

As Tanya had done for Chase, Devon had made all other women pale in comparison. She could fulfill his every need and make fulfilling hers a lifetime challenge that he would look forward to meeting.

The idea of his child growing inside Devon gave him goose bumps. It was probably the goose bumps, and the lump that had formed in his throat at the thought of making a baby with her, that convinced him it was love.

Hand in hand with love came honor. That was one lesson the Tyler children had been taught by both their parents. If you loved people, you might hurt them, disappoint them, anger them, but you never, ever, dishonored them.

It was that code of honor that had compelled him to drive through the gates of the country club prison to meet with her husband.

"Are you Tyler?"

At the sound of the voice, Lucky came around and got his first look at Greg Shelby. Mentally he sighed with relief. He'd dreaded meeting a Mel Gibson lookalike garbed in righteous martyrdom and prison stripes.

Instead, facing him was a tanned, nice-looking guy—but not one Sage would deem a hunk. It pleased him to note that Shelby's hair was thinning.

"Mr. Shelby?"

"That's right."

Carrying a chip on his shoulder the size of Mount Rushmore, he moved into the room and sat down on the sofa, laying his arm along the back of it. His nonchalance surprised Lucky. Surprised and provoked. Why wasn't the son of a bitch going for his throat? Didn't Devon deserve that?

Shelby said, "I don't have to ask what you want to see me about, do I?"

"I guess you don't. You read all about it in the news-papers."

"So did everybody else," he remarked bitterly.

Lucky sat down in a chair adjacent to the sofa. The two men squared off and eyed each other. "I'm sorry you found out about it that way," Lucky said, meaning it. "I know it couldn't have been easy on you, but it was a helluva lot worse on Devon."

Shelby snorted. "She's not in prison, though, is she?"

"She didn't commit a crime."

Lucky's bluntness momentarily took Shelby aback. Then he grinned slyly. "Some would think that what she did with you was a crime."

"I don't. And you don't either."

"How do you know what I think, Tyler?"

"If you were torn up over her adultery, we wouldn't be discussing it so casually."

Shelby gave him another wily grin and said sarcastically, "You're right. Devon's a veritable saint. Her only crime was marrying a guy destined for prison."

Lucky leaned back in his chair as though they were discussing the baseball season instead of an issue that, depending on the outcome, could determine his future.

"I wonder why she did that?"

Shelby regarded him shrewdly, then shrugged. He left the sofa and went to pour himself a cup of coffee from the dispenser. "Want some?"

"No thanks."

He blew on his hot coffee, then sipped. "Devon wanted an inside, in-depth story on a white-collar crime that most people would merely label good business. Because I claimed to be innocent, the victim of manipulators too smart to get caught, the case made damn good fodder for her column."

"She's got talent."

"She sure as hell does. She had everybody in Dallas rooting for me." He frowned into the Styrofoam cup. "Too bad the judge and jury couldn't read the newspapers. Maybe we should have put her on the stand as a character witness. She might have convinced them of my innocence."

"Like you convinced her?"

Again, Shelby shrugged noncommittally. He was too clever to admit anything or to be caught in a verbal trap. Lucky wanted to pound his complacent smile to mush.

"Devon got out of our marriage what she wanted," Shelby said.

"If you're suggesting that all she wanted out of it was a good column or two, you don't know her at all."

Shelby actually laughed. "Maybe you're right, Tyler. You probably know her at least as well as I do."

Lucky wasn't going to discuss Devon and their relationship with this man, whom he was despising more each minute they spent together.

Shelby finished his coffee and tossed the cup into the wastepaper basket. "I've been a model prisoner, you know," he said conversationally. "I don't complain about the food. I keep my quarters neat. I don't pick quarrels with the other inmates. I had a good chance for an early parole."

He turned a menacing stare on Lucky. "Then you banged Devon, and she didn't even have the good sense to keep it quiet."

Lucky's hands balled into fists, but Shelby was so caught up in his own wrath, he didn't notice that or the flexing motions of Lucky's jaw.

"I didn't want any wrinkles in my plan. My lawyer said I had a good chance to get out the first time I was reviewed for parole, if there wasn't a blemish on my record. Now this," he spat. "Of course, it has nothing to do with me personally, but they're bound to figure that our hasty marriage was a gimmick to try and keep me out of here by swaying public opinion in my favor."

"Which it was."

Lucky was fully enlightened on Shelby's character now. He had manipulated Devon into feeling sorry for him and marrying him on the spur of the moment, as girls marry soldiers on their way to the front trenches. He hadn't thought a man could stoop that low, could use someone so unconscionably, but Shelby didn't have a word of regret for how this scandal had affected Devon. All his concerns were for himself.

He was saying, "I mean, if my wife's bedding other men, it sure as hell doesn't say much for our marriage, does it?"

"No, it doesn't." Lucky came to his feet. "Tell me something. Did you ever love her?"

"Love her?" Shelby repeated scornfully. "That's the real joke on me. There was a possibility that Devon's stirring prose might keep me out of prison, so I milked that for all it was worth. It didn't work.

"Then I married her on the chance that would help, but lost that gamble too. So what have I got? A wife who's no use to me at all. In fact, she's a liability now that she's made her own notorious headlines. And the real kicker is that I haven't even availed myself of the consolation prize, her sweet body."

Lucky's heart slammed against his ribs. Only excellent control kept him from audibly gasping. His ears rang with Shelby's words. A shudder passed through his body.

"Stupid bitch. If she's going to pass it around, the least she could do is keep her affairs secret until I'm released."

Lucky, elated and furious in equal measure, had to get out of there or he was going to ram his fist through Shelby's front teeth. Over the last few weeks he had learned the wisdom of exercising self-control.

He stretched his arm straight out in front of him and aimed an index finger at the center of the prisoner's chest. His eyes were as cold and blue and still as a fjord.

"When you get out of here, I'm gonna beat the hell out of you."

Having made that promise, he pivoted on his bootheels and stalked toward the door. There, he turned and, almost as an afterthought, added, "Before long, it won't matter to you who Devon is sleeping with. She's getting an annulment."

When the office door was pushed open, Chase glanced up from the paperwork he'd been doing. He was surprised to see Tanya come in, followed by a tall, attractive woman.

"Goosey!" He stood and rounded his desk to greet his former classmate with a handshake, then a quick, hard hug.

"Hi, Chase," she said, laughing. "It's good to see you."

"Why haven't you been to any of our class reunions?" Smiling down into Marcie Johns's face, he said, "You look fantastic."

"I can't believe you're calling her by that horrid name!" Tanya exclaimed.

"You didn't take any offense, did you?" Chase asked.

"Of course not. If I could bear it as a sensitive, self-conscious adolescent, I can bear it as a mature adult. As for the class reunions, I lived in Houston for several years, and it was never convenient for me to make one."

Chase regarded her approvingly. "You're really looking terrific, Marcie. The years have been more than kind. They've been generous. I hear your business is going great guns, too."

"Thank you, and yes, I've enjoyed being in business for myself. The economy has slowed things down the past year or two, but I'm hanging in there."

"Wish I could say the same," he remarked good-naturedly.

"Oh, I understand you've got something very happy to celebrate."

"I told her about the baby," Tanya informed him. "And she's convinced me that even though our budget is tight, we can afford a house, and that now is an excellent time to buy. It's a buyer's market," she said, repeating Marcie's words.

"Should I be reaching for my checkbook?" he asked teasingly.

"Not yet. Marcie and I want you to come see the house she showed me yesterday. I think it's perfect. Will you come?"

"What, now?"

"Please."

"Sorry, sweetheart, but I can't." Tanya's animated face became crestfallen. "If it was any other time, I would, but I'm expecting a rep from the insurance company. He was supposed to be here right after lunch, but called to say he was running late. I need to be here when he arrives."

"I read in the morning papers that your brother had been cleared of those ridiculous arson charges," Marcie said.

"Is there another problem, Chase?"

"No," he said, reassuringly pressing Tanya's hand between his. "We just need to go over the inventory list of all the equipment we lost and discuss our claim."

She sighed with disappointment. "Well, maybe tomorrow."

"Or even later today," he offered. "Why don't you go look at the house again, and if you're still excited about it, call me. Maybe I can meet you there after he leaves. That is, if you're free, Marcie."

"I blocked out the entire afternoon for Tanya and you."

Tanya was smiling again. She threw her arms around Chase's neck and kissed him soundly on the mouth. "I love you. And you're going to love this house."

With his arms around her waist he hugged her tight. "I probably will, but not as much as I love you. Call me later."

Following them to the doorway, he waved them off.

"I know you're looking at me through the peephole. I'm not going to leave until I see you, even if it means climbing over your fence again. Save us both the trouble, okay?"

Devon unlatched the lock and pulled open the door.

"You shouldn't be here, Lucky. You're only making things worse by—"

Her words were stifled by his mouth, which swooped down to claim hers in a scorching kiss. With his arms locked tightly around her, he walked her backward into the nearest wall. Securing her in place by tilting his body forward at the hip, he cupped her head between his hands and held it still for his plundering mouth.

The kiss left her breathless and unable to speak. He used that to his advantage. "I drove straight here from the prison where I had a chat with Greg Shelby." Ignoring her sudden intake of breath, he doggedly continued, "Notice I didn't call him your husband, because in the strictest sense of the word, he isn't, is he, Devon?"

"Yes," she cried mournfully.

"No. I'm more married to you than he is."

He swept her into his arms and carried her into the bedroom, keeping his gaze riveted on hers, which was wide with disbelief. Depositing her gently on the bed, he followed her down.

"I knew there was something odd about that night, something I should remember." He spoke rapidly, the words tripping over each other. "But I could never pinpoint what it was. Now I can. You were a virgin. I was your first and only lover. Not Shelby. Not any man. Me. Right, Devon?"

She closed her eyes. Tears leaked from them and rolled

down her cheeks. She nodded. Lucky released a long-held sigh and bent down to rest his forehead on hers.

"Your marriage to him was never consummated?"

She shook her head no.

"Thank God." His breath ghosted over her tear-streaked features. He sipped a cloudy, salty droplet from the corner of her lips, then whisked them with his tongue.

Their open mouths sought each other. It wasn't as tempestuous a kiss as the previous one, but it was deeper, longer, wetter, more meaningful, their searching tongues conveying unspoken emotions.

Slowly, article by article, he removed her clothing, stopping occasionally to admire, pet, kiss areas of her body that up till now he had only imagined. He had explored them first in darkness and knew them only by touch. Now his eyes had a sensual feast as he marveled over each curve and contour.

Placing her hands above her head, he ran his fingers down the pale undersides of her arms. His hands brushed across her breasts, causing the nipples to peak, then down her belly, over her navel, to her thighs. He caressed the satin texture of each one, delighting in their slender shape. The muscles of her calves perfectly fit his palms. He stroked her slender ankles, the arches of her feet, and ran his thumbs along the pads of her toes.

She was lovely all over, but between her thighs she was so beautifully, wonderfully woman, it made his heart ache.

Palming her soft mound, he bent over her and made love to her mouth with his tongue, delving and withdrawing with a tempo that fired their imaginations and their blood.

With anxious longing, she quietly cried his name. He removed his expertly caressing hand and calmed her by dusting her face with light, airy kisses. Leaving the bed, he undressed.

The blinds were open. Afternoon sunlight streamed in, casting alternate strips of light and shadow across his flesh, limning his body hair with gold.

He had never known an ounce of modesty. Yet, standing at the side of Devon's bed, as he stepped free of his jeans and was left naked, he experienced a twinge of uncertainty and self-consciousness. Would his tall, lean body appeal to her? His chest was hairy. Some women didn't like hairy chests.

But when he returned to the bed and stretched out beside her, she allayed his misgivings by imbedding her fingertips in the crinkly pelt on his chest.

To his supreme satisfaction, she explored him with bashful but lustful curiosity. Her deft caresses were driving him slowly mad, but he forced himself to lie still and let her explore to her heart's content. Dying of pleasure wouldn't be a bad way to go.

At last, unable to take any more, he captured her hand. Keeping his eyes on hers, he sucked her fingertips while stroking her palm with his thumb. He then carried her hand down and folded it around his steely erection. He held his breath, wondering if she would accept or reject the gesture.

First with wonder, then with pleasure, then with desire, her hand explored and caressed his sex—the strong root, the smooth length, the bead of moisture at its tip.

Groaning his ecstatic misery, he lowered his head to her breasts. They were beautiful, and he told her so as he rubbed his open mouth over one flushed crest, then the other, until they were stiff. Wantonly he kissed her belly and that alluring delta of soft curls.

She murmured a low, throaty "Please."

He said that this time she had to be very ready, very wet.

She said she was.

He tested her to see.

He waited no longer.

As her body closed around him, milking him like a silken fist, he learned the difference between having sex and making love. This wasn't taking, but giving. It wasn't temporal, but lasting. It wasn't just physical, but emotional and cerebral. He was involved with her, totally involved, from the tip of his straining manhood to the outer perimeters of his soul.

They mated eye-to-eye, smile-to-smile, heart-to-heart, body-to-body, moving together with sublime compatibility. She matched his even strokes with a subtle undulation of her hips.

The closer they moved to climax, the tighter she clung,

the deeper he penetrated. Gritting his teeth, he held back until he felt the waves of sensation shimmy through her, felt her gentle contractions around his manhood, and saw the lights of ecstasy explode and glimmer in her green eyes.

Only then did he release the rigid control he had imposed on himself. He buried his face in the soft fragrance of her hair and gave himself over to the encompassing pleasure that erupted from within him and into Devon.

"Are you all right?" He felt the affirmative motion of her head where it lay next to his on the pillow. His lips grazed her ear as he whispered, "You're still so small." He kissed her throat. "It's wonderful for me, but I know it can't be very comfortable for you."

He was already becoming aroused again, and there was nothing he could do about it except withdraw, and that was out of the question. Readjusting their bodies slightly, he heard Devon whimper, but not with pain. With pleasure. He smiled into her neck.

"Did I hurt you that night in the motel?"

"No."

"I must have."

"Not much."

"I remember thinking that something wasn't right. Something was out of sync. But I was so sleepy and so caught up in you that I didn't stop to sort it out. I should have known. You were so tight. So sweet." Of its own acme. I used his story to help promote my column. That's when the Devon Haines byline really began to mean something to the newspaper. So I, as much as Greg, profited from our marriage."

"Devon, you've got incredible talent. Your column would have succeeded anyway. Why are you staying married?"

"Because I take my responsibilities seriously. I can't just wash my hands of a marriage because it's no longer useful, because it's inconvenient."

He shot down that argument with a curt, "Bullshit. You just don't want to admit that you were duped."

"That's not true!"

He knew by her instantaneous and adamant rebuttal that his guess had been right. "You always have to be in control, calling the shots. It's impossible for you to admit that twice your heart has overruled your head. Greg's sob story got to you, and you can't live with that. Rather than admitting to a mistake in judgment, you'll stubbornly stay married to him just to prove you were right."

"As long as there's the slightest chance that he's innocent, I can't desert him while he's in prison."

Lucky's oaths were vicious. "You don't believe he's innocent any more than I do."

"You said my heart had overruled my head twice."

He glanced at the bed. "You've fought it every step of the way, but you love me and I damn well know it. We connected the first time we laid eyes on each other. What you can't own up to is that you're as vulnerable between the thighs—"

"I won't listen to your lewd—"

"You don't want to be a weak nonentity like your mother was, totally dependent on her husband for everything. Okay. Fine. Guess what, Devon? I don't want to wipe my feet on you. I don't want a silent, submissive partner, in or out of bed."

"I have a husband."

"He's not the issue. He never has been, or so I found out this morning. You're just using him as an escape hatch. This is between you and me."

He gripped her shoulders. "You want a career. Terrific. Have one. I'm all for it. But have me, too. We can have each other and make both our careers worthwhile.

"I want babies. The burden of that responsibility falls on you, I'm afraid. But if you consented to have my babies, I'd put you on a pedestal and make it the most wonderful experience of your life."

He lowered his voice to a compelling, tempting whisper. "I've felt your passion for me, Devon. I've tasted it. I know it's there. Put your arms around my neck. Tell me you need me. Admit you love me."

"Twice you've persuaded me to break my wedding vows. Isn't that enough for you?"

"I want us to exchange our own vows, vows our bodies have already made. Vows you haven't made with Greg or any other man."

"I can't see you again, Lucky."

"Say you love me."

cord, his body stirred inside her and her muscles contracted reflexively, leaving them both breathless for a moment.

Panting, Lucky continued, "I didn't remember it later. Not until today when——" He broke off, unwilling to let mention of Shelby spoil the most pleasure he'd ever had in bed. God, it just didn't get any better than this.

"Today, when I realized that you were a virgin that night and that I was the only man you'd ever been with, hell or high water couldn't have kept me away from you, Devon."

Then he groaned her name again and sank deeper into the snug, liquid heat of her body, and they both climaxed. Her throat arched beautifully, and her limbs enfolded him as she experienced her long, sweet release.

Moments later, lying face-to-face, he brushed away the damp strands of hair that clung to her flushed cheeks. Her eyes were limpid and dilated, as though she had been drugged.

"Lucky," she said in a soft, sad rasp, lightly touching his lips with her fingertips.

"That's me." He smiled crookedly.

Without returning his smile, she rolled to the opposite side of the bed and got up. He appreciatively watched as her graceful body moved from bed to closet and she wrapped a robe around her slim nakedness. He was charmed, especially when she used both hands to free her sex-tousled hair from her collar.

But when she turned to face him, his enchantment dissipated.

"What?" he asked with perplexity.

"You've got to go now."

He would have thought he hadn't heard her correctly if her face weren't so pale and blank of all expression. Throwing his legs over the side of the bed, he reached for his jeans, thrust his feet into them, and pulled them on as he stood up. Tamping down his frustration, and a twinge of fear, he approached her calmly.

"That's the craziest statement I've ever heard you say, Devon. What do you mean by it?"

"Just what I said. You'll have to go now. And this time our parting must be final. You can't come back."

"Does the expression 'fat chance' mean anything to you?"

"Don't get angry."

"I'm not angry. I'm incredulous."

"Let's not make this difficult."

He laughed hoarsely. "It started out with a fistfight, Devon. It was difficult from the beginning, and got more so each time we saw each other. But dammit, we've just proved it's worth fighting for. Tell me you think so, too."

Gnawing her lower lip, she glanced away and began fiddling with the knotted belt of her robe. Her distress was plain. Lucky softened his tone. "Tell me what's wrong."

"I'm married."

"Not to him."

"To *him*," she said with emphasis. "Our names are on the marriage certificate. We signed it. In the eyes of the state—"

"What about the eyes of God? Who's more your husband? Him or me?"

"How dare you drag religion into this," she cried angrily. "Are you suggesting that since you've known me in a biblical sense, you have a greater claim on me than Greg?" She tossed back her hair. Her green eyes were stormy. "If you are spiritually married to every woman you've slept with, then you're a polygamist!"

The barb hit home, and Lucky knew it would be pointless to pursue that line of reasoning. It had been worth a try, however. This was one argument he had to win. He had to pull out all the stops.

"You don't love him," he stated flatly.

"No, I don't. But I'm still married to him."

"And why? Why did you ever marry him? He doesn't love you either."

"At the time it seemed right."

"I applaud your grand gesture, but, Devon, surely you don't plan to throw away your happiness and spend the rest of your life with a jerk like him?"

"I have to stay married to him at least until he gets out of prison."

"He used you."

"I know that."

"He's a felon."

"I know that, too."

"You know he's guilty?" he asked, his jaw dropping open.

She gave a terse bob of her head. "I lied to you before. I'm reasonably certain he did it. At first I believed he was innocent. Later, after he was incarcerated, I began to have my doubts."

"Why?"

"He refused to consummate our marriage. Oh, he told me it was for my benefit. That way, he said, if I wanted to get out of the marriage, I could more easily. I thought he was being self-sacrificing. He might still be."

Lucky was shaking his head. "He was thinking of himself. He wanted to be able to have the marriage annulled when you were no longer useful. I'll bet that even now, he's trying to figure a way to turn the scandal about us to his advantage."

She hung her head. "The afternoon I met you, I learned that he had been declining his conjugal visits, something that I hadn't even known was available until I heard another prisoner's wife talking about it. I confronted Greg. We had a big row. I couldn't understand why he would reject his marital rights."

"Unless he was guilty not only of the crime, but gross manipulation."

"Yes."

It was a tough admission for her to make, but it only frustrated Lucky further. He plowed his hand through his hair. "Why haven't you started divorce—or annulment—proceedings?"

"Because I had used Greg just as much as he had used

me. I used his story to help promote my column. That's when the Devon Haines byline really began to mean something to the newspaper. So I, as much as Greg, profited from our marriage."

"Devon, you've got incredible talent. Your column would have succeeded anyway. Why are you staying married?"

"Because I take my responsibilities seriously. I can't just wash my hands of a marriage because it's no longer useful, because it's inconvenient."

He shot down that argument with a curt, "Bullshit. You just don't want to admit that you were duped."

"That's not true!"

He knew by her instantaneous and adamant rebuttal that his guess had been right. "You always have to be in control, calling the shots. It's impossible for you to admit that twice your heart has overruled your head. Greg's sob story got to you, and you can't live with that. Rather than admitting to a mistake in judgment, you'll stubbornly stay married to him just to prove you were right."

"As long as there's the slightest chance that he's innocent, I can't desert him while he's in prison."

Lucky's oaths were vicious. "You don't believe he's innocent any more than I do."

"You said my heart had overruled my head twice."

He glanced at the bed. "You've fought it every step of the way, but you love me and I damn well know it. We connected the first time we laid eyes on each other. What you can't own up to is that you're as vulnerable between the thighs—"

"I won't listen to your lewd—"

"You don't want to be a weak nonentity like your mother was, totally dependent on her husband for everything. Okay. Fine. Guess what, Devon? I don't want to wipe my feet on you. I don't want a silent, submissive partner, in or out of bed."

"I have a husband."

"He's not the issue. He never has been, or so I found out this morning. You're just using him as an escape hatch. This is between you and me."

He gripped her shoulders. "You want a career. Terrific. Have one. I'm all for it. But have me, too. We can have each other and make both our careers worthwhile.

"I want babies. The burden of that responsibility falls on you, I'm afraid. But if you consented to have my babies, I'd put you on a pedestal and make it the most wonderful experience of your life."

He lowered his voice to a compelling, tempting whisper. "I've felt your passion for me, Devon. I've tasted it. I know it's there. Put your arms around my neck. Tell me you need me. Admit you love me."

"Twice you've persuaded me to break my wedding vows. Isn't that enough for you?"

"I want us to exchange our own vows, vows our bodies have already made. Vows you haven't made with Greg or any other man."

"I can't see you again, Lucky."

"Say you love me."

"I can't."

"It's because of the way your mother died, isn't it?" he demanded.

Devon fell back a step. "What?"

"You turned a deaf ear to her and she died. You take responsibility for her death."

"Yes!" she cried. "Wouldn't you?"

"Was she incapacitated? Bedridden? Homebound? Unable to drive?"

"What are you getting at?"

"Could she have gone to the doctor alone, Devon?" She hedged, and he knew he was on to something. "She laid that guilt on you because her life had been miserable, and in a warped way she wanted yours to be. She probably wanted to die, and going about it as painfully as possible was her way of guaranteeing your attention for the rest of your life. And in the same damn way, you've shackled yourself to Shelby."

"He might be innocent."

"He isn't."

"But if he is——"

"You will have done all you could do to save him from imprisonment." He clamped down on her shoulders. "Devon, you can't take on responsibility for the whole world. No one's asked you to. You can't sacrifice your present happiness because of what happened in the past or what might happen in the future. Let it go. Let them go. Focus on someone who needs you here and now."

He had never begged a woman for anything. It was difficult for him to do so now. It went against his nature as diametrically as snow in the jungle. But, as he had realized, this was one argument he couldn't lose. His life depended on it.

"Don't throw away the best damn thing that has ever happened to either of us. Not for the sake of pride or principle or anything else. Don't. I'm begging you, Devon, please don't." He bracketed her jaw with his hands and tilted her head back. Enunciating each word, he said, "Tell me you love me."

She stared him down, her features tortured and emotional. Slowly her head began moving from side to side, as far each way as his hands would allow. Then, voice tearing, she said, "I can't. Please don't ask me to again."

Chapter Twenty

Lucky's black mood didn't improve when he got caught in a traffic jam as he approached the outskirts of Milton Point. He cursed the summer heat, the gloriously setting sun, cruel fate. After sitting broiling in his open convertible for several minutes, he got out and flagged down a cattle truck that was driving past in the opposite lane.

"What's caused this snafu?"

"Helluva wreck ahead of you," the teamster shouted down from the cab of his rig. "Two cars. Ambulances. Highway patrol and local cops. The whole shooting match. You might be here for a while, buddy."

"Not likely," Lucky muttered as he climbed back into his Mustang. He was going to the place, where he would drown out all thoughts and memories of Devon Haines and her senseless, stupid stubbornness if it took ten gallons of Jack Daniel's to do it.

He was eventually able to maneuver the Mustang out of

the lane and onto the shoulder of the highway. To the fury of other stranded drivers, he breezed along the outside lane, slowing up only when he came even with the site of the wreck and the emergency vehicles.

He was hoping to crawl past without attracting attention, but his legendary luck had deserted him. One of the officers flagged him down and approached his car. Lucky recognized him as a local sheriff's deputy.

"Damn."

"Hey, Lucky, I thought that was you," the deputy called when he was still some distance away. "Stay put," he ordered.

"But—"

"Wait right there." The officer turned and jogged toward a cluster of other officials.

Lucky blew out a gust of breath. Why the hell was he being detained? He had just about decided to disobey the deputy's order when he noticed Pat Bush detaching himself from the huddled group of officers.

"Pat," he called, "get me out of this—"

"Lucky."

Pat's somber expression and hushed tone of voice were out of character under the circumstances. Pat usually commandeered this kind of situation with professional detachment. Lucky's impatience switched to curiosity. "What's going on?"

"Pull your car over there. I need to talk to you."

"What's the matter?" Lucky put on his emergency brake and alighted. Something was very wrong here. Pat was having a hard time looking him in the eye, and Lucky couldn't account for his strange behavior. He was off the hook as far as the arson charge went.

Alarmed, he glanced beyond Pat, toward the tangled wreckage, and slumped with relief because he didn't recognize either car involved in the accident. "Good God, Pat. You had me thinking that one of—"

Pat laid a hand, a consoling hand, on his arm. He and Pat exchanged a meaningful glance. Then Lucky shook off Pat's hand and broke into a run.

"Lucky!" Pat grabbed hold of his shirt.

"Who is it?"

"It's Tanya."

Lucky's chest caved in painfully, his ribs seeming to crack under the pressure of his disbelief. "Tanya?" he croaked. "She's hurt?"

Pat lowered his eyes.

"No," Lucky said in swift denial. What Pat's silent gesture indicated was unthinkable. He ran toward the ambulances, elbowing aside anybody who dared to block his path.

Parting the crowd, he saw that an injured woman was being worked over by paramedics. When he heard her groans, he felt a burst of relief. But as he drew nearer, he saw that her hair color was wrong.

Frantically scanning the area, he spotted another collapsible gurney. It was being lifted into the ambulance. A black zippered bag had been strapped to it. He lunged forward.

Pat stepped into his path and struggled to stop him. "Let go of me!" he shouted.

"It won't do any good to see her now, Lucky."

"Get out of my way!" Bellowing like an enraged bull, he overpowered the older man, shoved him aside, and charged for the back of the ambulance.

The startled paramedics put up token protests as he pushed them aside, but the ferocity of his expression was intimidating, and they fell back. Lucky reached forward and unzipped the black plastic bag.

After one long, disbelieving gaze, Lucky squeezed his eyes shut and spun around. Pat signaled for the paramedics to finish their business. Lucky didn't even respond when the ambulance doors were slammed shut and the vehicle drove off.

"You okay?"

Lucky looked at Pat, but he didn't really see anything except his sister-in-law's still white face. "It's not possible."

Pat nodded his head, as though agreeing. "I was just getting ready to notify Chase of the accident and tell him to meet the ambulance at the hospital."

Lucky's chest heaved. He felt as if a white-hot spike had been driven through his heart. He thought he might vomit.

"No. This is a family affair. I'll go. And nobody else tells my mother or sister either, got that?"

"Lucky, this isn't the time to—"

"Got that?"

Pat backed down. "All right. If that's the way you want it."

"That's the way I want it."

"As soon as this is cleared up, I'll come out to the house."

Lucky didn't hear him. He was already headed for his car. It was only a short distance from the accident site to the office of Tyler Drilling. On the one hand, it seemed the longest drive he'd ever made. On the other, he was there far too soon, before he had found the words he must say.

Chase's car was parked out front. Lucky pushed open the door of his Mustang. It felt as though it weighed a ton. On his way into the office he met Chase coming out.

"Hey, where've you been all day? Mother said you struck out first thing this morning and hadn't been seen since." He was obviously in a hurry, and didn't give Lucky time to answer.

"George Young called and wants to know when we plan to make that note payment. That s.o.b. is still putting pressure on us, fire or no fire. I heard from somebody at the courthouse that Little Alvin and Jack Ed both pleaded guilty to arson today and will be sentenced sometime next week. I also met with the guy from the insurance company for two and a half hours. Thank God we kept up those premiums.

I'll tell you all about that later. Right now I'm late. I'm supposed to meet Tanya at—"

"Chase, wait a minute." He laid his hand on his brother's shoulder, stopping him halfway down the steps. His lips began to tremble, and Chase's image blurred because of his tears. Lucky's voice faltered. He unsuccessfully cleared his throat. "Chase—"

God, how did one tell a man that the woman he loved and the child she carried were dead?

The following morning Marcie Johns was moved out of intensive care and into a regular room at St. Luke's Methodist Hospital. She had suffered a concussion, a broken arm and collarbone, and trauma, but none of her injuries had been critical.

She was considered fortunate, since the driver of the other vehicle involved in the accident, a Texas Tech student home for the summer, and Marcie's passenger, Tanya Tyler, had been fatalities. The student had run a stop sign and hit Marcie's car broadside. Most considered it a blessing that he and Tanya had died instantly upon impact.

Lucky had wanted to hit anybody he overheard saying such a thing, and was only glad that, so far, nobody had said it to Chase.

His brother wasn't himself. He was acting like a crazy man. A little unreasonableness was justified, but when he had announced that he was going to the hospital to speak with Marcie, the other members of his family had been shocked and had pleaded with him to reconsider. No amount of persuasion could change his mind, however, so Laurie had instructed Lucky to go with his brother and "take care of him."

Together they walked down the corridor of the hospital toward the room assigned to Ms. Johns. "Why are you so bent on seeing her?" Lucky asked quietly, hoping that even now Chase would change his mind. "If anybody catches us with her, they'll throw us out of here. She's still in serious condition, and not supposed to have visitors."

Chase was walking with the determined tread of a prophet on a mission. He pushed open the door and entered the shadowed room. Lucky, after a quick glance over his shoulder, went in behind him. He vaguely remembered Marcie Johns from high school, and knew her now only by sight. She was an attractive woman, but one couldn't tell by looking at her now.

In spite of the fact that she had been wearing her seat belt, she'd been thrown against the windshield with enough force to bruise and abrade her face. Both eyes were ringed with bruises. Her nose and lips were grotesquely swollen. On her shoulder was a cast designed to keep her broken arm elevated.

Lucky was moved to pity. "Chase, for godsake, let's get out of here. We shouldn't bother her."

He had spoken so softly that the words were barely audible, but she heard them and opened her eyes. When she

310 Sandra Brown

saw Chase, she moaned and made a move as though she wanted to reach out to him.

"Chase, I'm sorry," she wheezed. "So sorry."

Apparently she had been advised that her passenger hadn't survived. She would have had to know sooner or later, of course, but it seemed to Lucky that later would have been preferable. The additional mental anguish couldn't be good for her body's healing process.

"We . . . we never even saw him." Her voice was thin and faint. "It was just . . . a racket . . . and . . ."

Chase lowered himself into the chair beside her bed. His features were distorted by grief. Lines seemed to have been carved into his face overnight. The area beneath his eyes was almost as dark as Marcie's. His dark hair was a mess. He hadn't shaved.

"I want to know about . . . Tanya," he said, his voice tearing on her name. "What kind of mood was she in? What was she saying? What were her last words?"

Lucky groaned, "Chase, don't do this to yourself."

Chase irritably threw off the hand Lucky placed on his shoulder. "Tell me, Marcie, what was she doing, saying, when . . . when that bastard killed her?"

Lucky lowered his forehead into one of his hands and massaged his temples with his thumb and middle finger. His insides were twisted. He couldn't even imagine the hell Chase was going through.

Or maybe he could. What if Devon had been killed yesterday? What if, after he had angrily left her, she had gone out and needlessly been killed by a driver running a stop sign? Wouldn't he be acting just as unbalanced as Chase? Wouldn't he be damning himself for not telling her one more time that he loved her no matter what?

"Tanya was laughing," Marcie whispered. Pain medication had made her speech slow and slurred. Chase clung to every careful word she was able to speak. "We were talking about the house. She . . . she was so excited about . . . about it."

"I'm going to buy that house." Chase glanced up at Lucky, his eyes wild and unfocused. "Buy that house for me. She wanted the house, so she's going to get it."

"Chase—"

"Buy the damn house!" he roared. "Will you just do that much for me, please, without giving me an argument?"

"Okay." Now wasn't the time to cross him, although his brother's request made no sense at all. But was a man who had just lost his family required to be sensible? Hell no.

"Right before we went . . . through the intersection, she asked me what color I thought . . ." Marcie paused, grimacing with discomfort. ". . . what color she should paint the bedroom for the baby."

Chase's head dropped forward into his hands. "Jesus." Tears leaked through his fingers and ran down the backs of his hands.

"Chase," she whispered, "do you blame me?"

Keeping his hands over his eyes, he shook his head. "No,

Marcie, no. I blame God. He killed her. He killed my baby. Why? *Why?* I loved her so much. I loved . . ." His voice broke into sobs.

Lucky moved toward him and again laid a comforting hand on his shaking shoulders. Tears marred his own vision. For a long while they were quiet. He realized a few minutes later that Marcie had mercifully lapsed into unconsciousness again.

"Chase, we'd better go now."

At first Chase seemed not to have heard, but he gradually dragged his hands down his wet, ravaged face and stood up. "Order some flowers for Marcie," he told Lucky as they left the room.

"Sure. What do you want me to put on the card? Do you want them to be exclusively from you or from all of—" He came to a dead standstill when he spotted Devon standing at the end of the hospital corridor.

Chase followed his brother's dumbfounded stare. Devon came forward to meet them. Her eyes moved from Lucky to Chase. "Sage called me early this morning," she told him, surprising Lucky. He hadn't known his sister had phoned Devon. "I got here as soon as I could. I can't believe it, Chase." Extending her hand, she took Chase's, pressing it firmly.

"Tanya liked you. She admired you."

Devon's smile was sweet and tearful. "I liked her, too. Very much."

"So did I." Chase didn't apologize for the gruffness of

his voice or the tears he continued to shed openly. Indeed, he seemed unaware of them. He addressed the two of them. "I'm going to the apartment now."

"Mother is expecting you back at the house."

"I need to be by myself for a while, among Tanya's things. Tell Mother I'll come out later."

Lucky wasn't so sure that Chase should be alone, but figured he would have to wrestle him to change his mind. He watched him approach the elevator. Moving like an automaton, he punched the button. The doors opened instantly; he stepped into the cubicle. The doors slid closed.

"He looks completely shattered, Lucky. Will he be all right?"

Lucky glanced at Devon, who had been standing quietly at his side. "I doubt it. But there's not a damn thing I can do about it."

"Nothing you're not already doing. I'm sure it's a comfort to him just knowing that he's got your support."

"Maybe. I hope so. He needs to find comfort where he can."

Hungry for the sight of her, he unapologetically stared. Her hair looked a darker, deeper shade of auburn against her black dress and pale face. In the cold glare of fluorescent lighting, her eyes appeared exceptionally green. They were bright with tears.

"It was good of you to come, Devon," he said thickly.

"I wanted to."

"How did you know where to find us?"

"I went to the house first. Sage said that I had just missed you, and that you and Chase were on your way here."

He nodded toward the bank of elevators. "Since Chase took the car, can I bum a ride home?"

"Of course."

They boarded the next available elevator and rode it down in silence. Lucky couldn't take his eyes off her. It seemed like a million years since he'd held her, made fervent love to her, yet it had been only yesterday.

Yesterday. Twenty-four hours. In that amount of time lives had been irrevocably altered, dreams shattered, loves lost. Life was tenuous.

He came to a sudden stop on the plant-lined path that wound through a courtyard connecting the hospital complex with the parking lot.

"Devon." He took her shoulders between his hands and turned her to face him. "I'm going to fight whatever or whoever I must to be with you for the rest of my life, even if it means fighting you first. Life's too damn short and too precious to waste a single day on misery and unhappiness.

"Listen to me. I love you," he vowed, his hands tensing, gripping her tighter. To his consternation, his surging emotions manifested themselves in tears again. Grief over losing Tanya, pain for his brother's suffering, sadness over the Tyler heir who would never know life, love for Devon, all overwhelmed him. He couldn't breathe for the tightness surrounding his swelling heart.

She sighed when she saw his distress, then placed her arms around his waist and laid her head on his chest. "I need you," she whispered earnestly. "I love you."

They came together in a fierce embrace. And after they kissed, they wept.

Epilogue

Lucky entered the house by the front door. "Hello? Anybody home?" He received no answer. His mother was out. Sage was only home on holidays and an occasional weekend, since she was now in Austin at the university. But Devon's red compact was in the driveway, so she should be at home.

Then he heard the familiar click-clack of her word-processor keyboard. Smiling, he followed the sound past the stairway to the rear of the house. Laurie's sewing room had been converted into an office for Devon. The conversion had taken place while Lucky and she were away on their honeymoon; Laurie had surprised them with it upon their return.

"I can't sew much anymore because of my arthritis," Laurie had told Devon when she protested the generosity. "The space was being wasted."

Over the last several months Devon had made it her

room, filling it with periodicals and books, both fiction and nonfiction, which she used for reference material or pure reading pleasure. Sage's contribution had been a wall calendar featuring a semi-nude hunk-a-month. When Lucky had threatened to take down "the perverted eyesore," Devon had launched into a tirade decrying the double standard, and Sage had threatened to cut off his hand if he tried.

The tragedy of Tanya's death, and Sage's impending move to Austin, had precluded Lucky from even suggesting that Devon and he make their home elsewhere. Following their quiet, private wedding, they moved into the large house with Laurie. Lucky was pleased with the arrangement and, apparently, so was Devon.

The three women in his life got along very well. Devon loved having a younger sister, and Laurie showered on Devon the warmth and affection that her inattentive mother never had.

Lucky knocked on the door to the office, but when he got no answer, he pushed the door open anyway. As he had suspected, she was engrossed in the green letters she was typing onto the black terminal monitor.

Headphones bridged her head, blasting her eardrums with music. Her taste was eclectic; she liked everything from Mozart to Madonna. He thought it was nutty, using music to drown out distracting noise, but that was just one of his wife's idiosyncracies that intrigued him. Her contradictions had attracted him from the beginning.

He waved his hand, so his sudden appearance wouldn't

startle her. When she noticed him in her peripheral vision, she turned her head, smiled, and removed the earphones.

"Hi. How long have you been standing there?"

He crossed to her and dropped a kiss on her forehead. "Almost long enough for the rose to wilt." From behind his back he withdrew a single yellow rose. Her eyes lighted up with pleasure as she accepted it and rolled the soft, cool petals over her lips.

"You remembered."

"Six months ago today you became Mrs. Lucky Tyler."

"Only twelve hours after I ceased being Mrs. Greg Shelby."

"Shh! Mother frowns on foul language being spoken in this house."

Lucky didn't have any charitable thoughts toward Devon's first husband. True to his word, the day he learned that Greg Shelby was out on parole, he had driven to Dallas and, following a hunch, located him at Dallas/Fort Worth Airport, covertly about to board an international flight. Lucky engaged him in a fistfight. He had even maneuvered it so that Greg threw the first punch. He hadn't inflicted nearly as much physical damage as he could have or wanted to, but the ruckus had alerted airport security. When they were told Shelby was a parolee about to leave the country, the police were notified, thwarting Greg's plans to retire to Switzerland with the illegally obtained fortune he had banked there.

In the resultant confusion Lucky managed to slip away

unidentified. He never told anybody that he'd been instrumental in Greg's second arrest, not even Devon, though he would have liked for her to know he had avenged her. He had to be content with the personal satisfaction he'd derived from drawing Shelby's blood.

Now he pulled Devon from her chair, sat down in it himself, then drew her onto his lap. She asked, "Do you think I'm a brazen hussy for getting a quickie annulment one day and marrying another man the next?"

"Shameful," he growled into her neck.

"Stop that. I'm officially still working."

"What's this column about?" He had encouraged her to continue writing for the newspaper, so she had made arrangements with her editor to work outside the office and mail her columns in on a weekly basis. Lucky squinted into the screen, but the green symbols always looked like Greek to him.

"Bereavement."

Her softly spoken answer brought his eyes back to her. "Well, you've certainly got firsthand experience to base your theories on, don't you?"

"Did you see him today?"

Lucky nodded. They were all preoccupied with Chase and his steady emotional decline since Tanya's death. "He put in an appearance at the office this morning."

"And?"

"He was drunk again."

"Eight months, and he hasn't even made a start at healing,"

Devon remarked sadly as she studied the petals of her rose. "Do you think he'll ever get over it?"

"No," Lucky said candidly. "I think the best we can hope for is that he can learn to cope with his grief and lead a productive life again."

Her sad expression reflected the regard she had come to have for her brother-in-law. Lucky loved that about her, too. She had absorbed all the concerns of his family. Their sorrows and joys had become her own. She took them to heart. Family life, with all its blessings and drawbacks, was new to her, but she had blossomed within that environment.

Often she cried with Laurie over the loss of her first grandchild. Sage confided secrets to Devon that she kept from the rest of the family.

Devon celebrated with him the day he temporarily staved off the bank by scraping together a loan payment and lent moral support because business was still dismal despite the replacement of the equipment they had lost in the fire. Tyler Drilling Company hadn't had any new contracts since the one in Louisiana.

Chase was useless, immobilized by his grief. Lucky had been left with the responsibility of trying to save a sinking ship. Devon's faith that he could do it boosted his confidence when it flagged.

"It's awful for him to be so unhappy, to waste his life like this," she murmured now. "Awful."

"He's never even been inside that house he had me buy

for him. It just stands there empty. He wallows in filth and misery in that apartment he shared with Tanya."

"What can we do to help him?"

"I wish to hell I knew. Criticism and lectures only make him nasty and defensive. Sympathy makes him furious. And he's going to get killed riding those damn bulls. He's too old to rodeo."

"Maybe that's what he wants," Devon said sorrowfully. "To die. Bull riding is just a chancy form of suicide."

"God." Lucky wrapped his arms around her waist and nuzzled her breasts. "I can understand how devastating it must be for him. If I ever lost you—"

"But you won't."

"I lost you after our first night together. I nearly went berserk until I found you again. And that was only for a week."

She leaned back and gave him a quizzical look. "You nearly went berserk? You never told me that."

In spite of his brother's bereavement and the sorry state of their business, Lucky was still a newlywed, and frequently behaved like a groom. That included teasing his bride.

"There's a lot I haven't told you," he drawled.

"Oh yeah?"

"Yeah."

"Like what?" she asked.

"Like how damn sexy you look when you're wearing your glasses."

She crossed her eyes behind the lenses. " 'Boys don't make passes at girls who wear glasses.' "

"I make passes at all the girls."

"So I've heard."

He drew her closer and kissed her with increasing fervency, parting her pliant lips with his tongue. The buttons on her blouse were no match for his nimble fingers. As her breasts filled his gently reshaping hands, she reached between his thighs and caressed him. Freeing him from his jeans, she put the petals of the rose to prurient use.

"Thank you for my flower," she purred as she delicately twirled the stem.

"I taught you too well," he hissed, sucking in a quick breath at the tickling sensation.

"Meaning?"

"Meaning, I don't think we're going to make it upstairs to the bedroom this time."

Leaving his lap, she lay down on the rug and pulled him down on top of her. Moments later they lay panting together amid hopelessly wrinkled clothing, crushed rose petals, and dewy, naked limbs.

Propping himself up on his elbows, he smiled down at her. "Beats writing all to hell, doesn't it?"

Devon took one of his hands, kissed the palm, and laid it against her throbbing left breast. "Feel that? I love you with every beat of my heart, and I don't know what I would do without you in my life."

He gazed down into her eyes, seeing in their green

depths the love that mirrored his own. She was intelligent, sensitive, loving, gorgeous, sexy, and hotter than a firecracker in bed. And she freely and generously shared herself with him.

"Damn," he said, sighing with contentment, "no wonder they call me Lucky."

About the Author

Sandra Brown is the author of more than fifty *New York Times* bestsellers, with over seventy million copies of her books in print. She and her family divide their time between South Carolina and Texas.